MON

The
Midwife's Song

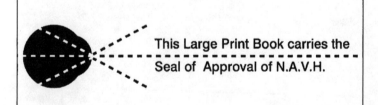

This Large Print Book carries the
Seal of Approval of N.A.V.H.

The Midwife's Song

A Story of Moses' Birth

Brenda Ray

Thorndike Press • Waterville, Maine

Scripture taken from the New King James Version. Copyright ©
1982 by Thomas Nelson, Inc. Used by permission. All rights
reserved.

This book is a work of fiction. Although some of the characters
are historical figures, their actions, thoughts, and dialogue are
products of the author's imagination.

Published in 2005 by arrangement with
Farris Literary Agency, Inc.

Thorndike Press® Large Print Christian Fiction.

The tree indicium is a trademark of Thorndike Press.

The text of this Large Print edition is unabridged.
Other aspects of the book may vary from the original edition.

Set in 16 pt. Plantin by Al Chase.

Printed in the United States on permanent paper.

Library of Congress Cataloging-in-Publication Data

Ray, Brenda.
    The midwife's song : a story of Moses' birth / by Brenda Ray.
        p. cm. — (Thorndike Press large print Christian fiction)
    ISBN 0-7862-7980-X (lg. print : hc : alk. paper)
    1. Moses (Biblical leader) — Birth — Fiction.   2. Bible.
O.T. Exodus — History of Biblical events — Fiction.
3. Egypt — History — To 332 B.C. — Fiction.   4. Midwives
— Fiction.   5. Religious fiction.   6. Large type books.
I. Title.   II. Thorndike Press large print Christian fiction
series.
PS3568.A875M54 2005
813′.6—dc22   2005015402

To midwives everywhere, who honor life,
giving safe, gentle care
to women and babies.

This is your heritage.

As the Founder/CEO of NAVH, the only national health agency solely devoted to those who, although not totally blind, have an eye disease which could lead to serious visual impairment, I am pleased to recognize Thorndike Press★ as one of the leading publishers in the large print field.

Founded in 1954 in San Francisco to prepare large print textbooks for partially seeing children, NAVH became the pioneer and standard setting agency in the preparation of large type.

Today, those publishers who meet our standards carry the prestigious "Seal of Approval" indicating high quality large print. We are delighted that Thorndike Press is one of the publishers whose titles meet these standards. We are also pleased to recognize the significant contribution Thorndike Press is making in this important and growing field.

Lorraine H. Marchi, L.H.D.
Founder/CEO
NAVH

★ Thorndike Press encompasses the following imprints: Thorndike, Wheeler, Walker and Large Print Press.

ACKNOWLEDGMENTS

This book wouldn't have been possible if God hadn't given me the midwife's calling. From an early age I knew I was destined to share in the miracle of birth. Midwifery isn't a job, but a divine assignment. I'm truly humbled for having been chosen. Although illness prematurely ended my career, I'm forever grateful to the families that let me share the miracle of their children's birth.

My wonderful family — how do I thank you? You gave me feedback and back rubs, washed dishes and laundry, tiptoed through the house, contributing to this project in a hundred different ways. You believed in me, encouraged me, and prayed for me when I was ill. You are the wind beneath my wings. I know how blessed I am.

John, my own precious husband, thank you for being there for me, and for your input into the plot of *The Midwife's Song.*

The story came from my heart, but the book came from countless hours of thoughtful review by my critique group.

Mike, Ric, Norris, Irma, Nadine — you guys are the greatest. I also want to thank Jean Ann Williams, Janet Barton, and Donita Thompkins for reading and critiquing the first draft of *The Midwife's Song* and encouraging me to tell Puah's story.

To my publishers, Mike and Karen Helms of Karmichael Press — thank you for allowing Puah's story to be told.

Finally, to all midwives everywhere. The world is a better place because of you. I am honored to be called "midwife."

AUTHOR'S NOTE

Fictional stories are born out of fascination with a character, a setting, or a plot idea. In the fall of 1997, shortly after my own nurse-midwifery career ended, I was reading the sketchy account of Puah and Shiphrah in the second chapter of Exodus. I had read this story many times before, but this time it grabbed my interest in a different way. My mind raced with questions. How did two Hebrew midwives come to be before Pharaoh's throne? Why would a king order his future workforce killed? Did the midwives lie to Pharaoh, or did a true miracle occur? That is, did the babies arrive before they could attend the deliveries? The midwife in me said, "Not likely." Out of these questions and my own conclusions, *The Midwife's Song* was born.

While researching, I grew increasingly perplexed. Sorting through the maze of facts on Biblical archeology proved to be a daunting task. Which theory about Egyptian chronology is correct? Even experts in the field do not agree. There are "late" theorists, and "early" theorists. This is further complicated by the fact that traditional Egyptian chronology does not seem to agree with Biblical chronology.

After many weeks of research, I settled on the work of Dr. David Rohl as a theoretical model. His "new" chronology of ancient Egypt is based on a lifetime of work in Egyptology. The book (also a PBS production), *Pharaohs and Kings: A Biblical Quest* (New York: Crown Publishers, 1995), is the result of his findings. I found Dr. Rohl's arguments fascinating and convincing.

Using Rohl's theory, we can place the birth of Moses around the third year of Khaneferre Sobekhotep IV's reign. (Thus, the Pharaoh of the Exodus would have been Dudimose.) In Moses' time, the capital of Egypt was located at Itj-tawy, near or at the site of the modern village of Lisht. Founded by Amenemhat I, Itj-tawy (meaning "Seizer of the Two Lands") was strategically located on the west bank of the Nile River at the border of Upper and Lower Egypt.

For the believer, whichever theory you embrace does not change history. Only names and dates change. Knowing which Pharaoh ruled at what time does not change the integral fact: the Exodus occurred;

Moses did indeed lead the seed of Abraham from bondage.

Jewish tradition tells us that Miriam and Yocheved were also midwives; I chose not to reflect this in *The Midwife's Song.* In the Brooklyn Papyrus (catalogue number Brooklyn 35.1446) a Hebrew slave named Shiphrah is listed (this is a Biblical name, not Egyptian).

Still, with all the facts and traditions, I never lost track that this is midrash, a "story behind the story." We weren't there; we can only speculate. So, realizing this is a work of fiction, settle back and enjoy. This account of the circumstances surrounding Moses' birth is held together by archeological theory and scriptural record. With God's help and a midwife's heart, I only added window dressing.

Brenda Ray
March 2000

PROLOGUE

For you are a holy people to the LORD your God; the LORD your God has chosen you to be a people for Himself, a special treasure above all the peoples on the face of the earth. (Deuteronomy 7:6)

Darkness descended with delicate grace. Puah reclined against soft pillows, thankful for the luxury. At ninety-eight years, her bones ached, especially after the previous night's grueling march across the seabed, which came on the heels of an equally trying journey in blistering desert heat the day before. Now, cool night air circulated freely past the flap of her tent, bringing with it the succulent aroma of roasting lamb.

Fears of the previous days lay at the bottom of the Red Sea with Pharaoh and his soldiers. Images flashed through Puah's mind. She shuddered, drawing a blanket closer around her.

This was a day of rest and celebration.

Earlier, she'd sat on a rocky prominence overlooking the vast Sinai Desert to the east. Craggy hills jutted from the tawny desert floor at irregular intervals. Behind her the setting sun blazed, an orb of fire as it sank slowly below the horizon. Egypt, the country of her birth, lay to the southwest. A bittersweet prayer formed in her heart. *LORD, do not let me see that land again.*

Now, as evening settled, Puah watched her people gather around cooking fires outside their tents. Stars appeared as daylight waned. Inside the tent soft light glowed from a single oil lamp, a breeze causing shadow play on the walls.

Puah picked up her indigo-blue mantle, now covered with powdery, alkaline dust. She folded it with the matching veil and set them aside. Leathery hands, gnarled with age, caught her eye. Darkened and dried by desert sun, it seemed impossible they could be hers. Coarse blood vessels wove splotchy patterns beneath delicate skin that bruised too easily these days. Where had the soft, well-oiled resilience of youth gone?

She touched a wrinkled cheek and sighed. The finely sculpted nose of her youth stood out sharply against the weathered planes of her face, giving the appearance of an ancient raptor. Miraculously, her vision was still sharp, with the exception of close work. She'd never liked needlework anyway. She cackled at the rebellious thought, the coarse sound echoing in the silence of the tent.

Puah's joints ached constantly now, her hands certainly no exception. Countless days throughout long years of midwifery had taken their toll. She accepted without bitterness the pain brought by old age. She'd lived to see God's hand deliver the Hebrews from Egypt, and for that she was grateful.

The children of Israel are free from Pharaoh's bondage. Will I live to also see the Promised Land? Puah's soul was torn asunder. Part of her wished to see and share that day with her family; another part yearned to be with her beloved husband again. She vowed to leave her remaining days in the LORD's sure hands.

Outside the tent and across the sandy plain, Joseph's descendants, her own extended family, stretched like a vast, living tapestry. Banners of the other eleven tribes waved across the distance in the evening air.

Daphne, her great-granddaughter, hovered over a grinding stone, crushing emmer for cakes to sustain them in their travels. With an easy rhythm she pushed stone against stone, all the while tending the lamb roasting on a spit above the fire. Occasionally Daphne brushed stray hair from her eyes, smiling as she watched children playing nearby.

Puah smiled at the gentle rounding of Daphne's abdomen. Perhaps it would be a son. Suddenly a new thought came to mind. *This child will be among the first Hebrews born into freedom in centuries!* A tightening gripped Puah's heart as tears formed in her thankful eyes. Yes, this new one would be free, born perhaps in the Promised Land!

Daphne's daughter, Hannah, played nearby with a small wooden crocodile, its jaws set on hidden hinges. Out of all her possessions, Hannah chose the crocodile to take to Canaan. She opened and closed the toy reptile's mouth, making growling sounds. Her nose wrinkled as it ate invisible prey in the desert sand. Would Hannah remember what a crocodile looked like when she was her great-great-grandmother's age? Would she ever see another crocodile other than this toy?

No, she wouldn't. Neither would she see her children beaten by a taskmaster, nor be forced to bow to graven images. As a child of Israel, she now lived and played free from bondage. How different would Hannah's life be in comparison to her elders?

16

A murmur rose among people gathered a few tents away, gaining Puah's attention. Moses cleared the crowd, taking to Ahiram, Puah's oldest grandson and leader of the tribe.

"Everyone, hear me!" Ahiram shouted. The dull hum of voices soon quieted, like a wave of summer wheat blown by the wind. Only fluttering tent flaps disturbed the silence. Everyone waited expectantly.

"Moses wishes to speak." Ahiram bowed and backed away.

Moses stood tall against the backdrop of cooking fire. Aaron, his brother and spokesman, stood nearby, leaning upon his staff. Moses retained the proud bearing of a son of Pharaoh. But the once smooth, oiled face of an Egyptian prince was now hardened by the years spent toiling in Midian, and covered by a hoary beard. He wore the dusty, multicolored robe of a Hebrew shepherd. He faced the people and pondered their countenances.

"My family, I . . . I do not speak well, but I must be . . . be heard this night. I will sing unto the LORD, for He has triumphed gloriously, throwing the horse and rider into the sea!"

Moses' voice rang out across the desert. He sang of victory, of battles won through

God's mighty hand, of victories yet to come in Moab, Edom, and Canaan. Faith poured from Moses' exaltation, flowing like poetry, mighty and beautiful.

He does not stutter! Puah was amazed. Moses had stuttered all his life. Tears welled in her eyes as the Deliverer sang a love song to the Holy One of Israel.

God had not forsaken His children. Since the death of her beloved Hattush, Puah's hope rested on two things: the promise of her fathers that someday the children of Israel would return to the Promised Land; and being reunited with her husband in Paradise.

When Moses' song ended, Miriam, the prophetess, sister to Moses and Aaron, could no longer contain her excitement. With more energy than most women her age, she arose and stood near Moses, singing, "Sing unto the LORD for He is highly exalted!"

Young women joined her in the inner circle, timbrels in hand, answering Miriam's call of victory with their own musical response. "The horse and its chariot has He thrown into the sea!"

Their song filled the air, repeating Moses' own praises to God. Harps, drums, and other stringed instruments joined the worshipful concert.

Soon celebration resounded across the desert floor as far as ear could hear. Above, millions of stars shimmered in a rhythmic dance of the heavens. A three-quarter moon gleamed, reflecting a soft glow onto every face outside the circle of fire. Its gentle light bathed the children of Israel, young and old, male and female, rich and poor.

Throughout the vast camp children's voices mingled with the music as young ones began playing and chasing one another. They laughed and sang, uninhibited by adult fears or cares. Their joy was contagious. After awhile they tired of their play. Puah watched as little Hannah gathered her playmates into a huddle, talking animatedly.

No sooner had Hannah pointed toward her great-great-grandmother's tent than an avalanche of children descended upon Puah.

"Grandma´ma, would you tell us a story?" Hannah asked breathlessly. "You tell such wonderful stories!"

"What story would you have me tell?" Puah watched the mixed expressions on the children's faces. The youngest seemed about three, while some could be as old as ten years. All stood reverently, waiting for her answer and invitation to be seated.

Hannah whispered behind her hand to her friend Tabitha, who in turn whispered back to Hannah. Both beamed a conspiratorial smile to one another and nodded their heads in union.

"Please, if you would, Grandma´ma, tell us the story of how you delivered Father Moses. We'll be quiet and help with the little ones. Please!"

Puah's heart smiled. How could she refuse? Hannah knew parts of the story. Did the other children not deserve to know the truth of God's plan? Shouldn't they hear how He orchestrated their passage to this great desert and out of the bonds of slavery?

"Very well, Hannah. I will tell the story. But first, please bring this old woman some water, if you'd be so kind."

"Yes, Grandma´ma!" A gleaming smile lit Hannah's dusty face and she scurried out, returning moments later with a gourd brimming with water. The children gathered around Puah like chicks under the great cloak of their mother's wings. Older children placed smaller ones upon their laps and settled back onto pillows. The rustle of activity soon settled into an expectant quiet. Lamplight revealed dozens of bright eyes, wide with excitement.

Puah drank her fill of the cool water. She

readjusted the pillows to ease some of the pressure from her aching hip. She missed the soft couches of Egypt. Oh, but the other things — she wouldn't miss them!

"It is a long story, my children. I cannot possibly tell it all in one night, but I'll tell as much as I can before bedtime. You may hear a bit each night until my story is finished. Is that agreeable to everyone?"

A musical chorus pealed the air as the children shouted a resounding "Yes!"

"Very well. Now, sit back and close your eyes so your mind can see the journey we're about to take. We go back many, many years, before any of you were born, or your mothers or fathers. I am just a young girl, barely fourteen. We are traveling to the village of Itj-tawy where the palace of Khaneferre Sobekhotep IV stands."

Puah sighed deeply as her mind drifted back to that day so long ago. Even after these many years the details were vividly bright. She could almost smell the marketplace.

With eyes closed, the children waited patiently for her to continue. Settling back deeper into the pillows, Puah shut her own eyes and traveled back to the common market outside the gates of Pharaoh's palace. . . .

I

He will fulfill the desire of those who fear Him; He also will hear their cry and save them. (Psalm 145:19)

"Puah, look at this linen. It's beautiful!" Behira, her mother, gently stroked the downy white fabric. "Wouldn't it be wonderful to wear such soft fabric instead of this coarse cloth?" Her mother glanced down at the thick, crude weave of her own woolen cloak. "Oh, listen to me. I complain too much. I should be ashamed. We are blessed."

"Mama, someday I'll buy it for you and dress you like a queen."

"Oh, daughter, you know we are destined for the servant's life. Don't torture yourself with things that are not to be." Behira wistfully stroked the soft fabric one last time, then admonished her daughter, "Let's be on our way. Your father will be meeting us soon and we still must find herbs for roasting the lamb."

A wide-eyed Puah followed her mother

through the crowded marketplace. Merchants hawked their wares beneath cotton pavilions supported by sturdy, rough-hewn poles. The awnings sheltered sellers and buyers from the scorching sun. Puah wanted to see everything. Unlike Avaris, a mostly Hebrew village and the place of her birth, the Egyptian market was vibrant and colorful.

All around, Egyptian men and women moved about, servants shuffling close behind carrying weighty purchases. Hebrew slaves, some in the traditional multicolored robes and some in linen kilts or sheaths of Egyptian linen, followed their masters as they shopped. Meat sellers displayed every kind of meat, fish, and fowl imaginable, while farmers displayed colossal papyrus baskets filled with onions, garlic, grain, and cucumbers. The sweet fragrance of fruit drew the wide-eyed girl's attention to melons, pomegranates, grapes, and dates that lay in baskets by the hundreds. Rare aromatic oils mingled with the odors of spices, fruits, and vendors' foods.

Puah found it all very exciting. She loved visiting her aunt and uncle in the bustling city of Itj-tawy. How wonderful it must be to live so close to the marketplace! If only her parents could purchase freely, and not worry about the weight and cost. . . .

A tug on the sleeve of her mantle reminded Puah of the purpose for their visit to the market. She hurried along to keep up with her mother.

It doesn't matter anyway, Puah thought, frowning. She would become a poor Hebrew's wife, just like her mother. She would marry, have children, and *they* would be her riches. It was her destiny. The children of Israel were slaves. She must never forget it.

Father Joseph was a hero to his people *and* to Egypt, but since his passing things were not the same. How quickly the royal family forgot how Joseph had saved Egypt from starvation. Now, his descendants were slaves.

Still, something deep within made Puah cling to her dream. Since childhood she'd been captivated by all things relating to the body. She found satisfaction in caring for the ill. She especially loved to listen to women talk of birth and the miracle of new life. Oft times she would happily volunteer to help her papa with the sheep, hoping to witness the miracle of birth as a new lamb delivered. It stirred something deep within, something so profound she seemed unable to share it with her parents. The calling to be a healer was part of who she was, just as the coarse threads woven into her multicolored wool mantle were an intricate part of the whole.

But this was not to be. Only the rich or favored Egyptians could become physicians. Yes, a farmer's wife, that was Puah's destiny.

"Stop! Thief! Thief!" A merchant's cry rang over the hum of the market.

From the corner of her eye Puah saw an Egyptian beggar flash by, scurrying through the crowd, a pomegranate clutched in his hand. He vanished into the throngs of shoppers, two Egyptian soldiers in pursuit.

Moments later a terrible scream rang out. As the crowd parted the soldiers came into view. One dragged an old Hebrew man behind him, the soldier's spear glistening with dark fluid. Blood covered the old man's garments, pouring rapidly from a wound in his side. The other soldier strutted alongside holding a pomegranate high in the air. His eyes danced with sadistic excitement, proud of their Hebrew quarry, proud of their recovery. The fruit was a trophy, a reminder not to forget who ruled this land.

A young Hebrew girl followed, beseeching them to reconsider, "No! It's a mistake!" she cried. "Please, please, my grandfather bought that fruit. It's a mistake!"

Growing tired of the girl's lament, the younger soldier whirled about, rage filling his dark eyes. With all his might he slapped the girl across the face, knocking her to the ground. He grinned wickedly, then spat in the dirt at her feet before turning on his heels and following his partner.

Puah gasped aloud. *Why? Why would he be filled with such hatred for an innocent child?* Suddenly she understood why her parents wanted her in Avaris, why they shielded her from Egyptian life in the city.

Behira grabbed Puah's arm. Fear danced in her mother's eyes. Such scenes were all too common in Itj-tawy. Pharaoh hated the Hebrews and his disdain trickled down from his throne into the streets. No Hebrew was safe in Egypt. For them, there was no justice or mercy. Only God listened to their cries.

Puah followed her mother, the day's joy stolen. *An old man falsely accused, probably murdered. Why, because he is of Abraham's seed?* Puah's mind swirled as she tried to understand.

"Behira! Is that you?"

A woman pushed through the mingling crowd toward them. Tall, regal, and richly dressed, the crowd stepped aside as she made her way toward Puah's mother. A Hebrew porter followed, laden with parcels of various sizes.

Puah was dumbstruck. What woman of such station would know her mother? In a strange city, no less.

The courtly stranger wore an elegant ankle-length linen sheath, as preferred by the Egyptians. At her waist a girdle of woven hair and cowrie shells glistened with an occasional thread of gold. Surprisingly, no kohl or malachite darkened her eyes. Her skin testified to its well-oiled care. She wore no wig; her own hair coiled carefully atop her head beneath a silken shawl. Her facial features, clearly Hebrew, glowed with good health and prosperity. Who could she be, this part-Egyptian, part-Hebrew stranger?

"Shiphrah?" Behira exclaimed, amazement lighting her face. "Is it really you?"

Could her mother know this woman of mystery? Puah wondered.

"Yes! It is I, my dear friend. Where have you been all these long years?" With that, the two women embraced. Behira's eyes filled with tears. They pulled apart and gazed at one another as only dear friends can do after a long absence.

"We live in Avaris. My husband's family

is there. Oh, Shiphrah, look at you! Where have you been? Indeed, the LORD has blessed you."

"Yes, I've indeed been blessed. I work here in Itj-tawy. I am a midwife, and many of my clients are Egyptian. They're very generous and most grateful for my services. With Pharaoh's court here most of the year, the wealth is great."

"A midwife? *You,* hoyden of the village? I cannot believe my ears!" Behira threw back her head and laughed aloud at this announcement. "You must tell me all about it, my friend. How I've missed you! Sadly, we have to return to Avaris tomorrow. We're only here to visit my husband's cousin and exchange lambs for some other goods that are hard to find in Avaris."

"Who is this delightful creature with you?" Shiphrah's lark eyes fastened on Puah.

Surely Shiphrah couldn't be talking about her! Her lips were too full and her long eyelashes shamed her. They gave her the look of kohl-painted eyes. Even now, at fourteen, she could sense young men staring. Their bold glances made heat rise within her. How she wished she still had the boyish figure of just a few months ago.

"Oh, forgive me, Shiphrah. This is my

youngest daughter, Puah. Puah, this is my dear friend, Shiphrah."

"It's a pleasure to meet you, Puah. Your mother and I were best friends when we were about your age. How old *are* you?"

Puah lowered her eyes, suddenly shy in this elegant woman's presence. "Fourteen years."

Shiphrah smiled. "Yes, that's just the age we were when we became close friends. We shared our deepest secrets. I think I was the first to know of her love for your father." Shiphrah glanced back at Behira. Her eyes brightened.

"Can the two of you come to my home? We can break bread and talk of old times. Say yes, please, Behira?"

"Well . . . I don't know. I must find Amiel and ask him. Wait! There he is now. I'll ask." Behira rushed off toward her husband as he made his way through the noonday crowd. Puah watched them talking for a moment, then turned her attention to Shiphrah.

"You are a midwife? I think that would be the most wonderful calling. It must be very exciting!" Suddenly embarrassed at her impetuous outburst, Puah felt flush in her face. Would she ever learn to keep her mouth closed?

Shiphrah didn't seem to notice Puah's discomfort. She smiled at her, the lines of her face softening.

"It *is* wonderful. There's no greater honor than ushering a new life into the world, to hear its first cry and to see the joy of the parents. I consider it a great honor and blessing. It's also a tremendous responsibility. Most of the time it's the happiest job on earth, but at times it will try your soul *and* your faith in God."

Puah had no time to ask further questions. Behira rushed back to them. "Amiel has other business to attend. He said he would call for us at your home later today if you'll give him directions. We'd be delighted to visit with you, Shiphrah."

Puah, Behira, and Shiphrah gathered around the noon meal, the two older women catching up on the years since their last visit. Puah listened intently, trying not to miss a single word, hoping the mystery of Shiphrah's success would be revealed.

She'd never seen such opulence. Surely this couldn't be the home of a Hebrew! There must be at least three stories, with beams as stout as the strongest man holding up the tall ceilings. Rich, vibrant colors typical of Egyptian homes dressed the walls with painted scenery. Lotus blossoms, fruit-laden trees, and fragrant flowers embellished the rooms. Cool air moved through the great hall from high windows. Beneath her sandals, smooth, cream-colored brick lay in ordered precision.

This was a palace compared to the mud walls and dirt floors of her family home. How did a Hebrew, even a midwife, come to possess such wealth? Dark questions plagued Puah. Could Shiphrah possibly be a courtesan? Surely her mother would not socialize with someone like *that.* Of course, Puah had no real knowledge of women of that sort, but she'd heard older girls whispering about women of questionable reputation.

Puah tried not to gobble the food, though the lavish assortment of fruits, breads, and cheeses seemed a feast. Even the pomegranate-flavored water was a luxury of which she'd only heard. Oh, to know this every day! The thought of such abundance overwhelmed her young mind. If a Hebrew woman lived this well, how extravagant the house of Pharaoh must be!

"I'm looking for an apprentice. I am no longer a spring ewe, and I must train someone to help me when I'm old and feeble."

Lost in pleasurable daydreaming, Puah almost missed Shiphrah's statement. The words hung in her heart, and she could have sworn it skipped a beat.

"Puah, is there a young man in your life?"

A bite of goat cheese caught in Puah's throat. She covered her mouth, coughed, and shook her head. "No, mistress, there is no young man, at least none I *like*." Oh, why did she say that? Seeing her mother's frown, Puah stared at the floor. Why did they insist on Deron? He was a nice boy, but she didn't feel any attraction to him. Of course, she'd never felt any such allure, but she'd heard the older girls talk of those feelings. She yearned to know this love that made one's knees weak, that caused one's heart to gallop with joy at the very sight of a special young man.

"Puah wishes to learn a trade," said Behira. "She thinks being a wife and mother is old-fashioned. Yet as impractical as it sounds, I'm sure it would be wise for a young woman to know other things besides caring for a family. It's certainly been a blessing to you."

"What do you think of midwifery, Puah?"

Shiphrah's pointed question caught Puah off guard. She tried to contain the excitement surging in her veins. "I . . . I'm not sure. I believe it would be . . . exciting, perhaps? Being a healer would be a great honor." Why would Shiphrah ask *her* such a question? Oh, she dared not get her hopes astir only to be disappointed.

"Puah, the garden is cool this time of day. Perhaps you'd like to explore?"

Shiphrah's invitation seemed more a command than offer. Surely Shiphrah's plans didn't include her! Waiting in the garden, Puah's curiosity grew.

By bedtime that evening she would be even more confused.

A heated discussion began shortly after the evening meal when Puah's father ordered her to retire early. From the rooftop she heard a muffled conversation in the sleeping chamber below. Her father's angry whispers and mother's anxious entreaties carried deep into the night.

Puah lay on a mat alongside two of her female cousins who were already asleep. The night air carried the emotional mumbling from below. Puah couldn't make out the words, but the sentiments rang clearly. Her mother was trying to convince her father of something, and her father contended strongly. Occasionally Puah was certain she heard her name. After a while she tired, the day's exciting activities taking their toll. She gave in to the mingling night sounds from the city and drifted into a restless sleep.

Morning brought a bustle of activity intrinsic to any household with five children. Her aunt and uncle, though poor in material goods, were rich in offspring, with yet another on the way. Etana's girth grew daily, the pregnancy pushing forth larger than any Puah had ever seen. Surely she couldn't grow much bigger else she would burst. Uncle Namir declared it would be triplets; Aunt Etana struck him playfully each time he made the laughing remark.

"Daughter, after you bring water from the well, your father and I need to speak with you," Behira commanded quietly. Puah lifted a jug to her shoulder and nodded before walking outside toward the well. Her stomach knotted. Whatever was wrong? Some great change had occurred in her family, and somehow it involved her. Her parents rarely argued. What could it be? Had they arranged for her betrothal? *Oh please, not yet!*

Puah's mind raced. She was not *ready* to marry! Besides, she wanted to pick her own husband. She knew it was unheard of, but it only seemed right. Why would anyone want to marry a stranger? Deron was a nice boy and she'd known him since childhood, but she couldn't imagine even being kissed by him.

Puah filled the jug as unbidden thoughts tumbled about, stirring the confusion she felt. With dread she returned to the house. She couldn't avoid her destiny any longer. Whatever her fate, she would accept it with some degree of grace, for she knew her parents loved her deeply. They would never intentionally hurt her, only wanting the best for her.

"I am finished, Mama."

"Good morning, daughter." Amiel stood at the window, looking out thoughtfully, stroking his thick curly beard. A scowl darkened his brown eyes. The serious inflection of his voice made Puah's heart quake. She felt a strong urge to rush into the protective circle of his arms. Her father was the most wonderful man she'd ever known and her tower of strength. His loving arms had soothed away night fears more times than she could count.

"Good morning, Papa. You and Mama wish to speak with me?" Her voice quavered. She wrung her hands behind her back, trying to renounce the rising sense of alarm at her parents' behavior. She waited, fearing their news.

"Yes, little one. Please, sit. We must talk."

Puah sat on a pillow near the window.

"Your mother and I have come to a decision about your future. At first, I must admit I was against the idea, but after discussing the issue, I see your mother is right." Amiel reached out and took Behira's hand, squeezing it gently. Puah watched unspoken words pass between them, a look replete with mutual love and agreement — and pain.

"Puah, since you were a small child you've been unlike your sisters and playmates. You are brighter than most, and yes, more headstrong. We had thought to arrange a marriage for you, but it seems none of the young men meet your favor. I admit, my heart is soft where your happiness is concerned. There is still time, and I see no need to force you into a marriage you oppose."

Puah breathed a silent sigh of relief.

Her father continued. "Your mother's friend has offered to apprentice you in midwifery. Although she is a widow, she runs an upstanding house that honors our ways and traditions. She serves the God of our fathers, Abraham, Isaac, Jacob, and Joseph. For you to learn, you would be required to live with her here in Itj-tawy."

"Shiphrah? Do you mean . . . Shiphrah?" Astonishment made putting words together difficult.

"Yes, whom you visited yesterday. She's a woman of much wealth. She cares for the Hebrew women particularly, but some of her clients are Egyptian. Their wealth has trickled its way into her purses through the years, but don't be deceived. She's one of us. After much thought, your mother and I have decided you should become her apprentice. To bring new life into the world is a most holy charge, and one you're well suited to pursue. What do you think, my child?"

"I . . . Father, I'm not sure what to say. I've only dreamed —" Thoughts tumbled through Puah's mind. So much so quickly she felt overwhelmed. "I'd like to learn from Shiphrah very much, but . . . what of you and Mother?"

"We'll return to Avaris. Once you are skilled at your craft, you shall return home and we'll arrange your marriage." The hint of a smile softened Amiel's mouth. He raised his eyebrows in amusement. "Perhaps by then you'll have found a young man who fulfills your requirements."

Tears sprang into Puah's eyes even as panic welled in her breast. "You . . . you'll leave me here?"

Behira reached out and drew Puah close. "Darling daughter, you'll be with my dearest friend in the whole world. Shiphrah will love and care for you as her own. She'll open doors for you that your father and I cannot. Just think, child, you'll be delivering the children of Israel. What an honor!"

Tears spilled unashamedly down Puah's face. Leaving her family and living in the home of a rich woman in a strange city — it was more than she could comprehend. At least if she were betrothed, she could be near her parents in Avaris.

"Will I see you often?" Puah asked with trembling lips.

"Yes, my dove." Amiel cleared his throat before continuing. "Your Uncle Namir and I have found a firm market for the lambs. I'll be bringing them to market regularly. I'm certain your mother will want to join me now more than ever. So yes, daughter, we will visit you often."

Puah tried to imagine life in Itj-tawy without her parents. Her chest hurt and her eyes stung to think of it. Still, with all the fears and uncertainties, she couldn't suppress the rising excitement of their proposal. To become a midwife! Live in a modern city, in a home fit for a queen. Would she be able to wear sheaths of fine linen? Would she be paid for her work? She envisioned presenting her parents fine gifts, the fruits of her own, honorable labor. Could this be the answer to her prayers? Oh, how she wanted to help her family! They had toiled so hard through the years. Always a struggle; that was their life. *With such a trade I can help them as they grow old. Having no sons, it will be a wonderful blessing.*

"Yes, I would like to become Shiphrah's apprentice!" Puah blurted, then fell into her mother's arms. The thought of being away from her family, all that she'd ever known, almost paralyzed her. But she must be strong. Such an opportunity might never come again. It would enable her to give back to her parents. She looked down at her mother's dry, worn hands, her coarse garments, and vowed silently that if God allowed, she would see her parents resting comfortably in their old age.

"Good! We'll notify Shiphrah immediately and make final arrangements." Rising swiftly, Amiel turned to leave, then seeming to have second thoughts he reached for Puah's hand and pulled her into his arms. He hugged her tightly, clutching her as if to never let go. Puah inhaled, trying to memorize the distinct scent of her father. She allowed the gentle roughness of his embrace to seep into her very being, striving to hold it there so she could take it with her. Finally he released her, cleared his throat and spoke.

"I cannot believe my little dove is becoming a woman. I want you to know, Puah, that I have great faith in you. You will make us proud. I've known this since the day your mother presented you to me. When I looked down at your red, screaming face I knew you were no ordinary child. Your mother and I have always known of your dream to be a healer. Even as a small child you ran to comfort the injured while other children fled at the sight of blood. Like our God, we want you to have the desires of your heart. You have our deepest blessing in your holy calling. Our prayers will ever be with you."

Puah gazed up into her father's watery eyes. She sensed his pain in letting her go, and for the first time in her life realized the true cost of love.

She couldn't stop her lips from trembling

as she spoke. "I'll make you proud, Papa." With more courage than she felt, she reassured her father. "And I promise not to pout when the time comes for my betrothal. I know you and Mama will find me a kind and gentle husband."

Amiel smiled, his eyes beaming. "Yes, daughter, I know you'll make us proud." He turned to Behira. "We must make preparations. Send one of Namir's boys to Shiphrah's home with the news. Today, our daughter becomes a midwife of the Hebrew people."

"And did you study hard, Grandma´ma?" Hannah asked after securing the tent flap against the chilling wind that drove sand into every crease and crevice. The children waited quietly. When Puah didn't answer right away, Hannah's ebony eyes widened in alarm.

"Are you not feeling well, Grandma´ma?" She held Puah's gaze, watching and waiting for an answer. The child licked her lips, still powdered from playing in the desert dust.

Puah dared not tell anyone of the pain coming more frequently these days. Like a beast of burden it sat on her chest, causing pain and shortness of breath. The herbs no longer eased it as they should. Hannah, the bright seed who spent much time with her, knew her well and suspected something wasn't right. Yet, how could she tell the child the truth?

"Yes, my child, I'm fine. To answer your question, it was indeed a very busy four years." Puah struggled to hide the evidence of pain from her face. "Now if you please, would you bring me water?"

"Oh, yes, Grandma´ma. I'll hurry. I want to hear the rest of your story."

II

Set me as a seal upon your heart, as a seal upon your arm; for love is as strong as death . . . (Song of Solomon 8:6)

(ITJ-TAWY, FOUR YEARS LATER)

A messenger delivered news of Aunt Etana's impending delivery just as Puah dressed for the day, sliding into her new linen sheath. She still loved the feel of fine linen and favored this dress in particular with its graceful pleats that fell from her shoulders, caressing her ankles. The soft leather sandals on her feet were likewise new. Sometimes she pinched herself just to be sure it was not all a dream. *This* was the reward of her work. There had been other purchases, but she sent most of the remunerations to her parents. The gold and silver would be saved to buy a home for her family; perhaps, someday, even one for herself and her future husband.

Someday? More likely it would be soon. Her parents' patience with her finicky ways was nearing an end. Her father wanted her wed before the eligible and desirable men all married. Amiel would announce his last offer forthwith if she didn't soon agree to a suitable spouse. Yet during Puah's four years in Itj-tawy, no one had appeared who moved her heart to sing.

From time to time Shiphrah also introduced her to eligible men. Puah tried hard to like them. Indeed, several she found favorable, enjoying their company and lively conversation. But she couldn't imagine spending a lifetime with any of them. Torn between a desire to please her parents, but still listening to her heart, there seemed to be no suitable resolution.

This much she knew — if she didn't decide soon, she may well wake up one morning married, and to a man she didn't desire.

With a servant's assistance, Puah completed her toilet, dressed, and rushed to start the day. She uttered a prayer leaving her sleeping chamber, the same supplication she offered each morning before work.

LORD, please guide my hands and my mind as I attend to Your little ones. Keep Your merciful hand of safety on mother and child.

After gulping a quick breakfast of goat

milk and fruit, she rushed out the door.

Aunt Etana would be anxious. The still-birth of twins four years earlier had deeply scarred her heart. This was the first pregnancy Etana had chanced since the loss, and she'd been unusually apprehensive during her entire confinement.

Puah hurried through the streets of Itjtawy, her medicine bag tucked under her arm. She halted before turning the corner onto the Avenue of Pharaoh to watch a group of men pass. They were headed for the palace gates. She'd seen them before, these builders of the tombs. One she recognized as the son of Heber, the Hebrew stonecutter. And there was Malachi, who made beautifully crafted furniture often inlaid with gold for the royal family. Another of the men caught her attention. Had she met him before? He wore a light shirt of linen and matching kilt. An Egyptian would not have worn a shirt. Modesty was not part of their ways. No, this man's coloring and features were clearly Hebrew.

Puah's chest tightened as she watched him pass. He stood tall and straight as the group marched by. His curly, auburn hair shone like polished cedar in the morning sunlight, and he smiled with an easy grace while talking to one of his companions.

Warmth crept to Puah's face. His eyes flashed as he threw back his head and laughed aloud at something his friend said. The sound of his deep husky voice caused her heart to flutter.

Puah groped for the nearby wall to steady herself. Blood pulsated in her ears. Did he notice her gawking at him like a silly baboon? Her face flushed deep scarlet at the thought.

Her innermost being screamed at his passing. *No! Stop!* She wanted to see him more closely, study the lines of his face, hear the huskiness of his voice, inhale his manly scent. Would his eyes twinkle when he spoke? She wanted to memorize what her senses could only guess at. Something deep within rebelled at his departure. Her heart cried silently for him to wait. *Who is this man?*

The sound of sandals scuffling down the street receded. They were gone. A barking dog competed with the distant murmur of vendors and shoppers to break the stillness of early morning. The aroma of freshly baked bread rode the slight breeze, filling Puah's nostrils and helping break the spell.

She wiped her brow, surprised to find a fine sheen of perspiration there. Never before had she reacted to a man in such a way. Surely it was how the sun illuminated his features or his attire that caused her heart to leap. Perhaps it was the proud yet fluid way he strode that set him apart. She shook her head in bewilderment, then reminded herself she must hurry. She drew in a breath, then released it in a deep sigh, trying to banish the feelings this tall, captivating stranger evoked.

Puah hurried around the corner toward her aunt's house. *Such a handsome man. If Father would betroth me to someone equally handsome, the idea of marriage wouldn't seem so unpleasant.*

The thought brought a sly smile to her face; without doubt it would bring a frown to her mother's face. Her father would probably smile, then scold her with no real conviction in his voice. Nevertheless, in spite of her wishes Puah would be faced with betrothal soon. There was nothing she could do or say to stay it. Already she'd delayed the matter too long.

Later that day Puah reclined in the bathing pool as she talked with Shiphrah. A servant rubbed fragrant oil over the older woman's body. The girl worked silently, massaging with practiced skill while the two women chatted. Shiphrah groaned with pleasure as the girl kneaded away a knot of pain.

"And what is the occasion for this dinner?" Puah asked.

Without warning Shiphrah dismissed the servant. Whatever the older woman wished to discuss would be in private.

"It is prudent we know how the wind blows with Pharaoh. It is said he's not happy, that he grows ever more restless. Some say he blames the Hebrews for his discontent. I say it's because he has more wealth than any man could ever desire, yet finds his heart empty. Anyway, forgive the rambling of an old woman. The dinner is to discuss news from the palace. Don't be naive, Puah. What happens in the king's palace will be felt throughout Egypt."

"Yes, I've also heard rumors about Pharaoh's moodiness. Some say he is unhappy with the progress of his tomb." Puah poured a pitcher of water over her long, dark hair.

"Oh, I almost forgot!" Shiphrah changed the subject. "Etana's delivery? How did it go?"

"It went well. She has a vigorous new son. He looks like his father. He's fat and healthy, but Etana has the swelling poison of pregnancy. I ordered her to stay in bed until I see her tomorrow. Her womb is tired,

Shiphrah. I worked harder than I liked to stop the bleeding after the birth. She shouldn't bear any more children. I worry for her if she conceives again. Perhaps I should ask Father to speak with Uncle Namir."

"Yes, that would be wise. Also, you should talk to Etana about ways to avoid conception. She may not listen, but perhaps she will. Your aunt has always been a practical woman."

Shiphrah began combing her hair. The long, dark tresses now boasted shiny streaks of silver that glimmered in the soft light. Puah watched in quiet admiration. Even in her advancing years she made a striking picture. With serious deliberation Shiphrah placed the comb on the couch, then looked pointedly at Puah.

"One of our guests tonight is an eligible young man of the house of Jacob."

The silence grew, leaving only the sound of water dripping into the tiled bath from the mouth of a stone crocodile.

So, yet another attempt to marry me off. "A young man, did you say? Hmm . . . now let me see, how many is that?" Puah stifled a giggle. How many suitors *had* Shiphrah and her parents invited for dinner or other poorly disguised occasions in the past year?

A score? Two score?

Shiphrah's frown warned that time for serious consideration was at hand. Her next words confirmed it. "Child, if you don't find a spouse soon, you'll be stuck with some dried-up old goat who needs a wife to raise his wild, hateful children. Is *that* what your heart desires?"

Puah watched as Shiphrah retrieved the comb and returned to the task of arranging her hair. The last four years had brought more gray hair to Shiphrah than Puah cared to acknowledge. Nothing harsh rode on the wave of her friend's scolding, just tender concern. The years with Shiphrah had taught her to love the midwife as her own mother, and indeed, she had become a daughter in return. To disappoint Shiphrah would be as painful as disappointing her own flesh and blood.

Puah rose from the water and wrapped a length of soft cotton about her body, then moved to the stone bench and began rubbing fragrant oil into her skin. It smelled of flowers and spice. Would she ever grow accustomed to the luxuries afforded by her new station in life?

"I truly *do* want a husband."

"I should hope so. Else, soon you will be called an old maid."

"Shiphrah, may I speak frankly?" Puah concentrated on the oil. The intimate nature of her question caused her to blush.

"Of course, child, what troubles you?"

"It's just that . . . when I think of . . . well, the more *personal* parts of marriage, I cannot imagine. Is it shameful to dwell on such things?" Again Puah felt the heat of embarrassment rise in her face.

"No, child, it isn't shameful, but perhaps the unknown is getting in the way. Love can grow with time, Puah. For most young women the intimacies of marriage are difficult to imagine. Believe me when I say that I was not the most eager of brides. In fact, I was terrified, but my husband was as gentle as a lamb. I think I fell in love with him that night. Like many things in life, that too, requires time, as well as love and respect for one another. The rest will work itself out."

Shiphrah's eyes glazed with a faraway look of sweet memories. She shook her head and turned away as if hesitant to say more.

"Yes? What, Shiphrah?"

Turning back, Shiphrah smiled. "You know me too well. I was only remembering. Your questions brought back my own memories of being a new bride." Shiphrah caressed Puah's cheek, smiling wistfully as she

51

continued. "When you truly love and are loved in return, there is nothing to fear. It is a gift from God. Does our God give inferior gifts?"

As always, Shiphrah's advice seemed fitting. Puah would just have to trust her wise older friend. Besides, there were no young men in her life she would consider anyway. *Was* she too picky?

"Well, I promise to be on my best behavior tonight for your dinner. That's all I can promise. I'll also be kind to your young man friend. What's his name?"

"His name is Hattush. I trust you will find him pleasant enough." Shiphrah stood and wrapped herself. "I'll see you at dinner." With that, she withdrew to her sleeping chamber. Puah hurriedly completed her own tasks and headed to her private quarters. She dared not be late.

The cold desert wind howled, blowing the flap askew and causing the lamp to flicker. Puah directed little Moriah sitting near the entrance to secure it.

"That's all for tonight, children. This old woman grows weary."

Collective sighs of protest and groans of disappointment filled the tent. Hannah's eyes grew wide. Brushing a sable ringlet from her eyes, she asked, "Did you fall in love with the stranger in the street that day, Grandma´ma?"

Puah could not suppress a smile. "Yes, child, I did."

"But Grandma´ma, from your words . . . you *loved* that stranger! Forgive me, but . . . is that not, um, wrong? Papa says that someday I will marry the man he chooses for me, like a good Hebrew girl. How is it you fell in love with a stranger? Was your father upset? And what of Father Hattush?"

"So many questions!" Puah croaked, her throat dry. She was weary from the day's journey and needed rest. "I will explain tomorrow."

The children began murmuring among themselves at Hannah's questions, looks of shock and confusion on the faces of the older ones.

Oh, *dear!* Puah sensed she must explain herself to clear up this troubling dilemma for the children before the night ended. If not, rumors would fill the camp and fathers of marriageable daughters would be up in arms with the old midwife.

"Quiet, children!" Puah said, above the growing clatter. "Very well, perhaps I should explain further. But first, Sarah, would you bring me water? This old throat is as parched as the desert floor."

After a long drink, Puah laid the gourd aside. "Now children, I'll try to help you understand what really happened to a naive Hebrew girl that day on the streets of Itjtawy."

III

*His mouth is most sweet, yes, he is alto-
gether lovely. This is my beloved, and
this is my friend, O daughters of Jeru-
salem! (Song of Solomon 5:16)*

"This will have to do," Puah mumbled to
herself as she tied the belt. She wore an attractive but discreet dress befitting a good
Hebrew girl. Not too elegant, but certainly
not the attire of a farm girl. Anyway, he was
probably another odd fellow. Would they
ever present a man to her that even closely
made her heart croon? Probably not. Parents
didn't view these matters the same as young
people. She sighed.

Puah slipped on her best sandals. What
would he look like? Guilt washed over her at
the question whirling through her mind.
Not only was it shallow, but she knew it
must displease the LORD. She couldn't help
it, though. Didn't God create the beautiful
flowers? Did He not paint them with a
boundless palette? Surely He understood a

young girl's heart in wanting a comely husband, one that delighted the eyes as well as the heart.

She finished tying the sandal strap encircling her ankle. Standing, she smoothed the lines of her dress, threw her shoulders back and headed for the dining hall. *I'll just have to make the best of this attempt at matchmaking. Perhaps I am doomed to be an old maid.* The thought brought her heart no comfort. At least she had her work. Many of those unfortunate women who didn't find husbands had little to fill the years as they watched others marry. *If I never marry there's still plenty to fill my life, isn't there?*

Puah walked down the long corridor. The aroma of richly spiced lamb, antelope, and quail fresh from the spit met her nostrils. Without doubt, Shiphrah spared no expense for the meal. With so many of the Hebrew community barely able to buy food, whenever Shiphrah was able to feed guests she made sure there was a bounty. Conversation from the dining hall drew ever nearer. A husky voice caught Puah's ear just as she turned the corner into the entryway.

It's him — Pharaoh's craftsman from the street! She froze, her heart seeming to stop with her feet. He sat next to Shiphrah, his deep voice ringing out as he laughed at the older woman's words. Thank the heavens they hadn't yet seen her!

Puah drew back behind the vine-covered screen, trying to memorize his every detail. His tunic, a simple style of fine linen, white and crisp, enhanced the olive gleam of his smooth skin. From behind she realized how powerful his muscled shoulders must be. *Much broader than most.* The thought made her feel vaguely disquieted.

He carried himself with the poise of someone of great self-assurance. Yet a soft humility rang out in the tenor of his voice. The arrogant haughtiness of so many men was missing from hi tongue. Perhaps this one *would* prove interesting to meet.

Well, avoiding him will do no good. He could as likely be a simpleton or bore. Though I must admit, a very nice looking simpleton or bore. Puah wiped the perspiration from her palms, bolstered her courage, and strode confidently into the dining hall.

"Here she is now," Shiphrah said, rising. "Puah, you know our other guests, but you have not met Hattush. Hattush, this is my associate and the daughter of my dearest friend. I would like you to meet Puah, daughter of Amiel of the house of Joseph. Puah, this is Hattush, son of Asa of the house of Jacob."

Hattush rose slowly, using only the power of his thighs to push up from the pillows.

So tall . . . will he never stop rising?

He turned to face the young midwife. Puah gazed into a solid wall of chest. She fought an impulse to avert her eyes, forcing herself to offer a hand which she prayed was not shaking. Slowly her eyes drifted upward to meet Hattush's. Her legs nearly buckled. A thousand tingles coursed through her hand and body at his firm but gentle touch.

Puah stared into the face of her dreams. Could this visage be God's answer to her many prayers? Her tongue was paralyzed, lips refused to move. She knew she must acknowledge the introduction but felt helpless to act. She could only stare into these hypnotic eyes of amber where tiny flecks of obsidian danced. Eyes that seemed to pierce into the secret depths of her very soul.

"It's my pleasure to make your acquaintance, Puah. May I assist you?" He dipped his head, indicating the soft pillows at their feet. His eyes tarried on the attractive young midwife, as though afraid she would disappear if he took them from her.

Still unable to do more than nod like a mute, Puah allowed him to guide her to a place beside him. As he lowered her with a strong arm, she caught the clean scent of sandalwood. She closed her eyes and inhaled deeply. *He even smells wonderful. How will I ever get through this dinner?*

Puah felt like a young girl still in the shadows of her mother's robes. *Of all the suitors through the years, only this one makes my knees feel like the mud of the Nile. His presence causes my heart to leap like the gazelle!*

When Puah looked up, feeling at last in command of her emotions, she saw Shiphrah biting her lower lip in surreptitious amusement. The gleam in her friend's eyes reflected the delight of what she observed in Puah's reaction to the handsome young man.

Puah blushed. She felt confused, out of control, like the rising river during spring floods. Nothing could stop the flow, nothing could hold back the powerful surge that threatened to overwhelm her in the presence of this man, this beautiful man.

The conversation during the feast indeed centered on the growing concern over Pharaoh's increasing hatred for the Hebrews. Rumors abounded that Pharaoh feared the Hebrews grew too strong, that they would rise up and rebel against Egypt. Hattush had heard of it for weeks now. Of late,

Sennerfer, Pharaoh's vizier, pressed the artisans sorely to hurry their work on the tomb, but one could only work so fast. After that, the quality of work suffered, and Pharaoh demanded only the very best. Given Pharaoh's current temperament, presenting less than flawless work was dangerous, especially if you were Hebrew.

"It's the Egyptian priests who create the rumors," Ethan, the carpenter, proclaimed. "They try to intimidate us. They'll never rest until we forsake the One True God and worship their graven images. I'll *never* bow to a crocodile statue!" He stuffed a morsel of roasted antelope into his mouth.

Ivara, wife of Heber, the stonecutter, always offered the voice of reason. "Perhaps Ethan is right, but I hear Pharaoh is nearly mad in his obsession to see his tomb completed. It was the same with the palace. Once he sets his mind on a project, he won't rest, or allow anyone else to rest, until it's completed. Since many of the artisans are Hebrew, it's convenient to blame us."

"Hattush, you work closely with the vizier," said Shiphrah, "what do you hear? Where do these rumors originate?" Shiphrah looked at Hattush as she sipped wine, concern of the rumors circulating Itjtawy evident in her eyes.

Hattush found it difficult to concentrate on such matters with Puah sitting beside him. She reminded him of a delicate flower. He found it necessary to force himself not to stare. Shiphrah hadn't warned him of her beauty, only that she wished him to meet her associate, an eligible maiden of good family. She had spoken of the parents' failure at finding her a suitable spouse. He truly expected a maiden far less comely. It seemed the girl was not only beautiful, but also of ardent will and independent mind. Strong in spirit — that pleased him.

Puah had spoken but a handful of words since he helped her to her seat, talking only when addressed. Only then did he hear the music of her voice, a sound that fell on his ears with easy grace, causing him to hunger for more. A midwife; she must be intelligent, so it surprised him that she didn't actively participate in the lively dinner discussion.

Even now she sat quietly, hands clasped in lap, occasionally placing a small morsel of food in her mouth. She seemed as nervous as a mouse chased by a cat. Hattush watched her from the corner of his eye, trying to memorize her loveliness. She wore her long hair in a simple braid down her back. He thought of how it would look loosened and free. The sleeves of her linen sheath fell near her wrists, and her only adornment, a girdle of colorful beads, drew in the soft fabric to outline the slim contour of her waist.

Her eyes were black and shiny as the rich ebony of Nubia. Feathery lashes adorned them. He could lose himself in those hypnotic spheres. They caused his chest to tighten each time he glanced at her. Nothing however, captured his attention like her lips. He could spend the rest of his lifetime and never again see the perfection of her fully sculpted mouth. Yet even as he admired her physical beauty, he felt drawn to something more, something almost indefinable. No princess of Egypt could compare with the beauty that glowed from within this woman.

Hattush shook off the new path his thoughts were taking and rejoined the conversation by answering Shiphrah's question.

"I have heard many rumors, but my work keeps me busy. It may be true that Pharaoh fears an uprising. I do know he rages at the workers to complete his tomb. Perhaps he fears he's near death. I don't know. I have a meeting with the vizier tomorrow about the next project for the tomb. Now it seems

Pharaoh wishes a golden throne to take with him into the afterlife. I'll try to find out more. Sennerfer is a man of reason. Truly, I wouldn't want to be in his position of trying to keep Khaneferre pleased."

Hattush wet his mouth with a sip of water. "If anything, the rumors are consistent. Some say he's mad. Others say he's vexed by fears of death. He suffers from head-aches, so says one of the palace slaves. I do know Pharaoh is a very unhappy man. We must all pray for him. Be assured of one thing, however. As long as Khaneferre is un-happy, all Egypt will be unhappy."

The conversation continued, but Hattush's thoughts didn't dwell on the rising unrest and instability in the palace. His introspection kept returning to the beautiful maiden by his side.

Hattush also felt pressure from his family to marry. He could surely understand how Puah must feel. His family presented many young women to him, but none had caused his heart to race like the cheetah, until now.

Later, as the guests excused themselves, Puah stood at Shiphrah's side, cordially bidding each goodnight. Only Hattush re-mained, at Shiphrah's request. She wished to discuss something with him in private.

"Hattush, thank you for coming. It was a

pleasure to meet you," Puah declared in a rehearsed, nervous announcement. She stared at her feet, shyly avoiding his eyes.

Did this demure beauty possibly share what *he* was feeling? Dare he think such? Hattush gathered his courage. "I'm very thankful to Shiphrah for the invitation. The food was, of course, delicious, and the conversation intriguing." He cleared his throat, fighting the lump rising in his throat. "But the company was exquisite." He realized his forwardness, but something drew him to her as nothing he'd ever known before.

Puah felt herself blushing even as her heart soared. "I, too, found the company most enjoyable," she said when she found her voice. "I bid you goodnight." After hugging Shiphrah goodnight, Puah hurried away.

Hattush watched until she disappeared, still trying to forge the memory of every detail into his mind. *Is this what other men mean when they speak of falling in love?* He wasn't sure if this was love, but he knew that if it were possible, he'd never let her out of his sight.

"She is beautiful, isn't she?" Shiphrah's words dragged Hattush back to present company, causing the heat of embarrassment to rise at being caught staring so

64

openly at her young charge.

"Beautiful? Much more than that. She's divine! Tell me, Shiphrah, is she always so quiet?"

A chuckle escaped Shiphrah's mouth. "No, I've never known her to be this quiet. I suspect she's as much in awe of you as you are of her. How far do I miss the mark, my young friend?"

"I admit, I'm taken by her. Do you suppose she'd be interested in getting to know me better?"

Shiphrah sighed, gazing at the stars twinkling through the open windows. "Puah is a headstrong young woman. She knows what she wants, and I have no doubt that when the right man comes along she'll make her desires clear. Would you like to talk with her more? If so, she often sits in the garden before retiring. You may find her there. I'd like to refresh myself. I'll join you before it becomes unseemly."

Hattush nodded and began walking toward the door that led to the garden.

"Hattush."

"Yes?"

"Puah is like a daughter to me. She is a godly woman and she deserves a husband of the highest order. I do not want her hurt. I'll say no more."

Again Hattush nodded, then turned and headed for the garden.

The alabaster glow of oil lamps cast wavering light across the pool's surface. Puah lay stretched upon her stomach beside the pool. Lost deep in her own thoughts, she swirled a fig leaf back and forth through the water.

Hattush didn't see Puah until he was almost upon her. "Puah?"

Puah gasped and scrambled to rise. As she did, her foot caught the hem of her sheath, causing her to sway precariously close to the pool's edge.

"Careful!" Hattush rushed to help, securing Puah's elbow safely in his grasp while she recovered her balance. Nervously she straightened her raiment.

"I'm sorry I startled you," said Hattush, regretting catching her unaware, "but I wanted to talk with you. Shiphrah suggested I might find you here."

Puah cleared her throat, then turned from him to take a seat on the garden bench overlooking the pool. With restless energy she swept back a stray lock from her eyes.

"Yes, you did startle me," she said, finding her voice. "I didn't expect to see anyone else here." A giggle escaped her. "Thank you for preventing my tumble into the pool."

"May I?" Hattush pointed to the bench.

"Oh . . . forgive my manners. Yes, please."

Hattush sat next to her, turning his body slightly to see her better in the soft lamplight.

"So, you're a midwife. Tell me about it. Do you enjoy your calling?"

Like a moth emerging from its cocoon, Puah came alive, eyes shining and face aglow.

"Oh, Hattush, it is *wonderful!* There are no words to describe the joy of hearing the first cry of a new life."

Hattush watched as Puah's delicate hands moved through the air, conveying the excitement she felt.

"And the babies — they're so amazing! Why, even their tiny nails are perfectly formed."

Suddenly aware of talking with more zest than a young woman should exhibit, Puah dropped her hands to her lap, took a deep breath and said as daintily as possible, "And you are a goldsmith?"

Hattush smiled warmly and nodded.

"Tell me, what is it like to work on the royal tomb? Don't you feel sad for Khaneferre? To worship statues of stone and wood, hoping to find eternity by storing up worldly goods for the afterlife — is that not reason for pity?"

Hattush was taken aback at the young midwife's words. How often in the three years of laboring for Pharaoh had he voiced the same question to himself? How often had he sighed at the senselessness of making things that would be sealed with Pharaoh's mummy for eternity, turning to dust while his soul knew not the Holy One.

"You read my mind. Yes, I *do* feel sorry for him. Like all men, he'll die and his soul will face judgment. If only the Egyptians could see the maat, the truth of One True God. So quickly have they forgotten the blessings brought by Father Joseph's faith and obedience to our LORD."

They both fell silent. Hattush aimlessly tossed a leaf upon the dark shimmering pool and began his own study of the water, content to listen to the night sounds and inhale the fragrance of Puah's soft flowery scent. He dared not speak his heart to the girl for fear he would scare her as surely as the jackal startles the grazing sheep along the riverbank. Oh, how he wanted to pour his heart out, to tell this comely young woman of the effect she had on him!

After several moments, Hattush spoke. "I should be going." Rising, he assisted Puah to her feet. For a moment he hesitated, holding her hand, wishing he didn't have to say goodnight.

Still, the young midwife remained maddeningly quiet. *If only I could read her thoughts! Does her heart soar as mine? Does she feel the same sense of wonderment as I?* Sandals tapping on tile interrupted Hattush's thoughts. Shiphrah approached.

"Yes, it's late. Goodnight, Hattush," Puah said, a tentative smile brightening her face.

Hattush felt his heart swell. Then, as Puah gently slid her hand from his, he sensed a part of him had been removed. Too quickly she was gone, the soft rhythm of sandals the only sound as she disappeared deep into the house.

"Well, young man, what do you think of my charming protégé?" Shiphrah asked.

Without taking his eyes from where Puah had vanished, Hattush spoke. "Do you suppose her parents would find me a suitable spouse?" Never one to mince words, he knew he must not delay voicing interest in the girl.

Shiphrah squeezed his arm. "I'll speak with her parents. You cannot know how delighted I am to see her interest in you. Her parents and I have worked unceasingly to find someone suitable. But Puah always says 'He does not make my heart sing.' "

Hattush couldn't help laughing, its echo ringing in the quiet of the garden. He'd told himself the same thing through the years. Indeed, none of the maidens made *his* heart sing either — until now. At this moment his heart rang with the music of celebration. He had found her, the love of his dreams! *Dear LORD, let her heart be singing, too.*

"Did you know Grandfather Hattush loved you that night?"

Puah listened to soft sounds of the camp settling for the night. Weariness covered her like a cloak. In the softness of the tent's lamplight, dozens of small, eager faces fixed their eyes upon her.

The old woman smiled, her weathered face seeming to grow suddenly younger at the thought. "No, child, I could only hope. And pray! I think I loved him from the first instant I saw him on the streets of Itj-tawy."

She sighed deeply. "But this old woman must rest now, so *shoo!* We'll continue the story tomorrow night."

With obedient reluctance they filed out, leaving only Hannah behind.

"I love you, Grandma´ma." Hannah

hugged Puah with gentle fierceness.

"Oh, my flower, and I love you. See the sky outside? My love for you is bigger than that!"

Wonder filled Hannah's eyes as she stared beyond the tent flap at countless dancing stars in the clear desert sky. She pulled her hands together and clasped them to her breast as if to protect a treasure, then flashing Puah her most brilliant smile, she ran out into the night.

IV

Hate evil, love good; establish justice in the gate. It may be that the LORD God of hosts will be gracious to the remnant of Joseph. (Amos 5:15)

Sennerfer, trusted and most esteemed vizier to Khaneferre Sobekhotep IV, ruler of Upper and Lower Egypt, sat patiently while attendants dressed his wig. At nearly fourscore years he no longer needed to shave his head to accommodate the odious thing. With each passing year it became more difficult to hide his repugnance for the ostentatious whims of royal fashion. Certainly, with shaven heads, fabric linings kept you cooler, much more so than one's own hair in ever-present heat, but since he'd lost most of his own hair years ago it seemed senseless. Still, he must maintain the image to maintain power. Without his voice of reason, Sennerfer feared Egypt would be destroyed.

He'd been at Pharaoh's side more years than he cared to remember, but the past few months revealed an intensification of irrational ideas making their way into Khaneferre's head. Pharaoh's obsession with the completion of his tomb overshadowed even the weightiest concerns of state. Attacks by Nubian forces at the borders of the Upper Kingdom didn't seem to disturb him, but the wrong paint color on a wall in his burial chamber sent him into a raging frenzy.

The previous day Sennerfer had bid the royal family farewell. A hunting party would keep Pharaoh out of his way while he tried to find a means of bringing the project to a timely completion. This morning Sennerfer planned to meet privately with the tomb's artisans. Perhaps then Khaneferre would settle down and attend to the grave matters of ruling a kingdom.

Pharaoh's rants about the tomb were the least of Sennerfer's concerns. The king's rising hostility toward the Hebrews caused a cold wind to pass through the aged vizier's soul. He had invested much of his life trying to protect his mother's people from harm. To blunder now would be tragic for all Egypt. Somehow, he must appease Pharaoh without seeming overly charitable to the Hebrews. He must move carefully.

Anyone who might possibly know of

Sennerfer's true parentage was long dead. The knowledge of his Hebrew blood was tucked safely inside his heart and mind. Now he worked hard to keep the secret as a sense of duty to his own people.

Sennerfer never knew his mother. Raped by an Egyptian overseer, the young maiden was forced into hiding. Ashamed to return to her own village, a kindly Egyptian couple took her in. She worked for them as a servant until giving birth. Soon afterward, the despondent young mother swallowed poison, leaving the infant to be raised as an Egyptian. The new parents were warm and loving, and provided well.

Heeding a solemn promise, Sennerfer's parents told him of his mother's true identity when he reached manhood.

As a young man, anger drove Sennerfer. Debating the power of the gods with Hebrew elders, he vowed allegiance to Amun. In private, he searched for his own truth, his own maat. Amun's stony silence did not bring flowing peace to Sennerfer's heart. The unseen God of Israel answered his silent, earnest prayers. Only in the quiet of his sleeping chamber did he pray to the God of his mother, the Holy One of Israel.

Holding this secret close to his heart, Sennerfer eventually rose to the position of chief priest of Amun at Thebes. Whether whispered in the darkness of his sleeping chamber, under the stars on a rooftop, or listening to papyri rustle in the wind along the shore of the Nile River, the God of Abraham heard *and* answered his prayers. He spoke peace to Sennerfer's heart and gave him a calling. One night as the priest walked in silence along the banks of the Nile, a star blazed across the heavens, lighting the eastern horizon with a thousand brilliant lamps. Sennerfer fell to his knees as the LORD spoke to him, commanding him to save His people.

Sennerfer struggled with this double life. One open, public, and altogether false; the other secret, true, and holy to the dictates of his heart. Thus far he'd avoided any compromise of conscience, but he feared Khaneferre's disdain for the Hebrews would someday require him to make a choice, a choice that would cost him his life.

Sennerfer realized Khaneferre did not hate the Hebrews as much as he feared them. Any ruler worth his weight in salt knew that a unified, loyal people were a worthy opponent. Joseph's remnant were not only unified by their unwavering faith, they were separated by their beliefs. They lived apart from the Egyptians, their self-worth manifested in their lives and dealings with others. Sennerfer knew well the power behind them. One far stronger and more powerful than Khaneferre, ruler over Upper and Lower Egypt.

"Hattush, it is a pleasure to see you again. Now that the others are gone, we can talk in private. I would like to discuss some things with you. Please, be seated."

Hattush bowed, then seated himself on the bench near Sennerfer's elaborate chair tooled in gold leaf and displaying delicate renderings of lotus blossoms. Sennerfer clapped sharply.

A serving girl quickly appeared with a cup of wine, then bowed and hurriedly disappeared. For that, Hattush was grateful. Although raised in Egypt, he still fought the impulse to blush at the nakedness of slaves in the royal palace. Usually dressed in nothing more than a narrow girdle, they lacked the modesty imparted to Hebrew women from childhood.

"Tell me my friend, how is your work progressing?" Sennerfer studied Hattush closely with wary eyes.

Hattush's throat tightened. Today no hint of amusement lit the vizier's ebony eyes. He girded himself. Whatever weighty matter Sennerfer deemed compelling enough to summon him to the palace must be important indeed.

"The work moves along. As you know, my lord, each major change slows our progress. Also, each time we lose a laborer to the taskmaster's whip, we must train another to take his place. Do you anticipate any further changes or additions that Pharaoh desires?"

"That, I cannot answer, Hattush. Who can speak for Pharaoh? Is he not the god-king of the mightiest nation known?"

Did Hattush discern a hint of sarcasm at his reference to Pharaoh's title? The old vizier rose slowly from his seat, using a staff to support his deliberate, creaking movements. His wrinkled bronze hand gripped the top of the staff shaped as the head of an adder, hiding its eyes of ruby.

"Come, let us walk in the garden. The heat of the day already oppresses my spirit."

Hattush offered his arm. He felt no surprise when Sennerfer accepted the unspoken assistance. There was much about Sennerfer that reminded him of his aging grandfather. In spite of being Egyptian, something about the old vizier fostered a feeling of trust.

Reaching the quiet coolness of the palace garden, Sennerfer lowered himself onto a cushioned bench, then bade Hattush join him. The musical warbling of tiny birds flitting among the treetops drew a smile from the old man, causing a fine labyrinth of wrinkles to appear. He inhaled deeply, the garden's lush perfume teasing his nostrils.

"We can talk freely here. The walls inside the palace conceal many ears. Do not be deceived, Hattush, even *I* am dispensable. Times grow perilous, I will not mislead you. Pharaoh blames the Hebrews for the slothfulness of the tomb's work."

"But —"

The vizier's upraised hand silenced Hattush's protest.

"Listen, my young friend, I *know* the truth. You do not have to explain to me. But our problem is Pharaoh's perception. How can I put this delicately?" He glanced around to assure their privacy.

"Pharaoh does not think clearly at times," Sennerfer continued quietly. "Blaming the Hebrews for the tomb's delay is but one sign of his increasing, shall I say, delusion. Nothing I offer changes his mind. I can only try to assist you and the others in seeing the tomb is completed as quickly as possible. What can I do to help you? Tell me what you need."

For a moment Hattush sat stunned. Had

he heard the vizier actually imply that Pharaoh was going mad? Were the rumors true after all? Quickly he gathered his thoughts.

"I'll need more goldsmiths. They can work on the smaller tasks as I supervise. That will free me for the more important tasks and shorten the completion time for my projects.

"But quite frankly, my lord, the delays are caused because each time we complete a project, Pharaoh insists it be changed. As hard as we try, there seems to be no pleasing him."

"In that, you are correct, my young friend. We will not be able to please him on every issue, but we must work together to get this project finished according to his decrees. Then perhaps all might know some peace."

Sennerfer rose slowly, as though the weight of the ages lay upon his wizened shoulders. Again Hattush offered his arm for support. Walking toward the palace, Sennerfer left him with a final thought.

"Truly, Hattush, I know not what each new day will bring in the palace. Be assured of this — I desire peace for Egypt. It is my home. I was born here and I will die here. We cannot defend our borders if we are fighting within. I have heard the stories of how the Hebrew Joseph saved our land. It seems many of our people have chosen to forget. *That,* I cannot change. What I can do — *must* do, is try to arbitrate and keep peace. If I fail, you must know it was not my choice. I will defend your people to the end."

With that, the meeting ended. Hattush knew the vizier's concern for the Hebrews would not undermine his ultimate fealty to Pharaoh. Of course, no one possessed the luxury of choice. To usurp the king's authority or question his judgments would mean certain death, perhaps even for his lifelong advisor. Apprehension gripped Hattush's chest. Instead of being reassured by the aged vizier's words, his sense of foreboding grew.

Puah sat under the awning of her tent. She watched Daphne bathe Hannah, whose happy squeals joined other children's voices ringing across the sheltered confines of the oasis. Elim, with its twelve springs and abundant palms, was heaven after the disappointment at Marah three days earlier. Still, here at this paradise, the vast Desert of Shur encircled them, an ever-present reminder of what they yet faced.

Perhaps the water will cool the fretful dis-

position of my people. Days of marching in unforgiving desert sun had taken its toll on the Hebrews. The confrontation at Marah had been inevitable. What had Moses expected? Upon arriving at the watering spot, bad news spread quickly.

"It's bitter! The Egyptians give sweeter water to their animals!"

"This water isn't fit to drink! Why would Moses lead us to such a place?"

"At least we had decent food and drink in Egypt. We should leave this foul wilderness and return!"

Soon an angry rumble reverberated across the desert as word traveled throughout the twelve tribes. The water wasn't fit to drink. After days of suffering, rationing precious drops of water, listening to fretful, whining children and braying animals, the water was so bitter as to be unpalatable.

Finally Moses grew tired of it all. At the spring's edge he cried out, "Holy God, hear your people's cry!" Uprooting a sapling, he cast it upon the water. He turned to face the anxious crowd.

"If you people will follow God's voice and do right, God will keep you free from the diseases that plague the Egyptians. For The Holy One says to you, 'I am the LORD,

Who heals you.' " Then he walked away.

A few at the crowd's edge approached the pool uneasily, filling their water skins and jugs. Soon new rumors rolled through the camp, but this time of a different order altogether.

"It's sweet!"

"A miracle! God be blessed!"

"This water is pure as nectar!"

God had touched the water, making it sweet, yet Puah knew that God's palate had not been so honeyed by the constant complaining of His children. *Why must man be this way, always contentious and unappreciative?*

Now, under the silky sway of date-laden palms at Elim, Puah rested and watched the women bathe. Beyond Hannah and Daphne, other women dipped, reveling in the cool, refreshing water, washing themselves and their children, scrubbing away days of grit and dust. Laughter and giggles filled the air. The women hadn't known such luxury since leaving Egypt.

Later, as the children gathered for the nightly story, Hannah voiced what the others wanted to know. "Grandma´ma, why did God send us to bitter water at Marah?"

Puah looked upon the freshly scrubbed faces and selected her words carefully. "Do you remember our story last night? How Grandfather Hattush was given news he didn't want to hear about Pharaoh's increasing madness?"

Most of the children nodded.

"Being given a nice gift after receiving something bitter makes the nice gift even sweeter, doesn't it?" Puah raised a gnarled hand and pointed through the tent's open door to the pool shimmering with moonlight.

For a moment puzzlement covered the children's faces. Then one by one, enlightenment brought smiles.

"Yes, you see, don't you? My little ones, it's only after the bitter water that we can truly appreciate the good, sweet gifts of life. Our Heavenly Father knew this. He's always known this thing. In life, we receive bitter as well as sweet. But after the hard lessons, the good gifts are oh, so much sweeter on our tongue."

Contentment warmed Puah's heart as she watched the children's faces glow with bright eyes and wide smiles. *Sometimes it seems the little ones understand God's lessons far better than their elders. If only everyone had such innocent expectation of the Holy One's plan for them. . . .*

V

You have ravished my heart, my sister, my spouse; you have ravished my heart with one look of your eyes, with one link of your necklace. (Song of Solomon 4:9)

"Finally, I shall have grandchildren — God be praised!" Hattush smiled, remembering his mother's parting words as he left their home earlier in the evening. With some degree of boyish reticence he'd spoken to his parents about Puah and his ardent feelings for her. He worried they might question his choice for a bride, but his mother's words dispelled all fear.

"My son, I've heard she may be headstrong, but she is bright and very pretty. More importantly, she's not a child. The young midwife knows what she wants, and if she accepts the offer, you'll have a wife who will bring you much joy instead of tears."

"Your mother is right," Asa, his father, added. "Younger brides are often unready for marriage in many ways. Your chosen is mature and wise. She'll make a good mother for our grandsons. I'll be honored to assist you with the bride's price, my son." With that, Asa heartily slapped him on the back and poured everyone a goblet of wine.

Now Hattush walked tentatively toward Shiphrah's home. The boldness brought by his parents' excited approval quickly wasted away to nervous quivers deep in his bowels. How would he approach Puah? Would words fail him? Could he tell her what he really felt in her presence? What if she favored another?

Hattush stopped on the dusty back street. He smelled the rich fragrance of meat rubbed generously with garlic and herbs roasting on cooking fires. A child giggled behind a wall. He took a deep breath and looked up at the stars, trying to calm himself. Without realizing, he'd allowed his heart to overtake him. When he thought of Puah's warm brown eyes, his objectivity flew out the window like a finch freed from its cage.

LORD, I do not want to be selfish and marry wrongly. If Puah is truly the one chosen for me, please send a message of confirmation. Above all else, I desire to please You.

The simple prayer, whispered to the twinkling night sky, released the coil of tension threatening to send his poorly settled dinner into chaos. Hattush knew the longer he delayed his quest for Puah's hand, the greater his unrest would become. So, lifting his chin and straightening his shoulders, he continued toward the moment of truth.

A young servant promptly answered Hattush's knock and led him to one of the cool rooms that fronted the garden. Surveying the surroundings, he realized his fingers worried nervously with the tassels of his leather girdle. He forced himself to still his hands, then took a deep breath and was instantly rewarded by the floral scent of Shiphrah's garden. The sweet pungence brought Puah's smiling face to memory. Somehow the vision calmed him and he felt a smile play across his mouth.

"Well, you seem very happy tonight," Shiphrah said, gliding into the room, then staying Hattush's attempt to rise, sat opposite him on the cushioned divan amid a generous collection of bright pillows. "What brings such a smile to your face?" she asked, settling herself.

"Shiphrah, I've come to a decision. I wish to offer a bride's price for Puah."

"I see." Delighted amusement shone in

Shiphrah's eyes. "But what brings you *here?* Shouldn't you be talking to her father?" Her face remained stoic.

"I would like to speak with Puah first. I tell you true, Shiphrah. She takes my heart, but I'll not have her unless she desires me as I desire her. I want my marriage to be a blessing, not a curse. To me, an unhappy bride would be as near a curse on a man as I can imagine."

"Ah. So you come here to find out what is hidden in her heart. How do you propose to do that?"

Hattush shrugged. "I don't know. I don't wish to frighten her, but I believe I must let her know how I feel."

"And you are right." Shiphrah rose slowly with Hattush's assistance. Turning to face him, she reached out and touched his cheek. "I'm delighted, my young friend. You'll make a wonderful husband for Puah, because you put *her* heart first. You will have a long and happy marriage."

Hattush cleared his throat. "Shiphrah, how . . . do I ask? I feel like a hapless boy."

"Tell her what is in your heart, Hattush. She would have to be made of stone not to be warmed by your honesty and concern for her feelings. And since Puah is definitely not made of stone, I suspect your worries are for nothing. I'll send her to the garden."

Shiphrah smiled and placed a hand upon the goldsmith's strong forearm. "You won't have to tell me how it goes. Knowing Puah as I do, she'll surely inform me immediately. I will pray, but truly I believe in my heart this is already an answer to prayer. Goodnight, my friend."

Hattush stood with lead feet, his mind awhirl. As Shiphrah's footsteps echoed down the tiled hall, he willed his feet to obey the command to walk. Swallowing his fear, he entered the cool sanctuary of the garden to await Puah.

When Shiphrah announced Hattush's visit, Puah repressed the desire to run full gallop to the garden. Instead, with great resolve and deliberation, she slowed her steps. As she approached the garden, her heart's pounding increased until it seemed a roar in her ears. She knew her hands trembled. As the garden came into view, Puah stopped, breathing deeply to calm herself.

Hattush stood at the pool's edge gazing at the evening sky. Puah thought she'd never seen such a lovely man. He seemed a statue, straight and tall. Yet there was nothing cold or lifeless in the glow of his smile or in the way his amber eyes settled on her face. The night suddenly grew warmer as she moved closer to the source of heat.

"Hattush, what a pleasant surprise." She steadied her voice by speaking slowly.

For a moment Hattush was silent, speaking only with his eyes, their message causing her to inhale sharply. She could only stare back at him as the pools of liquid fire burned a hole into her heart.

"Puah, you are more beautiful than I remembered." The husky tightness of the voice hinted at his nervousness. The casualness present at their first meeting was gone, replaced with a weighty undercurrent of emotion.

Puah felt the warmth of a blush rise to her cheeks. Finally she managed to find her own voice. "Forgive my poor manners. Please, have a seat." Motioning to the bench, Puah led the way. She sat, hoping her quaking knees didn't betray her.

"What brings you here?" A most ordinary question, but tonight it was loaded with allusion. Did he hear the galloping of her heart, like the horses of Pharaoh's chariots? Or detect the heat rising within her?

Taking a seat beside her, Hattush gazed at the stars mirrored in the pool. "Puah, I've come to tell you something." Having said that much he rose, and with hands locked behind his back, walked to the pool and stared at his own reflection.

Turning, he said, "All my life I believed that someday I would marry. But I've never found anyone who made my heart soar like the falcon. For one reason or another, the young women my family and well-meaning friends have introduced have not appealed to me."

A sob locked in Puah's throat. She wanted to cover her ears. He didn't feel the same as she! He was here to tell her he wasn't interested, to dispel any notion for marriage she might hold. She fought back welling tears, steeling her heart for the bitter words to follow.

At least she would know *this;* she would know the rush of joy that flooded her heart in his presence. But would she ever be able to give herself to another? Would Hattush always be in the back of her mind, tempting her heart's loyalty?

Slowly Hattush approached the bench, then reached for Puah's hand. Gently, he pulled her to stand before him. She felt dizzy and ill being this close to him, so out of control. His scent was of leather and spice. The warmth of his strong, broad hand covering hers sent waves tingling up her arm. She felt as if she were close to collapsing.

Hattush was speaking, but she couldn't

hear the words for the blood pounding in her temples. She turned her face and dabbed at a tear with her free hand.

What did he say? "What . . . what did you say?"

Hattush held tightly to her hand, drinking in her beauty. "I said, until you, no one has caused my heart to soar. You make me feel like the eagle, strong and boundless."

He hesitated a moment, then placed a finger lightly below her chin, lifting her face until their eyes met. "Puah, would you allow me to offer the bride's price for your hand? Would you make my heart complete by becoming my bride?"

Puah trembled, her knees nearly buckling. Her lips quivered, she couldn't find her voice. *He asked me to be his bride! Oh, LORD, he truly did! You have heard my cry and answered my prayer. He wants me for his bride. Thank You, my LORD, thank You! Oh, how my heart praises You!*

"I suppose you wonder why I came to you first, and not your parents," Hattush said, not knowing if he had offended the young midwife by his forwardness. He'd gone too far to back away now. Mustering his courage, he continued. "The answer is a simple one. When I take a wife, I want her to desire me as I desire her. I want to be the husband of her heart, not of a marriage contract."

Tears flowed freely from Puah's eyes. Hattush's honesty unraveled her heart. *Please God, let me find my tongue, let me speak to his heart!*

Rapture poured over her. She smiled up at Hattush's nervous face. Involuntarily her hand crept up to smooth away the tension lines on his bronze face, to brush away the erring curl of hair from his forehead. New tears of humble gratitude mixed with girlish excitement gathered in her eyes, and for a moment his form swam before her in the pale lamplight. Drawing all her strength, she placed the palms of her hands on the broad expanse of his chest and met his eyes.

"I would consider it a great honor and joy to be your wife, Hattush, son of Abraham. For you see, like you, no one else has ever made my heart sing. Now I know it will sing forever."

One moment she watched glorious surprise cross his face, the next she was pulled into the shelter of his warm, strong embrace. As his lips covered hers, the last thing she saw before she surrendered to the heaven of his kiss was the twinkle of a lone star. Brighter than all others, it smiled down at her, daughter of Abraham.

VI

Many waters cannot quench love, nor can the floods drown it. (Song of Solomon 8:7)

"Stand still, child. I cannot adorn your hair to please your husband while you fidget so. He will be here soon!"

"Yes, Mama, and that's why we must hurry. Besides, I know Hattush. He doesn't care about those silly baubles; he told me so himself."

"Well, I care! I won't have you going to your husband's home half-dressed."

Puah sighed and surrendered to her mother's determined efforts. What did it matter anyway? The veil would hide it. At least she'd been able to convince them to allow her wedding dress to be made of soft, feather-light linen. The thick nubby woolens of her people were stifling in the heat.

Putting the finishing touches in place, Behira stepped back and appraised her handiwork. Her hand flew to her mouth. Shiphrah ran to her side as Behira began sobbing.

"Look at her! Have you ever seen a more beautiful bride? My baby . . . my baby is a woman this day!"

"Mama, please don't cry. You'll make *me* cry and my eyes will be red and swollen. Hattush will throw me back!"

The women roared with laughter. Puah's nervous titter diffused her high-strung emotions. It was much easier to laugh than cry in the confusion of emotions. The joy of becoming Hattush's bride was tempered with reality. No longer would she be her father's "little dove," but Hattush's wife.

Puah's stomach churned. She was legally his bride since the night of the betrothal feast when they'd signed the marriage contract. Soon Hattush would be here to take her to their new home. Then she would become his wife in every way.

Oh — she mustn't think too much about it or she would flee out the back door! What if he didn't find her pleasing? She knew nothing about how to satisfy him. *I mustn't think of that either.* The thought of disappointing Hattush made her truly ill. More than anything, she wanted to be perfect for him in every way. *Oh, LORD, please let him find me pleasing!*

"Mama, would you please go and see if he's coming?" Puah began pacing, then stopped to check her dress again for adjustments.

"Why do you frown, beautiful one?" Shiphrah stood before her, fussing with the collar of her wedding gown.

Puah dropped her eyes. Denying the truth to her dear friend was unthinkable.

"Oh, Shiphrah, I'm afraid!" Her lips trembled.

"I understand."

"Do you? Were you afraid like this? Afraid you wouldn't please your husband?"

Shiphrah smiled. "And more. I thought my ankles too skinny, my face too fat. What you're feeling is what every bride feels, my child."

She lifted Puah's chin until their eyes met. "Hattush loves you. In fact, he's beguiled by his love for you. Your fears are normal, but they are unfounded. You don't see how he adores you when you're not looking. He caresses you with his eyes, the same way you caress him with your eyes when you think no one sees."

Puah blushed. Her abashment brought a playful smile to the older midwife's lips.

"Yes, child, we old ones can still see. We

were young once, also. We, too, have felt the glow of youthful love." Shiphrah placed a gentle kiss on Puah's cheek.

"If you wish to please your husband, then love him. Follow your heart this night. He is probably as nervous as you. Your heart won't lead you wrong. Now, let's place your veil. I think I hear the revelers."

Indeed, a cacophony of cymbals, horns, and other instruments melded with the voices of Hattush's party that would escort them to their new home. They drew nearer until Puah knew they stood outside the gates of Shiphrah's house. Taking a calming breath, she followed Shiphrah down the tiled hallway to the courtyard and her new life with Hattush.

Puah dreamed she lay nestled in Hattush's warm embrace, protected from the night's chill; with arms locked tightly about her, his head rested in the curve of her neck.

Something tickled her nose. Sleepily, Puah forced her eyes open. Dark auburn ringlets fell into view. *It wasn't a dream!* She lay locked in the embrace of her husband. In a rush she remembered their wedding night. A shy blush crept up her face to join her sensuous smile.

Shiphrah was right. Nothing could have prepared Puah for the beauty of her husband's love. Gentleness and patience guided his every touch, and in the end they found sweet fulfillment together. They slept little that night, exploring the fullness of marriage with all their senses.

Through the window, sounds beckoned and the warmth of midday quickly smothered morning's coolness. A deep moan pulsed against the softness of her throat, and in the next moment amber eyes met hers.

Hattush smiled. "Good morning, my wife." He lifted her hand to his mouth and gently brushed it with his lips. "Wife — I love the sound of it. I'm the happiest man alive this day. You've made me happier than I ever thought possible, my beautiful wife. I'll have to practice saying it for, oh, let me see, perhaps seventy or eighty years. Then if I don't like the sound of it, I'll divorce you. Fair enough?"

"You!" Puah playfully pummeled him on his back, but soon found herself on *her* back, ensnared by the wrists. As they struggled she laughed, her heart spilling over with joy that bubbled deep inside.

"You'll never divorce me!" She ran her fingers through his thick curls, becoming suddenly contemplative. "I'll make you so deliriously happy you'll swoon each time you see my face."

"Indeed?" His eyes teased her, then the smile faded and his face grew serious. "You already have, my love. I adore you." He kissed her gently, as dew kisses the fragrant early morning blossom.

Puah felt she would faint as she sank into the ecstasy of his magic. Finally she pushed away and smiled.

"I'd love nothing more than to wrestle with you all day, my husband, but the women will be here soon to collect proof of my purity."

"You're right. Besides, I can't live on love alone. My stomach growls. Shall we break the fast and have some bread and cheese?"

"Hmm. That doesn't sound nearly as tasty as your kisses, but it will have to do."

Later, as they ate, the playful conversation of lovers turned to Hattush's work.

"I must return to work tomorrow. I'm sorry, but Pharaoh's temper grows shorter each day." Hattush took a sip of palm wine and stared past Puah through the door leading to a small garden, his brow furrowed.

"I don't wish to alarm you, my love, but I sometimes think all Hebrews are in danger.

Even the vizier grows more nervous by the day. Although he's Pharaoh's closest advisor, Sennerfer doesn't seem to share the king's hatred for our people."

Apprehension coiled in Puah's breast. "Surely once the tomb is finished he'll stop his royal grousing." The bread suddenly felt like lead in her stomach.

"Were the situation so simple! It seems to be much more than Pharaoh's impatience with our, as he says, 'slothfulness.' Some say he's mad. That's far more dangerous than hate. We must complete the tomb with all haste, but I tell you true, I don't believe it's enough."

Hattush chewed on his lower lip, deep in thought, his worried look sending dread through Puah.

"Husband, what are you thinking?"

Hattush looked at her, and for the first time she saw fear in his eyes.

"Pharaoh hates our people with a vengeance. He despises the fact we keep ourselves separate and worship the One True God instead of paying homage to their many gods. I don't think he will rest until we are all dead."

Those words haunted Puah in the weeks that followed. She and Hattush soon returned to the routine of their respective labors. When the workday ended, they fell gratefully into each other's arms, blissful in the love they found in one another.

Puah made rounds each day, some stretching far into the night as babies arrived. She'd promised to see Yocheved today. Amram's wife was with child, and concerned about some spotting. Indeed, it was an ominous sign. Puah sent word for Yocheved to remain in bed until she could be examined.

At the bedside her fears were relieved. It was nothing more than a minor inflammation. The child grew active within the womb.

"So, you're not concerned?" Yocheved's brow creased with anxiety.

"I'm more concerned that you're fretful. It's not good for the vigorous child that grows within you. I'll leave some herbs. Make a tea twice daily and drink it after it cools. That should take care of the inflammation and stop the spotting. I'll see you in three days. No lifting or heavy work until I see you again, just to be safe. Agreed?"

Yocheved smiled and nodded. "Agreed."

Playful yelling from the courtyard brought Yocheved's circumstance into practical light. "Who will help you with

Aaron?" Puah asked. "He's quite a handful these days."

"Oh, Miriam is wonderful with the boy. She'll watch over him when he's outside. When he comes in, I'll keep him occupied with stories and games."

Satisfied that Yocheved had things under control, Puah left, storing any concern for her patient in the recesses of her mind. Intuition told her Yocheved and the growing baby would be fine, but sometimes instincts failed. She prayed this would not be the case.

As Puah turned the corner onto the street leading home, a sight greeted her, bringing dread to her breast — soldiers! Four of Pharaoh's royal soldiers stood by her gate wearing the scant linen kilts of the infantry. Each brandished a copper-bladed spear and shield exhibiting the soldier's own personal emblem. They wore the standard, cropped haircut of Pharaoh's army that ended just below the ear with blunt-cut bangs running high across their bronze foreheads. Like statues they stood, giving no hint of the reason for their presence.

Puah's steps slowed as she tried to think of what this meant. *What could they want?* For a Hebrew, regardless of station, the king's soldiers seldom bore good news. She should spin around, head in the other direction! Ridiculous. It would be senseless.

The soldiers were regally tall, heavily muscled, accustomed to running in full gear for miles. She wouldn't make it around the corner before they overtook her. No, it would only add to her predicament. By the time she stood in their shadow, Puah's pace had slowed to a halting crawl. Her heart raced, making it hard to catch her breath.

"Puah, the midwife?"

Suddenly terror struck as she realized this might have to do with Hattush. Had something happened to her husband? She felt her knees go weak. Unable to speak, she could only stare at the soldiers as she grabbed hold of the gatepost to brace herself.

The soldier who spoke gave no sign of emotion. He wore the heavy Gold of Valor around his neck, a chain bearing three flies in purest fine gold, the reward for extreme bravery on the battlefield. It was a badge of great honor in Pharaoh's army. This man wasn't a casual foot soldier, but a hero of the highest caliber, trained to carry out any order unquestioningly. Even to kill.

Puah swallowed, the dryness of her mouth making it difficult to speak. She slowly lifted her eyes, finding no information in the soldier's stoic gaze. Pushing past the fear threatening to overwhelm her, she spoke. "Yes, I am Puah, the midwife." Her voice sounded raspy and foreign.

"You have been summoned by Princess Batya, daughter of Khaneferre Sobekhotep IV, Pharaoh of Upper and Lower Egypt. You will come with us."

Even with such a formal summons, one that would have struck fear into her at any other time, she almost felt like laughing in relief. *It has nothing to do with Hattush! The princess desires my services.*

"What does the princess require? What supplies should I carry?" Never before, to Puah's knowledge, had a member of the royal family requested the services of a Hebrew midwife.

"I was not given that information. I was told only to escort you to her palace. Quickly, go and gather whatever supplies you may need. We must hurry."

"Of course."

Rushing through the gate, Puah hurried through the coolness of her home. She added more supplies than normal to her bag, unsure of what the princess might need. Within moments she stood ready before the soldiers.

Puah's mind whirled as she struggled to keep up with the soldiers' long, steady strides. Two flanked her while the other two led the party, forming a circle of protection as they hurried through the dusty streets of the Hebrew section. Late morning activity halted as they passed. Wide, anxious eyes stared from gateways and alleys. Children hid behind their mothers' skirts, while those near doorways quickly ducked inside.

Pharaoh's army was not a welcome sight in this quarter. No doubt, Hattush would quickly have word of this. The Hebrew community, although growing rapidly, was well organized. Few secrets existed among the people, presenting both a curse and a blessing depending on the circumstances.

Just when Puah thought her legs would give way, they stopped before a high stone wall near the shore of the Nile River. The wall surrounded a large, ornate structure, more palace than home. She'd seen it many times before, and had heard Khaneferre's eldest daughter lived there.

Unseen hands opened a massive wooden gate. They entered a large courtyard, but Puah was not offered the luxury of inspecting it other than noticing the walls were adorned with likenesses of several Egyptian goddesses. The soldiers dropped back and a waiting servant signaled her to follow. They hurried through tall, airy hallways that led into the heart of the lavish estate. After numerous turns the servant ushered her into a sleeping chamber.

A young woman lay on a bed of carved ebony. Pain etched her exquisite face into a mask of misery and she cried out as Puah entered the room. Dark stains shadowed her dress of softest panther skin. When she saw Puah, her slim hand reached out through the air toward her.

"Please, help me. I think I am losing my baby!" Just as she spoke another pain seized her and she groaned, squeezing Puah's hand. Finally the cramp ended and the young woman looked up at her through pain-glazed eyes.

"I know you will not let me die. I did not want the Egyptian midwives. Their patients die of the fever."

Behind Puah an older Hebrew servant spoke.

"I am Zayit, Batya's nurse since infancy. Her monthly ceased two moons ago. She began bleeding during the night. She was panic-stricken at the thought of the Egyptian midwives. I knew of nothing else but to summon you. Please, help her. She's a good woman and like a daughter to me." Tears formed in the old woman's eyes.

"I'll do what I can. First, bring hot water.

We must brew tea for her pain. And I'll need fresh, clean water for washing." Puah signaled to a servant standing beside the bed. "Remove her clothes so I can examine her. Then we'll bathe her and put some clean clothing on her. Has she been fevered?"

"No, but she cries with pain since daybreak."

Zayit hurried away, barking orders to a host of slaves hovering near the chamber door. Puah set her bag on the polished stone floor and knelt at the princess' side.

"I know you're hurting. The first thing I'm going to do is try to ease your pain."

Tears streamed down the princess' dusky face. Even in such an unsettled state, she was a striking young woman. Her long, regal neck hinted of Nubian ancestry as did her dark, smooth skin. Long boned and graceful as the gazelle, she indeed struck a demeanor of royalty.

"Thank you for coming. I do not want to lose my baby. My husband and I desire a child very much. Can you can stop this?"

"I don't know. I'll do everything in my power to help you." Puah looked into the princess' eyes and smiled. "I'll also ask my God to answer your prayer. He knows you want a child, my princess."

When hot water arrived, Puah prepared

an infusion of herbs. One would ease the cramping and induce sleep; the other would fight fever. After that, she could only wait. It was in God's hands. She uttered a silent prayer for her patient, trying to allay her own fear. If the princess lost this child, Puah might be blamed. *I won't think of that!* She would do her best. The rest was God's will.

Between cramps, Puah was able to get most of the tea into the princess. Then with the help of the nurse and a servant girl, they undressed and cleaned the royal patient. Puah spoke soft, soothing words, encouraging her to relax. The princess' brow smoothed, her body relaxing. Puah took her hand and prayed aloud.

"God of Abraham, God of Joseph, look down this day on your child. Grant the answer to her prayer. Reveal yourself to her."

As quickly as the prayer ended, the thought came to Puah that if the princess lost the child, she might blame the God of the Hebrew people. Puah entreated God in silence. She'd done all she could. Heaven's divine hands held the answer.

As the heat of the day grew, the sun peaked in the sky, then descended slowly across the heavens beyond the hills of the western desert. Evening twilight painted a soft mural of pinks, blues, and softest crimsons against the backdrop of the tawny hills. Puah continued her vigil.

At times she paced, sometimes praying. Finally she dozed. When she awakened, the princess slept peacefully, her groans having ceased. Batya's brow remained dry and cool as she rested in the clean, soft cotton shift. A gentle breeze blew from the river, wafting through the high vents in the roof of the royal sleeping chamber. Time, only time, would answer the question.

The old nurse entered quietly, concern for the princess covering her wizened face. Like Puah, Zayit had not left her mistress' side except for a few moments during their day long vigil.

"She's a strong person and she loves people. It is a shame," Zayit said quietly. The old woman straightened Batya's covers. "Her mother was a beautiful princess of Nubia, brought here as a captive from a war campaign. She found favor in Pharaoh's eyes not long after he ascended the throne. Batya's mother became his favorite. Pharaoh has always indulged the child's every whim, but stays far away from her in the ways that are important. Perhaps that's why she so strongly desires children. They would offer the love she's been denied. I fear for her heart if she loses this baby."

The nurse's words touched a chord deep within Puah's breast. How sad to have been raised within the opulent walls of Pharaoh's palace, yet hunger for the simple hug of a loving father. Puah thought of her own father's tender face and thanked heaven once more for the blessing of loving parents.

"I can't make promises full of false hope. She's bled much and her womb is very irritable. We can only wait and trust God to help her now."

By nightfall, no fresh bleeding appeared and the princess awoke, seemingly free of pain.

"Hello, my princess." Puah smiled. "You slept well. How are you feeling?" She checked Batya's brow, relieved to find cool, dry skin.

"The pain is gone. My baby! What —"

"The bleeding has almost stopped. Perhaps we're through this crisis. For now, you must rest. The weeks to come will tell the truth. I've seen no evidence that you've lost the baby. For now, God is smiling on you, my princess."

Batya closed her eyes, her head falling back with relief. She searched for Puah's hand, and when she found it, gave a firm squeeze.

"I owe you much, Hebrew healer. When will we know how the baby fares?"

"In about two moons you should feel the quickening of life. We'll know more then, as long as there is no more bleeding. For now, you must stay in bed. I'll check on you tomorrow. I've left enough of the herb tea to last you through the night. Your nurse knows what to do. Are you hungry?"

A radiant smile lit Batya's face. "Starved."

"Good. I'll summon the servants. You may eat anything you like, but you must stay in bed. I'll see you tomorrow. God be with you."

Hattush met Puah at the gate of their home, his eyes dark with concern. He didn't give her time to drop her bag before gathering her into the shelter of his embrace.

"Oh, thank God you're all right!" he said, burying his face in her hair. "I was terrified. Where have you been? Where did they take you? Did they —"

"Shh." Puah silenced his barrage of questions. "I'm fine. Let's go inside and I'll explain everything."

Hattush's concern didn't ease until Puah told him the entire account and he seemed reasonably assured the crisis was over.

"I don't like it. You can't win if there's an-

110

other crisis. Is there no way you can withdraw your care?"

"Hattush, that's not possible! You know a Hebrew cannot refuse the commands of the royal family. I understand what worries you. I have the same thoughts."

Puah rose from the pillow and gazed up at the moon rising above the window's high sill.

"How can I explain to you?" She turned and looked into her husband's worried eyes. "As I approached Batya's palace, I had all the same thoughts that you've uttered. But when I knelt at her bedside, watched her writhe in agony, she was just another woman needing my care. That's what I do, my husband. It's as much a part of me as my eyes or my hands."

Hattush looked at her. Would he *ever* understand the mystery of women?

She smiled gently, knowing he could never fully comprehend the bond women share at such moments.

"You see Pharaoh only in his commanding role. And perhaps you've seen the princess on her dais, wearing royal finery. What I saw was a woman in horrible pain, bleeding, frightened, a woman who wants her baby as much as I would want your child. I couldn't help but minister to her. I cared for her as I would want to be cared for."

Slowly Hattush rose, sighed deeply, and drew her into his arms. "That's why I love you."

Puah inhaled his masculine scent, a mixture of spice, metal, and his own unique essence. She dared not tell him how truly frightened she would be if she allowed herself to dwell on the day's events. Had the princess lost the baby, it might have gone badly. And the danger was far from over. Perhaps the princess would forgive, but her father might use just such a thing to vent his growing rage against the Hebrews.

An involuntary shudder raced up her back. She pushed deeper into Hattush's embrace, trying to still the gnawing voice of fear that whispered doubt to her. She wouldn't listen to it. She would trust God. What else could she do?

Lost in thought of long ago, Puah didn't hear Hannah slip into the tent. A petite hand on her spotted forearm broke her reverie. "Can I get anything for you, Grandma´ma?"

Hannah held a gourd of water, patiently waiting to be acknowledged. Already the child reminded her of Daphne. Quiet and thoughtful, Hannah reflected innate grace and a servant's spirit, always eager to please. This little one held special favor in Puah's heart. Not love only, but a special bond, perhaps something in their inner being that drew them together.

Puah rolled from her position facing the back of the tent and sat up with unusual slowness.

"Are you feeling well, Grandma´ma?" Hannah's eyes stared with innocent concern, holding Puah's own gaze, watching and waiting for a cue from her aged ancestor. The child licked her dry lips, powdered with dust. It had been a long day's march, and as soon as her tent had been struck Puah sank gratefully into the soft bed of pillows.

"Yes, my love, I'm fine, but tell me this. How did you know this old woman needed a drink? Could it be that you also are thirsty?"

Puah watched emotions play across Hannah's face. First, surprise at her great-great-grandmother's discernment, then delight as Puah gently pushed the gourd toward Hannah, offering the first drink to her. A wide smile broke across her energetic face, and for just an instant Puah thought the child would start gulping greedily. Then without warning, Hannah pushed the water back to her grandma´ma and shook her head adamantly.

"Oh, no, Grandma´ma. I cannot! You must drink first. Mother would be most upset with me if I dishonored you in such a way."

"Well, what if I said that disobeying your elder by refusing my command to drink would be less than desirable?" Puah tried hard to hide the smile itching to break forth at the child's dilemma. How would she respond? She watched Hannah's forehead knit tightly in deep thought.

A wide grin broke across Hannah's face, revealing her acknowledgment of the game her beloved elder offered. Biting her lips in serious thought, she hesitated to respond. Hannah would rarely win against her great-great-grandmother's wisdom and advanced years in such loving games. The lessons, always rich with life's truths, taught Hannah many months ago that age meant wisdom. She was learning, however, growing sharper by the day. It always thrilled Puah when youth won out and they could share a laugh together at the victory.

"Then, with all respect to you, Grandma´ma, I would say my elder wouldn't want me to disobey my mother by drinking first. She forbade me to drink until you take your fill." Satisfied at her retort, she waited for Puah's response, her tiny bow-shaped mouth trying to hide the grin.

Puah's cackle of laughter sent the child into peals of giggles at their impasse. It pleased Puah to know Hannah was bright like her father and caring like her mother. She would go far in the Promised Land, a prize for her husband and a joy to her family. Who could know, perhaps someday she would wish to become a midwife also?

The thought satisfied a need in Puah. Already Hannah asked about healing herbs, always listening attentively as Puah showed her the art of making infusions and poultices to ease the pains of womanhood and lower the fevers of illness. Perhaps she should talk to one of the midwives about teaching the girl when she came of age. Long ago she'd left the lengthy days of strenuous work to younger women, but she would find joy in seeing Hannah fellow in her footsteps.

Puah accepted the gourd from Hannah's small hands and took a small sip. She swished it around in her mouth to loosen the grit, then spit it onto the sand beneath her blanket. The next swallows she drank deeply. She savored the coolness as it washed slowly down her parched throat. When the biting thirst departed, she offered the gourd to Hannah. The child drank thirstily, her small gulps eagerly receiving the blessed liquid so fast that some spilled down her chin. It formed a trail in the dust on her neck, ending at the neckline of her robe. When Hannah had her fill, she wiped her mouth with the edge of her apron and offered the gourd once more to Puah.

"Are you sure you've had enough, child?"

"Yes, Grandma´ma, for now. My belly feels as if it will burst. It's good, isn't it?"

Guilt washed over Puah at Hannah's simple thankfulness. She regretted her grumbling throughout the harsh day. They were on their way to the Promised Land. If the LORD allowed, she would be laid to rest among her ancestors. There was much to be thankful for. Standing before her, part of Puah's own inheritance stood, delighting in a simple drink of water.

"Yes, Hannah, it *is* good. Now go and eat. I'll be there shortly. I want to rest my weary bones a bit before I continue our story."

"Yes, Grandma´ma." Hannah darted out to her mother's side as Puah settled back onto the pillows.

Her mind traveled back to the early days of her marriage to Hattush. How could they have known such sweetness as the world around them grew ever more ruthless?

VII

From the end of the earth I will cry to You, when my heart is overwhelmed; lead me to the rock that is higher than I. (Psalm 61:2)

"Mistress! Mistress!" Alarm propelled the servant's words as she awakened the young midwife. Rubbing sleep from her eyes, Puah attempted to orient herself. Beside her, the bed was empty. Dawn approached, a faint blushing in the eastern sky. Hattush would already be at the foundry.

He worked such long days now. Driving himself even before daybreak and returning home late at night. She was concerned about him. He looked haggard and troubled these days, spending himself trying to please the crazed Pharaoh. Such foolishness to worry about his tomb. As if the dead really cared about such things!

"Yes, Anna?"

"Mistress, soldiers are at the gate! They wait for you. It's the princess! She's in

118

need of your service."

Suddenly the remnants of slumber departed and Puah jumped up. She wiped the heaviness from her eyes and stifled a yawn. Already Anna stood holding her dress in readiness. After helping with her clothing, Anna hurriedly assisted Puah with her sandals. As Puah fled the sleeping chamber into the hall, Anna pushed the medicine bag into her hands.

"God be with you, mistress." Anna's call echoed as Puah's sandals clattered across the tile toward the front entrance.

"And you, Anna," Puah called as she ran out the door. "Be sure to send word to Hattush that I'm at the palace so he doesn't worry."

"Yes, mistress."

The soldiers wasted no time in explanation. They marched briskly through the streets. Puah pushed forward at a near run to keep up. As they approached the palace she gave thanks. Her thighs ached with the unexpected activity, her breathing rapid and hungry for air. Often she hurried to deliveries, but never had she been forced to pace herself with soldiers.

Gates and doors swung open as if by magic. As Puah neared the sleeping chamber, she could hear the cries of the princess. Cries of pain and fear, like some poor trapped and injured animal.

"Aiee . . . have mercy Bes! Have mercy Tawaret!" Batya's cries for the stone gods of childbirth rang through the corridor as Puah rushed to the side of the sleeping platform and fell to her knees.

"I am here, my princess."

Another pain seized the princess and a shrill scream rang through the air causing the hair on the back of Puah's neck to rise. *Please, God, don't let it be!*

Batya's slim hand reached out and grasped Puah's and she sank back into the bedding. Her dark almond eyes glistened with fear and sought the midwife's like a hare snared by the hunter's trap. A fine sheen of perspiration covered her silky skin, her light diaphanous gown clung to her, twisted and damp.

Flashing a look of alarm to Zayit, Batya's nurse, Puah tried to compose her jangled nerves and set her mind to the task. With no time to ask questions, Puah washed her hands in the basin of clear water presented to her by the nurse. As she pulled back the cover, any hope she had harbored died.

"Hot water. Bring hot water for tea and for cleaning. Linens, clean linens."

Busy with her work, Puah at first didn't

notice the princess watching her. Only when she sensed it did she look up. Dark eyes questioned her, questions Puah knew she must answer. How she hated this part of her work, this moment of truth, a truth that could tear the heart asunder. Puah put down her cloth, washed the blood from her hands and dried them. Moving closer to Batya, she leaned down and took the princess's hand, caressing it and studying the fine map of indigo vessels beneath the skin. She admired Batya's dusky skin, untouched by toil. Yet these hands would now be empty. Puah searched for words, words she'd uttered too often before. They never came easily.

"I'm sorry, my princess. There's nothing I can do. You've lost your baby."

Silent tears trailed down Batya's cheeks and she clung to Puah's hand all the harder. Puah cradled Batya's head in her lap, caressing the damp hair and whispering softly, "Your pain should lessen now, for the worst is over."

Batya's silent tears became sobs of helpless resignation and anguish, then grew to the wail of unbound grief. A great barrier fell. No longer were they servant and princess, but two women embraced in the ancient dance of mourning.

They rocked, clinging to one another. Puah found strength in giving the princess comfort; Batya poured forth her grief, drawing strength from the midwife's quiet presence. The sobs slowed to tearful hiccups and quiet sniffling.

Puah prayed for words that would comfort. "It is good to cry. Allow yourself to feel the pain. You've suffered a great loss. I pray my God will comfort you, for only He knows your pain. I cannot imagine how your heart aches."

Puah continued rocking the princess. No words could ease the woman's pain. She'd lost her child. Though Batya never felt the soft flutter of quickening, her mother's heart had bonded with the life within. She'd readied herself to welcome the precious gift of new life into her arms and home, but now it had been snatched away. Although too small to see, unidentifiable, it was still a precious, sacred being. Though it would never experience life on this earth, its spirit rested safely in the arms of God. Now only the quiet presence of those who cared for Batya could offer comfort.

Puah's throat tightened. Images swam as tears filled her eyes and spilled onto her bodice, leaving telltale stains. *How would it feel to lose Hattush's child, my child?*

Where would I find comfort? How would I resign myself to God's will with such pain? Would I ever feel anything but pain again?

Finally Batya's anguish abated as a gentle morning breeze wafted through the room. Dawn beamed across the sky, striking the distant hills that lay to the west. They glowed with nuances of gold and rich bronze, mixing with deep purple and gray shadows. Somewhere in the nearby garden a bunting trilled its first melody of the day.

Now the silence of acceptance entered the room. For a time Batya lay spent, her head resting on Puah's lap. Then slowly, she pushed herself up. She brushed her hair from her face and looked into the midwife's eyes.

"Thank you," she said, her voice a bare whisper. "I thank you for all you have done."

"I did everything I could do, my princess. It was in the hands of God." Puah's voice quavered. She was at a loss for further words of comfort. "Would you like me to clean you now?"

"Yes, I think perhaps I would feel better."

Silently Puah washed away the blood and other fluids. Soiled linens disappeared in the arms of a servant, replaced by fresh, clean bedding. When all was done Puah prepared a rich herbal infusion.

"Drink. This will ease your cramping and allay fever."

Batya received the cup without comment and sipped quietly. Servants hovered outside the door, whispering quietly among themselves as if not sure what to do next. They knew their duties well, but now in the midst of tragedy seemed frozen with indecision like children awaiting instruction. Only Zayit stood by, anxiously awaiting orders from the midwife.

When Batya seemed at ease, Puah turned her attention to the aged nurse. "Zayit, the princess needs quiet and rest. Also, when she awakens she'll need food to build her strength, perhaps some broth of meat or fish. Keep visitors to a minimum. She's not ready for an influx of kinsmen. Only those closest can comfort her now. Any others will only tire her."

"Yes, mistress, don't worry. She will rest. I'll see to it."

Puah glanced up at the hoary head of the servant, the face lined with deep wrinkles earned from years of service. No one, save those Zayit allowed, would cross the portal into this chamber.

"I know you'll serve her wisely, Zayit.

Batya is blessed to have you."

"Indeed, Zayit has been like a mother to me." The clear voice of the princess came as a surprise. Love, in the form of a soft smile, lit her coppery face, erasing some of the ashen effects of bereavement. "I do not know what I would do without her."

Zayit returned Batya's loving gaze. A slight trembling of the old nurse's lip betrayed the deep emotions held in dignified constraint. The royal house was not noted for nurturing their children. In the end, they bred cold distant leaders whose hearts were of stone and whose only pleasures were the powers they wielded and the coffers they filled with gold. Fortunate was the child to have a caretaker like Zayit.

"Is there anything more I can do for you, my princess?" Puah asked as she reached up to feel Batya's forehead. The brow was cooler now, and dry, a good sign. Fever was always a dreaded development, for the herbs could only do so much. "You will grow drowsy soon and sleep for most of the day. When you awaken I want you to eat. Even though your heart is broken and you won't feel like eating, you must."

"I will try to honor your instructions, healer. I can only try."

Puah smiled warmly. "That's all I expect.

Now rest. I'll return this evening to check on you."

She turned to the nurse. "Zayit, send for me at once if there are any signs of fever. Bathe her frequently with fresh, clean water and change the linens each time. The fever abides in filthiness."

"Shall I bind her breasts, mistress?"

"No, her loss was too early. She won't require it."

As Puah turned to leave, the princess cried out, "Puah!"

Puah whirled around. Batya's look of abject abandonment grabbed her heart. Forgetting her patient was the daughter of Pharaoh, the young midwife leaned down and embraced her. She could do no less for this woman in her season of grief. Hers was a high calling. Puah couldn't allow the royal family's distorted sense of propriety to change the way she cared for those in need.

Soon sleep overtook the princess. She sank back onto the clean linens, breathing calmly. Puah left, her heart heavy. Would she ever be able to dismiss the feeling of failure at the loss of a mother or baby? There was so much to know, so much she had yet to learn. Truly, it was all a great mystery, all in the hands of the One True God.

★ ★ ★

The sun sank toward the distant hills as Puah walked to the palace for the second time that day. Pharaoh now knew of the princess' loss. Did he also know of the Hebrew midwife's part in the circumstances? Her involvement might bring a stormy wind, but Puah knew there was nothing she could do to prevent it. In retrospect, she would not have done anything differently. She'd ministered to the princess with all her training and knowledge, of that she was certain. Egyptian magicians and midwives might have killed Batya with their nonsense of mysterious cures and incantations. At the very least they would have induced the dreaded fever.

Batya slept peacefully most of the day, awakening in time for the midwife's visit. Puah breathed a sigh of relief and uttered a silent prayer when the examination proved normal.

Still, grief tinged Batya's wan face. She remained quiet as Zayit fed her sips of broth. Like an obedient child she allowed her nurse to hover about, straightening linens that didn't need smoothing and coaxing sips of tea and broth when it was obvious she wasn't interested. Like a mother hen Zayit fluttered about, hiding her concern with ceaseless activity. Finally even Batya tired of it.

"Zayit, would you *please* sit. You are making me weary. I am fine. There is nothing more you can do for me now."

The princess' petulant order brought a smile to Puah's lips. The poor old woman was probably exhausted.

"Zayit, have you slept at all?"

A stony shake of the servant's head indicated what Puah suspected.

"Zayit, you won't serve the princess well if you become ill yourself. You must sleep. Others can offer her broth and check her brow. Go! Get some rest."

"Yes, Zayit, I order it. You must rest." With the stern finality of royal decree, Zayit nodded her assent and withdrew from the chamber. Moments later a young Nubian girl with large frightened eyes entered, wearing only the decorative belt of a slave.

"My princess, I am here to serve you," she said, bowing. "Do you have any needs?"

"Make certain Zayit sleeps. That is my only need at this time."

Though Batya seemed much better after her long rest, Puah was still concerned. "I'll go now and allow you to rest, my princess. I'll return in the morning. If you feel feverish or develop chills, please send for me immediately."

Batya managed a smile. "You have been wonderful, Puah. I thank you for your care. When you come tomorrow I will make arrangements for your payment."

"Don't concern yourself with such matters now. Your task is to rest and heal in body and spirit."

Puah turned to go. As she reached the doorway, a hesitant whispered question stopped her.

"Is it normal to feel so empty and dead?"

Puah turned to face the princess.

"Yes, it *is* normal. In the weeks to come you'll feel many things, including anger. Expect to feel great sadness, also. I pray you'll find your place of peace soon. The pain will be with you always, but others say it grows less harsh with each passing day."

"I pray that also."

Puah returned home only to find Hattush still at the foundry. She needed him home this evening. She wanted to rest her head against his strong shoulder. She wanted to release her own grief and hide herself in the safety of his arms. He would know what to say. He always seemed to find the words to comfort her, words to give her strength.

Each loss cut Puah deeply. Yet each

forced a strengthening of her spirit by putting her in touch with her own grief. Somehow, sharing those feelings helped bring healing to the women. God forbid, were she to ever suffer such a loss, she'd want someone caring enough to grieve with her. She wouldn't want a midwife capable of coldly performing tasks for her body but forgetting medicine of the heart.

Puah dined quietly, allowing her body to release some of the day's tension. Shadows grew short as sounds of children playing in nearby courtyards floated through open windows. Their capricious voices carried on the wind as they conquered kingdoms or slew lions within the confines of walled domains. Soon their mothers would call them in for the evening as night settled in.

Puah sighed, hoping she and Hattush would soon be blessed with a child. Although she cherished their time alone, she'd gladly share him with a small, amber-eyed version of her husband. Most of her friends already had children, some even two or three. Holding an infant took on new meaning these days, and at times her arms ached to cradle her own.

Marriage to Hattush was all she had dreamed it would be. He embodied everything she could ever desire in a husband. He worked hard, and even though he came home tense and exhausted from Pharaoh's demands, he never discussed the particulars. When he entered the gates of their home, that world fell away. It was just the two of them. They laughed and talked, planning and dreaming about the children they would some day have. As one day melted into another, they learned each other's tiniest nuances and ways.

For Puah, the greatest surprise of all was Hattush's deep abiding faith. On nights when the heat of the desert hills swept down, making their sleeping chamber like a baker's oven, they would escape to the roof and make their bed there. The soft sounds of late night would soon quiet, leaving only the gentle rhythm of their breathing as they lay in each other's arms beneath the vast ceiling of stars.

It was during those special moments that dreams were shared, souls bared. Hattush held strongly to the promises made to Abraham.

"God promised our seed the land of Canaan. If we're not there, it's because the time isn't right. Father Joseph's faithfulness brought our people here and saved us from famine. When God is ready, He'll make a way for us to leave."

Such childlike faith escaped Puah, her rational mind too logical to accept it. She knew what she'd heard from childhood, but since Father Joseph, the children of Israel were little more than despised slaves.

"But, my husband, when? When will this be? After the taskmasters have killed all the young men? I've heard the stories of our fathers, but my heart cannot believe. If I'm wrong, I pray God will forgive me."

"Oh, my love, you *must* believe! If God provided the sacrifice for Abraham, He'll provide a Deliverer. Of that I'm certain." He pulled her closer, looking deeply into her eyes, his own warming with unspoken passion. Conversation ended. There under the stars they would love each other, marveling in the gift of one another.

How many times had she thanked God for Hattush? How often had she been grateful for following her heart and waiting for the one who made her heart sing? And sing it did. Sometimes, when he wasn't looking, Puah found herself studying the manly planes of his visage until it stole her breath. The tender way Hattush beheld her often swelled her heart until she thought it would burst from sheer ecstasy. The music of her soul surged into a song of delight known only by those who have experienced true love's miraculous light.

Puah finished eating, then washed the day's dust from her tired body and slipped into a soft cotton gown. A brief rest would be pleasant while she awaited Hattush's return. She settled back onto the pillows. Soon fatigue surrounded her like a heavy cloak. Keeping her eyes open became a battle which she quickly lost, succumbing to the temptation of sleep.

VIII

Deliver me from my enemies, O my God; defend me from those who rise up against me. (Psalm 59:1)

In her dream, feathers tickled her nose. Puah swatted at them and rolled over to sink down once more into the bliss of deep slumber. Instead, warm strong arms slipped around her. Hattush snuggled close, placing soft kisses on the nape of her neck. She smiled and rolled over to nestle into his loving embrace.

"Mmm . . . what a wonderful way to awaken. We'll have to rid ourselves of the rooster. He's far too noisy and obnoxious."

A husky laugh rumbled from Hattush's throat and he pulled her even more tightly to him. "I'm sorry. I couldn't resist. When I awakened and saw your hair spilling across your body and your dark lashes caressing your cheeks, I grew jealous. I wanted my turn."

This time it was Puah's turn to laugh. Reaching up, she kissed Hattush softly.

"I adore you, my husband, but be warned — if you love me too well, I won't let you leave for work!"

"Indeed. I've shared the same thoughts." Hattush planted a feathery kiss on Puah's lips, savoring it like the sweetness of the pomegranate. "Have you ever thought of how nice it would be to laze about in each other's arms for a whole day?"

"Mmm, yes, that would be wonderful." Puah leaned away and reached up to brush an errant curl from his forehead, then placed a kiss there.

"But we can't. It will be light soon and we both have work to do. What I *will* do is have a special dinner awaiting you this evening. And, if you're a very good boy, I'll allow you to lose to me in a game of senet. The new game board Ethan carved for us begs to be used. What better way to spend an evening than for me to conquer you in a game of senet?"

"Agreed, my willful wife, but I wouldn't boast of winning so quickly. I've studied some new moves and I might surprise your pretty little head."

With that, Hattush pulled her once more into his arms and kissed her smiling lips. His eyes threatened more than a kiss, but a sudden pounding on the outermost gate in-

135

terrupted. Shouting voices jolted them from the bed.

"I'll see who it is," Hattush whispered. "Dress quickly. It might be someone in distress." He hurried toward the sounds reverberating from the street.

Puah dressed as rapidly as possible. As she slid her other sandal into place and began tying the ankle strap, Hattush appeared in the arched doorway. His ashen face stilled her hand. *Was someone dead?* Whatever news he bore, it couldn't be good.

"Wh . . . what is it? Mother? Father?"

"No, my love, they're fine. Khaneferre has summoned you. You are to go with the soldiers immediately. Shiphrah is already with them."

Hattush slammed his fist against the doorpost, his face drawn in anguish. "I knew your dealing with the princess could come to no good." He spoke with self-recrimination, as if he could've prevented the events of recent days.

Puah swallowed tightly, unable to speak for the moment. Hattush voiced her own unspoken fears. But no! She wouldn't think about it. It would do no good to worry. She'd done the best she could and the princess held no blame. She would face Pharaoh and tell him the truth. How bad could it be?

"I'm going with you."

Puah ran to her husband and sought his eyes. "No, Hattush, you must not! Your presence will only remind him of the tomb and increase his anger."

"I am going!"

The finality of his words and the glare in his eyes convinced her it would do no good to argue. They clung together in silence. *Please God, protect us from Khaneferre's madness!* How had they come to be so intimately entwined in the king's life? Would that they lived anonymously in the countryside. There they'd still have each other *without* the fear.

Hattush stroked her hair and spoke calmly. "It's my place to go. You're my wife. Besides, I know Sennerfer. The vizier will surely be there. Whatever Pharaoh wants, I may have some sway. I am his chief goldsmith, after all."

In the end Hattush had his way. During the hasty march to the royal palace they dared not speak. Now he, Puah, and Shiphrah stood outside the door of Pharaoh's throne room waiting to be announced. They were not allowed the luxury of pacing. Around them an escort of eight armed soldiers stood like silent pillars, gleaming swords at the ready.

Never before had Puah been inside the royal residence. It was more a walled city than a home. The opulence was stunning. From every direction dazzling color leaped at her, demanding her eyes follow its seductive pull. As she stared at countless murals adorning the walls along the maze of corridors, the gleaming reflection of gold caused her to shield her eyes. *There must be cubits of it!*

The polished stone floor shone like a mirror. Its rich pinkish hue matched the hideous granite statue of Khaneferre he'd seen many times in Avaris. Pharaoh had ordered the likeness of himself erected, and it now stood in the main courtyard in Father Joseph's village. *How many slaves died needlessly for this floor? How many of our people sacrificed for Pharaoh's luxury?*

Sentries opened the massive cedar doors as the announcement echoed through the great hall:

"My lord, the Hebrew midwives — Shiphrah and Puah."

At Pharaoh's silent admonition they nervously approached the dais, an ornate raised porch within the massive room. Four thick columns, painted in cobalt and trimmed with gold leaf resembling lotus leaves, supported the roof of the structure. Hieroglyphics, the "language of the gods," decorated the wall behind the thrones where Ra's ever-seeing eye looked out over all who dared enter the chamber.

Khaneferre sat silently with his crook and flail, symbols of his power and kingship, crossed tightly against his chest in stony contempt. Puah's mouth, now dry as dust, locked silently as she kept her eyes down, carefully avoiding Pharaoh's stare. If she dared look up would she discern the ruler's intent in his heartless eyes?

The assembly watched as the trio silently approached the dais, their sudden arrival interrupting the business of royal court already in session. Servants hovered about, awaiting the slightest nod or cut of the eyes to send them scurrying to bid their master's will. Two scribes wrote furiously on papyrus tablets, dipping their quills into inkwells and quickly recording the spoken words. Armed sentries surrounded the platform, unmoving, unblinking, yet missing nothing with their hawkish eyes. Sworn to protect Pharaoh, their spears would fly as fast as the adder's strike to stop any attempt to harm the royal family.

Nearing Pharaoh, a figure caught Puah's attention. He stood next to a pillar of the dais holding a walking staff in the form of the deadly adder. Though aged and withered, he bore the quiet dignity of one with authority. *Could he be Sennerfer?*

The smaller throne to the Pharaoh's right was empty, the queen absent. Perhaps she was with Batya. The thought made Puah's chest tighten in terror as she remembered why she must have been summoned here. Surely they didn't blame her for the princess' miscarriage! *God of Abraham, protect me!*

Unsure of what to do, Puah followed Hattush's lead and fell in obeisance at the foot of the raised platform. Her heart fluttered, leaving her breathless. She tried to still the trembling of her hands by clutching them tightly together. She froze, face down, waiting silently. The rustle of clothing preceded the ominous quiet tap of sandal leather on the steps. She counted them. One. Two. Three. Four. At five, a foot fell into her line of sight below the bare, shaven calf of a man's leg. Still, she waited.

The god Amun, engraved in the wide gold ankle bracelet on Khaneferre's shaven leg, glared at her. The royal blue and gold crook slapped angrily against Pharaoh's thigh as he stood silently above her. A moment of faintness swept over Puah, and she realized she was holding her breath. She gasped for

140

air and froze again.

"Sennerfer!"

Puah flinched at the molten anger in the voice.

"Why have they brought the goldsmith? I did not summon him!"

Puah heard indistinct muttering between Hattush and the old man. The vizier then whispered something into Pharaoh's ear.

"Rise, all of you!" Khaneferre commanded.

As gracefully as she could, Puah forced herself to her feet. She reached out to assist Shiphrah. They clung, hand-in-hand, waiting.

Slowly Puah's eyes rose to face Pharaoh. Khaneferre's youth startled her. He was much younger than her father, yet he had a daughter old enough to bear children. Of course, the royal families bred early, producing heirs for their ever-changing throne. Not yet revealing the reason for his summons, Pharaoh turned and strode back up the steps to his throne. He sat and placed the crook and flail across his chest once more, glaring at the trio through kohl-painted eyes dark with unspoken anger.

"So, goldsmith, the young midwife is your spouse?" It was more a smirk than question.

Hattush stood silently and nodded in assent. His back was straight and proud, but he kept his head bowed respectfully.

Until this moment Puah had not fully understood her husband's constant anxiety about Pharaoh. Now it bolted at her with dreadful clarity. One word, even a nod of the head, and her beloved would be killed, so great was the power of this man, this one who called himself god.

After an interminable silence, Pharaoh spoke. "I have summoned the midwives for one purpose. The Hebrews are becoming a problem. They multiply like rats." Khaneferre spat the words like sour milk.

"The solution is clear. But before we attend to that matter, I wish to show my gratitude to the Hebrew midwife for the care of my daughter." Pharaoh turned his head to stare at Puah, his eyes slits of malice. "She sings your praises, midwife, even in her time of grief." He hissed the words, soft and silken, but with all the hypnotic threat of a cobra.

With a nod of Pharaoh's head, a female servant hastened to Puah, clutching a small golden box bejeweled with dark blue stones. She bowed and presented it to Puah. With shaking hands Puah received the gift, unsure of what to do next. *Should I look inside? Is the box the gift?* Still uncertain, a hasty response rushed forth.

"My lord, I thank you. My heart breaks for your daughter's loss. I pray for her quick healing." Puah kept her eyes down, afraid to see what she might find in Pharaoh's icy glare.

Again Khaneferre rose from the throne and approached Puah, stopping just a hairbreadth away. He smelled of pungent spicy oils and wine. He raised his crook and she flinched, preparing for a strike. The reaction brought a sly twinge of amusement to Pharaoh's full lips. Instead of hitting her, he placed the curve of the crook under Puah's chin and forced her to look directly at him.

The god-king smiled, but what the young midwife saw in his eyes sent chills of dread through her very soul. Pharaoh stared through her like the cobra's deadly gaze. His leer rang of madness.

"You do *too* good a job, midwife. Now *this* is what you will do." He sprayed the words in Puah's face, then spun on his heels and quickly ascended the steps to his throne. Instead of sitting, Pharaoh stood defiantly. He glared at the scribes and spoke.

"Record this decree for posterity." His eyes tracked to the elderly vizier standing quietly at the front of the dais, daring him to interfere. Whatever unspoken words passed were enough. Sennerfer lowered his eyes in acceptance.

"I hereby this day order the Hebrew midwives of Egypt to kill every male Hebrew infant born in all of Upper and Lower Egypt. Failure to follow my command will mean death!"

Gasps coursed throughout the room, then faded into stone cold silence. Puah could utter no sound. She didn't believe her ears. *Surely I heard wrong!* She looked to Shiphrah for confirmation that she'd misunderstood Pharaoh's words. The wide-eyed horror on Shiphrah's face told her what she didn't want to know. She spun around in panic to Hattush, then turned back quickly at her husband's unspoken warning.

The elderly vizier started to protest. "My lord, I —"

"Silence!" Pharaoh's roar halted him in mid-sentence. "The decree has been given. Anyone who fails to follow my command shall die!" The sentries were poised, swords and spears ready, bristling like beasts smelling blood before the kill.

Puah glanced at Hattush. The pain she saw there caused a wail to form in her throat. Her husband knew this man, this one who thought himself god. The abhorrence on Hattush's face told her all she needed to know. The sons of Abraham would die. By decree of Pharaoh who wore the double crown of Upper and Lower Egypt, she and Shiphrah were to kill every male child born to the children of Israel!

Puah's gaze fell on Pharaoh's crown. It was appropriate. The inner white crown symbolized death, while the outer rim of blood-red was the same color of the precious life force that would flow by his ungodly decree, the decree he expected *her* to fulfill.

Pharaoh rose and quickly departed. All eyes followed him as if in a trance, like prey of the cobra stricken into silence by cold, hard fear. The door boomed as it closed behind him, echoing across the stone walls of the throne room. For a strained moment no sounds were made, as if waiting would cause the nightmare to end. Then it began — the softest, gasping whimper of a young Hebrew slave. Suddenly chaos broke out. Other slaves wailed, clinging to one another. Foreign visitors at court watched in wide-eyed disbelief, chattering in a cacophony of languages. Egyptian servants clustered together, whispering, faces ashen with fear.

Puah's ears began ringing, a distant humming moving ever closer. It was far too warm. An encroaching dark tunnel surrounded her. The last thing she saw before sinking to the floor was Shiphrah ripping her sheath and wailing in deepest despair. Then the jeweled box clattered onto the mirrored floor and everything was black.

Silence lay heavy inside the tent as the desert wind murmured quietly against the walls. Innocent eyes watched Puah, waiting for her to break the stillness brought by her story. No matter how many times the story was told, it still caused her heart to skip a beat.

Puah looked down at Hannah. Tears rimmed her great-great-granddaughter's dark eyes. Puah felt moisture in her own.

"But, my children, that is *not* the end of the story. Our God was not yet finished. He was, and as you know *is,* more powerful than *any* man, especially a man who thinks of himself as god."

"What did you do, Grandma´ma?" Hannah asked not for herself, but the others. She'd pried the story from Puah on more than one occasion. Now, with Egypt behind them and the Promised Land ahead, it seemed even more precious.

"I'll tell you more tomorrow evening. For now, this old woman must rest."

"Yes, Grandma′ma." With quiet obedience Hannah planted a tender goodnight kiss on Puah's wrinkled cheek and ushered the children from the tent.

Soon only the sounds of camp settling down for a night of rest filled her ears. The tribes of Israel were prepared for the next day's trying march. Weariness assailed the old midwife, down to the marrow of her bones. Gently she eased upon the pillows and drifted into a deep, dreamless sleep.

IX

Behold, I send an Angel before you to keep you in the way and to bring you into the place which I have prepared. (Exodus 23:20)

Hattush stood in the sleeping chamber watching Puah pace back and forth like a caged animal. Her face was perfuse with the blotched redness of suppressed rage. She wrung her hands, then swept a stray strand of hair from her eyes.

"We must call a meeting of the elders and find a way to resist. We cannot do this, do you hear me? Pharaoh is insane! We'll go to Goshen. I refuse to be a part of this . . . this *slaughter!* Pharaoh cannot —"

"Stop it!" The harshness in Hattush's voice drew her up short. She turned and stared at him, wide-eyed and trembling.

Hattush saw her lips were quivering. She seemed near breaking. He must find some way to comfort her. "Puah, come here, my love," he said gently.

Puah rushed into his arms, clinging like a frightened child. Deep tormented sobs poured forth, his strong, independent bride reduced to disconcerting terror by a madman's decree. The unthinkable had been commanded, an act so hideous that surely God's judgment must soon fall on Egypt. Jehovah would not allow the senseless slaughter of innocent babies.

Thoughts rushed through Hattush's head as he held tightly to his shaking wife. Puah's anguished cries soon faded to soft gasps and exhausted moans. Perhaps she was right, they could hide in Goshen. But if they were ferreted out and returned, the outcome was unthinkable. They could openly refuse to honor the decree, but that would mean certain death. *Oh, God, there must be a way to avoid this slaughter without falling victim to Pharaoh's wrath, but how?*

Something stirred within Hattush, and the feeling frightened him. He would fight to the death to protect his bride. Her heart, though willful and strong, was full of good for others. How many nights had she rushed out to help women at their most vulnerable season? For long periods, days even, she would wait diligently at bedside, praying and ministering, forgetting to eat and take proper care of herself. Even when all seemed hopeless, she prayed. Many of those prayers were answered and her reputation grew throughout the community with each passing day. Increasingly, Egyptian women called for her at their time of confinement.

Yes, Hattush knew he would die protecting her. There was no doubt the LORD God did not intend for his innocent ones to be hurt. He also knew fully that Puah would choose death before she hurt *any* child. For that reason it was imperative he find a way to circumvent Pharaoh's maniacal order.

Was Goshen the answer? Her family would have no difficulty hiding her there. But what then? The decree would stand. Pharaoh would find a way to kill the babies. No, somehow they must find a way to hide them. It would be far more dangerous than he dared consider, but the alternative of walking away was not acceptable. With Puah and Shiphrah involved, there was assurance of saving some of the infants. Hope flared in Hattush's heart as he considered the alternatives, however few.

How would Puah and Shiphrah feel about a plan to hide the babies? If her family could hide *her* in Goshen, then certainly they could hide babies. *Yes, that's it! We'll form a human network and smuggle the newborns to Hebrew families away from the cities.* Pharaoh's soldiers would be sorely pressed to search every Egyptian village for babies. Why, the infants were so small they could be easily hidden in baskets!

Hattush slid an arm from around Puah, brushing her disheveled hair away from her tear-streaked face and placed a solemn kiss on her forehead. The kiss, a seal of promise to himself and to the LORD, gave him new strength and resolve that he would protect her and the babies with everything within him.

"My flower, let me dry your tears. We'll figure this out. God won't allow this evil to happen. I'm sure of His infinite mercy."

Hattush led her to a basin of water. Anna stood by quietly, her own eyes wide with fear and concern for her mistress. Taking a soft cloth, he dampened it and wiped away the salty traces of Puah's tears. She surrendered silently to his gentle ministration. Only her questioning eyes revealed the emotional jumble still reverberating in her exhausted silence.

"Anna. Prepare some sleeping herbs for the mistress. She must rest."

Anna nodded and rushed out, relieved to have a task to perform.

Hattush led Puah to their bed and coaxed her to lie down. She followed woodenly, like a submissive child. He pulled a light linen throw over her. She shivered, still somewhat in shock. She would make herself ill if she did not rest.

"Hattush, what —"

He halted the question by gently placing his finger over her lips, stilling the words.

"Not now, love," Hattush whispered. "We'll talk when you awaken. You rest now. This has been a terrible shock for us all. With God's help, we'll find a way out of this.

"While you sleep I must go to the foundry. There is a problem with one of the new molds. I'll be back soon after dark." He leaned forward and lightly kissed her forehead. "While I'm away you are to do nothing but rest. Do you understand?"

"Yes, but —"

"No! You are to rest! When we meet later at Shiphrah's your mind must be clear and refreshed."

Dear Shiphrah! Puah had almost forgotten her beloved friend's stricken face as they consoled each other after arriving home from Pharaoh's palace. For the first time, the young midwife noticed lines of age creeping across her mentor's face. Shadows of despair lay beneath the reddened eyes. Too shocked to speak of the morning's events, they'd simply sat together, drawing comfort from each other's presence. As Shiphrah departed, they agreed to meet at her home after dark.

Puah sighed and pulled the light covers closer. She rolled onto her side in quiet submission to her husband's mandate and nodded her head in affirmation.

Hattush took her hand and once again marveled at how small Puah's felt in his own callused one. Gently he brought it to his lips, placing a light kiss on her palm.

How he loved her hands! Though soft as silk, they were strong from laboring in the miracle of birth. Often he'd seen her return from a delivery, her clothing wet with perspiration and stained from the demanding physical work of a difficult delivery. Puah's hands echoed the strength of her quiet dignity and stamina.

We will survive this together. Oh, LORD, show us the way!

Anna returned with a warm infusion smelling strongly of herbs and wine. Hattush held the cup to Puah's lips as she drank. He stroked her hair, talking softly until her breathing slowed and a tiny shudder signaled her surrender to sleep.

"No one is to disturb her."

"Yes, I'll see to it," Anna whispered.

Hattush headed for the foundry and his own yoke of problems. Deep weariness filled his bones, and he wondered if Father Joseph could have foreseen the trials his people would face in this land of many gods. Could he have known the throne would someday become bondage for the children of Israel instead of a haven from famine? *How many more generations must fall under the taskmaster's whip before the promise to Father Abraham is fulfilled?*

Hattush passed the brickyard where the many bricks used in the tomb's construction were cut, dried, and stacked. Workers dotted the yard, their skin browned deeply by the ceaseless rays of the unforgiving sun. Some of the newer laborers bore blisters on their naked shoulders and backs.

The sun was at its zenith, heat beating down mercilessly. How many times had he passed here and offered silent prayers for the men who toiled from early morning until darkness forced them to stop? Nearby a haughty Egyptian guard glared at the workers. With muscled arms crossed at his chest, he clutched the detestable whip. The sight of it made Hattush's jaw tighten and his hands clench in righteous anger.

It was inhuman. The Egyptians treated pack animals better than they treated the children of Israel. Heat hammered down, yet they toiled on. When one collapsed, the others labored on. To stop would mean a beating, even to help a fallen friend. If the whip didn't bring the exhausted worker to his knees, he was dragged out of the way. How many had died there in the heat where the guards watched over their charges, eyes gleaming sadistically? It was almost as if they hoped someone would falter. Only when the last drops of water fell from the ceramic jug marking time, did the guards allow the workers precious moments to rest and drink.

Hattush hurried past. He had too much to consider. The brick workers' plight wasn't one he could concern himself with right now. At least they were men. They could run and hide, fight if necessary, though it would do little good. But innocent babies — that was another story.

At the foundry his foreman, Jareh, rushed to him.

"Is it true what we've heard? About Pharaoh's decree? Has he ordered the death of all male babies? My wife is with child. Hattush. I *must know!*"

Jareh's eyes ploughed into Hattush. No good would come of downplaying the danger they all faced. Yet he feared a general panic. *Oh, God, give me the right words.*

"You heard true, Jareh," Hattush said, placing a hand on the man's shoulder. "We'll find a way to stop Pharaoh's madness. For now, if possible, don't let your wife know. It will only cause her to be fearful, and that's not good for the baby. The midwives will be meeting with the elders soon. Be strong and trust God. Somehow we'll find a way."

Hattush's words appeased Jareh. He turned his attention to the work at hand. "Sennerfer just left. Pharaoh will inspect the tomb tomorrow morning. I cannot leave now. We're completing the mold for the outer mask. Perhaps you should go and inspect the work at the tomb one last time?"

"What did Sennerfer tell you?"

"He wants to meet with you as soon as possible. You are to be at the palace tomorrow morning after you see the priests leave the gates. A servant will tell you where to go."

"Is that all?"

"He seemed distracted. His mind wasn't on the details of our work."

Hattush walked toward the door, then as an afterthought turned to face his foreman. "Jareh, about Pharaoh's decree. I've already thought of one possibility. We'll speak more of it later. For now, I must go to the tomb. Ask the men to work as late as possible tonight. Pharaoh is in a mad rage. I don't want any of his wrath to fall on our people here."

Jareh nodded and Hattush left. He decided to take the mule kept at the foundry. Used for carrying goods back and forth between the tomb and the foundry, it would allow him to finish his business and return home more quickly. Tonight, Puah's needs must come before Pharaoh's obsession with his burial chamber.

The tiresome, dusty trek from the city gave Hattush time to think. As Itj-tawy fell behind, the mule accepted its fate, settling into a predictable rhythm.

Former dynasties had used Memphis to the north and Thebes to the south as governmental centers. The current royal family preferred Itj-tawy, conveniently located near the border of Upper and Lower Egypt. Because of its strategic location, Itj-tawy grew into a bustling capital.

With royal business moved here from the older centers, Pharaoh's family chose the rugged western hills to construct their final resting places. For generations Khaneferre's family had laid their dead to rest in tombs chiseled deep into the rocky cliffs.

157

Now Khaneferre himself oversaw the tomb construction. Driven by an obsession to see eternal life, he accepted nothing less than absolute perfection, a definition that changed with his every mood and the season.

The way grew steeper as Hattush left the flats, veering south toward the base of the looming hills. Soon evening shadows would offer blessed relief from the stifling heat covering the foot trail leading to the tomb's entrance.

Hattush scanned the horizon. Far to the southwest lay the Great Inland Sea, actually a large lake. A canal connected the lake with the Nile. Partially manmade, it followed the wadi's ancient natural bed. Under Father Joseph's direction, architects widened the canal, reinforcing its banks to accommodate the worst inundation years.

Somewhere along the canal lay Father Joseph's khenret, a huge mud-brick storage labyrinth. Now in abandoned disrepair and partially buried by the desert's ever-shifting sand, it stood as a legacy to Joseph's part in saving Egypt from seven years of famine. It was a wonder Khaneferre had not ordered it destroyed, for its silent presence would stand forever as a reminder of the Hebrew patriarch's role in saving Egypt. More importantly, it stood as a testament of God's hand in the affairs of man.

Already much of Father Joseph's story had been stricken from public record by Khaneferre's grandfather. No sound reason could be found. Truth be told, the stories enraged him. He considered them fantasies of a weak and addled predecessor. So, he'd ordered them removed from public records and court documents. Within a year, the king was dead. . . .

Once, then twice, the mule stumbled before Hattush finally surrendered and slid off. He led the panting animal by the rope harness. A triumphant bray almost sent a smile to his face, but today not even a near-human mule's antics could bring joy to his aching heart. All he could muster was a pat on the neck for the faithful mount and a date he had hidden in the pocket of his robe. The mule accepted it eagerly, chomping with relish as they ascended the ever-steepening path.

At the next natural landing along the path, Hattush tied the mule to a rock and continued toward the now visible overcrop which marked the tomb's entrance. Once nothing more than a small natural cavern, the chamber now comprised many rooms, hewn out and reinforced with bricks by Hebrew slaves.

The main rooms were heavily decorated with hieroglyphics and elaborate paintings proclaiming praises of Khaneferre's mighty deeds. Hieroglyphics — the language of the gods, according to the scribes. Would they record the slaughter of infants by Pharaoh's hand? Would they record his madness for generations to come? Would they tell of the abuse of Father Joseph's descendants? Not likely. Tales displayed on the walls spoke only of victory and greatness. In a thousand years, when future generations gazed in awe at the beauty and riches of the tomb, they would think Khaneferre accomplished it all by his own hand.

Bitterness surged through Hattush. The anger he felt and squelched through the years boiled within. *Why does such evil flourish? How much do God's people have to endure before He delivers us? And now, the babies? Why, LORD?* It was too much, much more than he could fathom.

"Goodnight, Hattush."

Lost in thought, Hattush glanced up in surprise as two workers exited the tomb. He nodded and stepped aside, watching the men retreat down the steep winding trail. As they passed from sight their laughter echoed, bringing more sadness to Hattush's

160

heart. *They'll be going home to their families now, home to learn the news of Pharaoh's decree. Are their wives with child?*

At the tomb's opening Hattush halted and listened. A slight whistle of wind caught his ear. Finding himself alone, he felt a faint disquiet. Had the workers already heard of the decree and rebelled? No, the two men who'd greeted him gave no such sign. It was probably just one of those days when the projects reached a stopping place at the same time. With stonecutters, goldsmiths, painters, and scribes all laboring on the tomb, such an occurrence was unusual, but it did happen.

The cave's dry musk reminded him that this was indeed a tomb, however ornately decorated. Khaneferre's first wife rested here in her own sealed chamber. She had been his sister, a marriage not uncommon among royal Egyptians, but considered an abomination to the Hebrews. Still, with all the contempt Hattush felt at this time for Khaneferre, he couldn't bring himself to hate him. This place would one day receive Pharaoh's body. If the young goldsmith felt anything for the king, it was pity.

Hattush lit a torch and entered the dark recesses beyond the entrance. After making a couple of turns he moved into what he knew would be complete darkness but for his torch. He'd been here hundreds of times, most often when dozens of other workers teemed about and the chambers were ablaze with light.

He entered the burial chamber, placed the torch in a holder and went straight to the pillars where the newest work appeared. It looked to be in order. The support pillars' golden crowns gleamed in the torchlight. This was the royal chamber where Khaneferre's sarcophagus and mummy would rest for eternity. Hattush surveyed the work carefully. It was flawless. Heaven only knew if they would please or enrage Pharaoh. No one could know. Khaneferre grew more unpredictable with each passing day.

Hattush struggled with his thoughts. *Perhaps Khaneferre will occupy his tomb sooner than later. That would silence his ungodly decree. But then who would rule?* Pharaoh's son was still a child. At least for a time Sennerfer would stand at his side, but how long would the vizier live? Who then would take Sennerfer's place as regent — one of the evil priests?

Hattush knew his thoughts were wicked, but he couldn't help it. Pharaoh was insane. Did his wicked decree not prove it? And all brought on by groundless paranoia that the Hebrews would rise up against him.

Deep heaviness weighed Hattush's soul. He needed answers and he needed them now. All his life he had heard of God's promises to Abraham, promises of a Deliverer who would someday lead their people out of bondage to Canaan. Yet today it didn't seem even God could make *that* come to pass.

Suddenly weary, Hattush felt like an old man. The stressful day had begun early after little rest the night before. Now it was taking its toll. He leaned against the column and closed his eyes. Oh, if only he could rest for a moment! But Puah's tortured image filled his mind. *I must hasten home and check on her.*

Hattush took a deep breath and exhaled. It echoed like a rushing wind throughout the dim chamber. *That's strange.* He opened his eyes. The torchlight flickered and almost went out. He turned to leave, but as his hand touched the torch its light waned again, then died. He stood in total darkness, hand frozen on the torch. He shuddered and caught his breath and tried to gather his bearings.

Light suddenly shimmered behind him, subtle at first, like the soft blush of dawn.

Soon it filled the chamber with a strange, warm radiance, bright as the midday sun.

With trembling hands Hattush steadied himself against the wall at the room's entrance. He summoned his courage, then turned slowly to find the source of this implausible light. A cold chill ran through him and his gasp broke the chamber's stillness.

Before him stood a giant of a man, at least a cubit taller than he. Dressed in pure linen that shone as if woven from fine, white gold, his right hand clutched a great sword which sparkled like cut diamonds. But it was the man's face that commanded attention. It glimmered as if dusted with the powder of precious metals, a light from within causing the illumination to fill the room. Deep in the mysterious being's eyes was the most powerful manifestation of love he'd ever witnessed.

Hattush sank to his knees as endless questions flooded his mind. *Who is this? How could he have gained entrance without my knowledge? Why didn't I see him until now? What does he want? Does he intend harm?*

"Fear not, Hattush, son of Abraham." The voice was deep but soft, like a resonant horn.

"Who . . . who are you?" Hattush asked,

clasping his hands together to stop their trembling.

"I have been sent by the Most High God, the God of Abraham, Isaac, Jacob, and Joseph. I come with comforting words."

No, this cannot be happening! Surely he was dreaming. The past day's events had driven him to madness. He was seeing and hearing things. Why, he was as deranged as Pharaoh!

"Hear me! Do not doubt that God knows where you are. He has placed you here at this time for *His* people. Events may not transpire as you plan, but do not be deceived. The Most High is in command, even in Egypt. By your wife's hands the Deliverer shall be born. He will lead God's people out of bondage."

"My wife?" *What could all this mean?* "But Pharaoh has ordered all male babies killed!"

"God will blind the eyes and stop the ears of Pharaoh's soldiers. Take the babies to safety. It is for that purpose you are here, Hattush. Your work with gold means nothing to He Who Created All Things. By your courage and pure heart you will save many, and great will be your reward. So hear me. Be of good courage. Be strong in the LORD and in the power of His might.

Trust not your own strength — it will surely fail you. Rely upon the LORD thy God. His arm is mightier than ten thousand times ten thousand of Pharaoh's mightiest armies. Rise. Go now, and comfort your wife with these words."

"Wait!" Even as Hattush spoke the messenger disappeared. He struggled to his feet and once more found himself in total darkness. Yet this time it was immensely different. Peace like he'd never known flowed through his veins as surely as his own life-blood. He felt like shouting with jubilation — God had heard his desperate cries!

Tears welled in his eyes as he again fell to his knees. He wept deeply and unashamedly. He cried out to the LORD in repentance for his disbelief and fearful heart. As he prayed for the LORD's forgiveness, he felt surrounded by an impenetrable wall of peace and joy.

Like most men, Hattush had lived life without realizing the importance of his own existence. Now in the midst of adversity, the Most High sent forth His messenger, declaring he was here for a purpose. Warmth rushed through him and he rose quickly. *I must hasten home to Puah. What was it the messenger said? By my wife's hands the Deliverer will be born!*

As Hattush rose and turned to feel his way toward the spot where he thought the wall to be, the torch ignited and its soft glow filled the chamber with golden incandescence. The likenesses of Egyptian gods stared at him with unseeing eyes. All the futile prayers and offerings to stone statues of jackals, alligators, and women who were part lion seemed so pathetic. *Oh, that these people could know the One True God who heard my people's prayers!* For the second time that day, tears welled in Hattush's eyes as he made his way down the long corridor.

Silence fell as Puah finished her story. Brisk desert winds whistled outside the tent this night, the flap long closed against the chill and blowing sand.

"Who was the messenger who spoke to Father Hattush?" Lemuel, Hannah's older cousin, asked.

Puah smiled. "Hattush believed he was from God, a heavenly messenger. I didn't see him, but I do know this. Everything he told my blessed husband came to pass."

A young girl sitting near the doorway spoke with assurance. "He was an angel! That's what he was!"

"Do *you* think he was an angel, Grandma´ma?" Hannah asked.

Puah coughed and grimaced as yet another pain stabbed her chest. How she hated to think of leaving Hannah behind. Such a joy, the child's smile would brighten the darkest day.

"At first I didn't," Puah said, shaking her head. "Sadly, I doubted my husband. I was very wrong. It was *my* faith that was weak. Father Hattush always believed God would keep his word. And you children are evidence of His promise. Don't ever forget that.

"And now, let us get some rest. Our journey to the Promised Land is far from over."

X

The Spirit of the LORD shall rest upon Him, the Spirit of wisdom and under-standing; the Spirit of counsel and might, the Spirit of knowledge and of the fear of the LORD. (Isaiah 11:2)

Puah awakened to her own startled cry. Dreadful fragmented dreams dissipated as she bolted upright and looked around. Late afternoon sunlight painted the walls opposite the sleeping chamber's window. Why was she still in bed at this time of day? Had she been up for a delivery? As suddenly as a slap it all came rushing back. The anguish of those recent memories caused pain in her belly as surely as if someone had struck her there.

Nausea swept through her and the next moment she hovered over the wash basin trying to wipe away waves of sickness. She blotted a cool wet cloth over her face and neck until the queasiness passed. Her hands shook. She couldn't remember ever feeling this ill.

What were they to do? She and Shiphrah would surely die if they refused to honor Pharaoh's decree. She would gladly choose death before intentionally harming a baby. Question after question flew through Puah's mind, yet no clear answer came.

Not only was she accountable to the mad king for her actions, but now Pharaoh knew Hattush was her husband. If she failed to carry out the maniacal decree in any way, Hattush could be punished. Nothing Khaneferre might do would surprise her. It all seemed hopeless. Why had God allowed His people to come here only to be punished by such wickedness? Had they not been faithful and kept themselves separate from the Egyptians' ungodly ways? They marked their males for Him by circumcision. And for what? So they could all die at the hands of a maniac who thought himself god? Could Pharaoh not see his heart could never be pure if he had the blood of innocent children staining his hands?

Falling to her knees, Puah tasted the salt of tears. What would God have her do? She couldn't kill the babies. She thought of a newborn's soft rounded face, its tiny puckered mouth, wide dark eyes staring up at her. *How could anyone possibly hurt such an innocent? There must be another way!*

Suddenly the room seemed to close in and her head began to pound. If she stayed here alone with her thoughts, she'd go mad. She threw a woolen shawl around her shoulders and headed for the kitchen. Though the afternoon was still warm, she felt chilled to the bone.

Anna worked diligently, patting cakes into shape and baking them on flat stones. Normally Puah would've stolen a bite, but this afternoon the mere thought of food made her insides wrench.

"Mistress, may I prepare something for you?" Anna, her ever-faithful helper and friend stood waiting, her face drawn with concern.

"No thank you, Anna. I'm feeling ill. Perhaps later. I'll be on the roof. Hopefully some fresh air will ease my nausea."

From the roof, Puah scanned the distant eastern horizon past village roofs. She wanted to be out there somewhere, running and running and running until the entire nightmare lay far behind. Yet even as she indulged herself in the childish fantasy, she knew the truth. No one could outrun Pharaoh's chariots and armies. They would surely find and kill her.

A call from a nearby courtyard brought her thoughts closer to home. Even the children's games sounded different today, the usual squeals and calls of happy, rowdy play absent. They were subdued, as if sensing the great heaviness weighing their parents' shoulders. Would Pharaoh vent his anger on *them* next?

Deep melancholy filled Puah's heart. She turned and sank onto soft cushions beneath the shade of the awning. Afternoon breezes fluttered the fabric's edges, a sound that normally relaxed and stilled her spirit. Often she allowed the sound to lead into a fantasy of sailing on great ships like she'd seen on the Nile, with wide sails dancing to the rhythm of unseen music. Today it seemed only mockery. Nothing could bring peace. Tears welled up once more and she surrendered to the pain, allowing deep sobs to escape as she cried out to heaven, "God, why are you allowing this!" It no longer mattered if others heard.

"LORD, what am I to do? Do You want me to hide? I cannot harm Your little ones. I *cannot!* You called me to be a healer, not a murderer! Please, show me the way. I am weak. Give me strength to do your will."

Finally spent, no more words formed, only her heart's cries. The tears dried but her throat was parched. Eyes swollen and red, and with no further insight than before, she fell back exhausted onto the pillows and watched clouds drift by. Numbness overcame her, and she welcomed it. . . .

That was how Hattush found her, reclining, staring emptily at passing clouds, trying not to think of anything, for there were no answers.

"Did you rest?"

Puah closed her eyes at the sound of his voice. If only she could memorize its deep, soothing resonance. Here in life's wilderness, he was her oasis. He'd put himself at risk for her today. The love she felt for him swelled greater in her breast.

"Not well." She was afraid to look at him. To see pity in his face would only bring more tears, and that would accomplish nothing.

The cushions sank as Hattush joined her. A strong, warm arm slid behind Puah's back and pulled her close. She lay against his shoulder and marveled at the sense of peace she found there. Hattush's tender presence could calm any storm. She adored his heart's deep drumming. Her head rose and fell to the rhythm of his steady breathing. She sought his hand and held it tightly, allowing his strength to seep into her. They rested for awhile without words.

Finally she turned and looked at him. "What are we to do? You know I cannot harm the infants. Yet if I disobey Pharaoh, I'll surely die."

Hattush smiled, his amber eyes shining with a brightness that surprised her. "Let me tell you a story, my bride." He pulled Puah closer, but his apparent lack of consternation caused anger to surge within her breast. She tried to rise, but strong arms held her in place.

Twisting to face him, she spewed, "A *story?* This is no time for fables! Didn't you hear me?"

Hattush laughed like a parent who's caught a child's hand in a dish of sweet treats. "Not *that* kind of story, my love," he said in a gentle voice. "Something happened today at the tomb. I think you'll want to hear it, so smooth your feathers and lay your lovely head here on my shoulder and listen. When I've finished, you be the judge of my *fable*."

His calming voice assuaged her anger and piqued her curiosity. Could Pharaoh have possibly changed his mind? What could've happened at the tomb today?

"Very well, tell me your story. But then we must talk seriously about this matter."

Hattush began to recount the story of the

mysterious visitor. Puah listened quietly, and as the encounter unfolded a shudder coursed through her.

"I've never seen anything like it!" Hattush exclaimed, his eyes drifting to the fiery glow beyond the distant hills. "His clothing was spun of the purest gold thread. His face and eyes shone with the most guileless love I've ever known. The sword he carried was nearly as long as I. Had he chosen to use it, I would've been utterly destroyed!"

"You say he appeared in the dark? How did he get into the room without you seeing him?"

"Not only did he appear in the room *after* the torch died, he lit the entire chamber with his countenance. Truly, if he'd never spoken a word I would've fallen to my knees by the sheer power of his presence."

"He spoke?" Amazement flooded Puah's mind.

"Yes, about many things, and he also spoke of you, my love."

Hattush clutched both her hands in his, and his eyes danced mysteriously. Hope? Joy? She couldn't tell. "He spoke of *me?* What could this stranger know of me?"

"Who he was I cannot say, but I do know who sent him. He told me he was delivering a message from the Holy One of Israel. He said that you and I have been put here in this time and place by the God of Abraham, Isaac, Jacob, and Joseph. The LORD has heard our prayers. He will keep His promises to our people."

Hattush paused. Tenderly lifting her chin with a finger until their eyes met, he whispered, "The messenger said by *your* hands the Deliverer will be born."

Profound silence passed as Puah tried to assimilate this. A heavenly messenger? She'd heard of such things, but to her husband? And to speak of her work as a midwife? Surely the days had taken their toll on Hattush. Still, he seemed so convinced of his story.

"Me? The messenger told you *I* would help the Deliverer be born? Is that what I heard?"

"Yes, that's exactly what he said. He also commanded me to come home and comfort you with those words." Hattush drew Puah closer. "Don't you see, my love? It's our confirmation of what to do. You're to continue your work as before, but we *must* find a way to hide and protect the babies, for out of these births will come the one who'll lead our people to freedom!"

Never had she seen her husband so animated. Everything in her being was convinced Hattush believed this. But could it really be true?

"Then what happened?"

Hattush laughed, then rose and pulled Puah to her feet. He cupped her face in his hands and planted a firm kiss on her lips.

"He disappeared as quickly as he appeared, while I stood there and watched him dissolve like vapor. I was left in total darkness once again."

"How did you find your way out of the tomb?" Perhaps it was all a dream. Her solid and practical Hattush wasn't one to dwell on frivolous things. Yet dreams were not to be discounted. After all, it was by his dream interpretations that Father Joseph saved Egypt and the children of Abraham.

"After he disappeared I could only stand there for a moment trying to collect myself. Then I felt along the wall for the torch. As soon as my hand touched it, the torch reignited as spontaneously as it died."

Hattush brushed her hair back from her face, capturing her gaze. "I know you must think I'm as mad as Pharaoh, but I tell you true. This was surely a message from the LORD. God *is* in control. I truly believe if we trust in Him, He'll provide a way to protect the babies *and* us. The messenger said that God would blind the sol-

177

diers' eyes and stop their ears."

Puah turned her face away. "Hattush, I don't know what to say. Could you have been . . . dreaming?"

Hattush smiled lovingly. He shook his head as if she were a small child. "No, my flower. It wasn't a dream, it was a message. We'll meet with the elders tonight to form a plan to protect and hide the babies. The messenger said we weren't to be in fear, but to trust in God and the power of *His* might. He warned me that our strength might fail, but God would not."

Hope quivered through Puah. Her beloved was convinced of the mysterious visitor's reality, certain a message had been delivered to them from the God of Abraham. If that was true, it was an answer to her prayers. Had she not prayed this very day for an answer?

But what was it God's messenger had said? That *she* would deliver the promised one? Puah could scarcely believe the words. No logic accounted for such a wondrous thing. She would reserve her judgment until after the meeting with the elders.

Even as Puah qualified her excitement, she studied Hattush's exhilarated face for signs of madness. She found none, only the glow of someone who'd seen something

178

wondrous or miraculous.

Puah and Hattush met Shiphrah at her home, then accompanied her to the house of Heber, the stonecutter, where the elders had chosen to meet. It stood on the outskirts of Itj-tawy, set back from the main road. Word traveled like desert wind throughout the region, and before the evening moon rose, people from all corners of the land descended upon Heber's home.

The room was packed with older bearded men, leaders of their people. Sitting was impossible. The air bristled with suppressed rage and fear. It smelled of leather, sheep, and sweat. Puah and Shiphrah were among the handful of women there.

Few spoke, and only in hushed tones. The palace's eyes and ears could be anywhere. Like troubled bees the men whispered excitedly, anger threatening to erupt any moment.

Puah stood between Hattush and Shiphrah, holding tightly to their hands, afraid to let go. The stifling heat brought nausea to her empty stomach. Hattush had encouraged her to eat some of Anna's flatbread, but it stuck in her throat. Finally, in desperation Hattush insisted she sip some wine. Now she regretted doing so.

The heat, her aversion to the fruit of the vine, and the mixed earthy odors all pressed in on her. Her stomach pitched and rolled. Perhaps the wine wasn't the cause at all. Perhaps it was the simple animal fear brought by impending death.

Stop it! She rebuked the thought. Before she could continue frightening herself, Heber called the meeting to order.

"We begin. Hattush, son of Asa and Pharaoh's chief goldsmith, tell us what has transpired in recent weeks."

As Hattush described Pharaoh's irrational behavior, an angry murmur began, growing louder with each passing moment. Heber finally quieted them, allowing Hattush to continue. When Hattush uttered the final words of Pharaoh's godless decree, shock and dismay filled the room.

Pharaoh's words struck like a fiery dart to the heart of every man there, for each could name at least one woman with child in his family — a wife or daughter, sister, aunt, or cousin.

"Shall we leave Egypt, then?" a man muttered from the stairway that led to the roof.

"And have Pharaoh's army hunt us down like frightened hare?" another interjected from near the back wall. "Slaughter *all* our people?"

"To stand against Pharaoh means certain death," someone hissed from the front near Heber.

Uncle Namir lifted his hands above the crowd and spoke with quiet conviction. "I say we must protect our women and keep those with child in hiding. Once the children are born, we will send them to our people in Goshen for protection."

"And what of the babies in Goshen? Will the army not find them there?"

"He's right! They'll hunt us down. We have no recourse but to fight!"

Puah couldn't see who spoke, but a tremor surged through her at the implication. Uttered in public, those words would mean instant death to anyone speaking of such rebellion or resistance to Pharaoh's orders. To act on it would mean full-fledged slaughter.

"Please, may I speak?" Hattush's husky voice silenced the room. The rumbling faded, a cough or two, then quiet.

Fervor tinged Hattush's words. "I believe that any open resistance will mean disaster for our people. We have little choice in this matter. I agree with Namir. We should hide all women with child from Egyptian eyes. We must find a way to secrete the midwives to each home for births when needed. Once the babies are strong enough to travel, they should be smuggled to the countryside to our people."

"But they'll be discovered. You're as mad as Pharaoh!"

Around the room quiet gasps followed the insult. The words failed to move Hattush. He stood straight and tall, turning slowly to the voice. Power emanated from him as never before. Perchance Puah was prejudiced and blindly in love, but beside her this night stood a true leader of men.

"Perhaps *some* will be discovered, but if we don't try to hide the little ones, *all* will die. With or without the midwives, Pharaoh will hunt for them. We know the risks. But there's something more that we haven't considered. . . ."

Puah gazed up at Hattush. His eyes shone brilliantly in the light of the oil lamps. Indeed, something unique *had* touched her husband. She squeezed his hand tightly. He blessed her with a loving smile, then looked about the room full of questioning eyes.

"The Holy One of Israel didn't bring our people here to abandon us. He will guide and protect us in our work. Did he not promise Father Abraham the land of Canaan? Is our God a liar?"

A communal gasp erupted at this blasphemous thought. The rumble of voices again filled the room. It seemed to have had the effect Hattush desired. To Puah's amazement a smile played across her husband's face. He waited a few moments until the crowd quieted before continuing.

"Of *course* not. Our God is true and just. He will keep His word. We must do our part and trust the LORD to do His part. As Abraham believed in Him for the sacrifice to replace Isaac, so must we trust the LORD for protection. If He is not true, if He is not just, if His word is not sure, then we must join the heathen now and abandon our ways. Why else would we live separate, awaiting the Deliverer? Either God is for us, or He is against us!"

Hattush paused, scanning the spellbound audience. Then placing one strong arm around Puah, he lifted the other toward heaven and declared, "As for me and my house, we will trust God. We will do what needs to be done to save our children. Who will join Puah and me in saving our children?"

At that moment all angry voices of dissent and insurrection faded. Calm but earnest conversation infused the room. Soon, goodwill and cooperation became the rule. With quiet nods, the most venerable elders signaled their assent to Hattush's plan.

The meeting carried on far into the night as the Hebrews devised ways to hide both midwives and infants. Many volunteered to transport the babies to Goshen. They would hide them as they transported livestock, or in carts holding goods for trade. Others offered to enact diversions for Pharaoh's soldiers. Still more agreed to relay messages around the city. A network of communication would be set up throughout the land. When the time came, a planned diversion on one street to occupy the soldiers might save a baby on the next street as it was smuggled away to safety.

Puah's fears were calmed. With God's help they would save the babies, and right under Khaneferre's nose. Did they really have any other choice? Besides, with the Hittites challenging the borders on the east, and the Nubians warring constantly in Upper Egypt, Pharaoh would be hard pressed to keep soldiers at the task of following women and assuring they were not in labor.

The thought brought a bitter smile to Puah's lips. She could picture the ridiculous scene: Pharaoh's strapping warriors tagging along behind women in the marketplace, trying to determine if they were with child, much less near labor. It was likely the soldiers would tire of the craziness sooner than later. They were trained for war, not following after Hebrew women's skirts. Their tastes in female matters took a different track, more likely to include the loose women who pursued the soldiers' encampments.

The half-moon was far below its apex as Puah and Hattush escorted Shiphrah to her gate, then hurried home. With her stomach calmed, they dined quietly on light goat cheese and cold bread before falling into the sleeping platform's welcoming softness.

The decision stood. They would do the work and trust God for the rest. Together they would find comfort. For now they would live fully, loving one another as never before.

"So, you and Shiphrah defied Pharaoh?" Adam, one of the older boys, asked in quiet admiration from his seat near the tent's entrance. The camp was quiet now. Stars rose in a moonless sky, twinkling through open flap.

Was it so strange to him that a woman could have courage? "Yes, the plan was made and we smuggled the baby boys to Goshen. As God's messenger promised, we were able to hide the little ones. I was terri-fied, but sometimes we're not given easy choices. Sometimes we must use all of our courage to do the right thing, even if it costs our lives."

A tiny hand snaked out and found Puah's. It was Hannah's, and when Puah gazed down, her little face gleamed up, pride shining in her soulful eyes.

Puah looked across the tent at Adam. "Courage is much more than an arrow or a club, my son."

The boy nodded in silent understanding.

XI

You who fear the LORD, trust in the LORD; He is their help and their shield. (Psalm 115:11)

Puah lay in Hattush's arms the following morning. Too tired the previous night to address the logistics of hiding the newborns, a multitude of questions now flooded her mind. And with the questions came renewed doubt.

"What are we to do if we're found out?" Puah asked. "How are we to conduct ourselves? What if someone speaks to Pharaoh of our work?"

"Our people won't betray us, not over the safety of their own infants," Hattush said. "We *do* have to be concerned about palace spies. You must never leave without letting others know where you're going. Diversions must be in place, and our lookouts must be watching for anyone who might follow you."

She snuggled deeper into the covers and

Hattush's arms. The noble plan to save the babies existed far from the harsh reality of openly defying Pharaoh. Getting caught meant certain death, not only for her, but now also Hattush. She wouldn't allow herself to dwell on it, but his next words forced her thoughts in that direction.

Hattush rolled onto his side and faced her. "I love you. You are my all in this world, my very breath." He gently drew his finger along her cheek in deep thought. Then like the softest touch of a butterfly, he kissed her.

Tears formed in Puah's eyes. She reached up and drew him to her, swallowing the tightness in her throat and allowing herself to draw comfort in his embrace. He pulled back and met her eyes.

"We must face the reality of our work. We might be detected. Everyone's at risk. Pharaoh could punish all of us for the mistake of one. But we can't allow ourselves to become paralyzed by our fears. If ever we placed our trust in God, it must be now."

"It's too much, Hattush! I cannot think of losing you! Perhaps we should try to hide." Panic reared, her heart racing at the thought. If they were found out, it would be brutal. The Egyptians were peaceful in many ways, but extreme in their punishment for open defiance of Pharaoh.

"Puah, look at me." Never had Hattush seemed so serious. "If I am caught, you are to deny any knowledge of my doings. Do you understand me? I don't demand this for myself, or even you. I demand it for our people. Your work must go on no matter what happens. Don't you see? You *must* continue your work. Remember what the messenger said? You, my dear wife, will help birth the Deliverer, the one who'll lead our people to Canaan!"

Hattush truly believed this. The fervor she saw in him yesterday still lit his eyes. Perhaps he truly had been visited by a messenger from God. But surely the LORD wouldn't expect her to sacrifice her beloved for this. Would He?

A vision of Abraham holding the knife above Isaac rushed into her mind and she almost cried out from the pain of it Yes, God *could* ask for the sacrifice most precious. Yet He had provided a substitute for Abraham. *Would God be so generous again?* Anguish knotted her bowels as she contemplated the possibilities. How could she find the strength to stand quietly by while someone accused her husband of a crime punishable by death, an act *God* demanded of her?

Would she be able to deny their accusations? Keep knowledge to herself? What if they tortured her? She'd heard horrible stories. *Surely they dare not do that to a woman!*

"Puah, I need your solemn word. Promise me now before the Living God that you'll not weaken if we're faced with accusation. You are not to betray me and I am not to betray you. There must be no room for exception."

"I cannot! How can you ask such a thing of me? You ask me to stand by silently while they accuse you of a heinous crime. Do you really think I could watch them drag you off while I stood by holding my tongue?"

"Yes, Puah, think about it! What do you think will happen if you confess the truth? We *both* die! And not just us, many others. You must determine in your heart and mind that this is how it will be. Now promise me!"

Hattush feared for her. Of that, she had no doubt. He was trying to protect her. Yet he asked for something she doubted she possessed strength to do. How would she summon the courage?

"Sweetest, listen to me. I know you think you're not strong enough. I also wonder if I can honor my own agreement and remain silent. But God gives us strength when we

190

need it. Look at the men who work the brickyards."

Hattush stood and walked to the eastern window. He scanned the horizon as traces of pink diffused the indigo of dawn.

"What about the men in the yards?" said Puah. "What could they have to do with this?"

"I once talked to Benjamin, son of Kedem, the onion farmer. He's forced to work the brickyards in fallow time. I asked him how he endured the backbreaking work in the heat day after day. Do you know what he told me?"

"I cannot imagine." Puah had seen the brick makers. Such a life seemed far too harsh to endure. With little doubt, she'd be dead within a day under the taskmaster's cruel whip.

"Benjamin said he gets renewed strength when he needs it. If he doesn't dwell on the work ahead, but simply concentrates on the load he shoulders at that moment, he can get through. God somehow gives him the strength, one brick at a time."

There did seem to be some truth there. How often had she been called to attend several deliveries when the moon waxed full and wondered how she could walk another step without sleep? Yet somehow she man-

191

aged, one baby at a time. In retrospect, she didn't know how she did it; the strength simply appeared when needed most.

"Are you saying God will give us the strength to remain silent in such a circumstance?"

"Exactly. I believe He'll protect us and provide what we need when we need it, just as He did for Abraham and Father Joseph."

Puah rose and walked to him, encircling his waist with her arms. *Oh, that I had such faith, such unwavering belief.* For a time she simply held him close, feeling his quiet strength as he stroked her hair. She wanted to hide away there, but the day wouldn't allow such luxury.

Instead, she sought his eyes. "I promise. With all that's in my power, I'll try."

Puah pulled away and grabbed his hand, attempting to lead him. "Now, come, I want to test my hand at cooking."

Hattush balked. When she looked back, his mouth betrayed his amusement at the thought of her cooking.

"No, don't *dare* laugh! I'm quite serious. I shall bake you a flat cake." She grinned at his feigned dismay. "Perhaps not as tasty as Anna's, but certainly enough to fill your grumbling stomach."

Hattush's teasing lightened her spirits.

After sending Anna to the market so they could talk privately, Puah prepared an acceptable meal. During breakfast they examined every possible scenario of their dilemma. When time came to kiss Hattush goodbye for the day, it didn't come easily. Today Pharaoh's tomb would be inspected. Even without the horror of his latest decree, the king's moods were too frightening, too unpredictable. Puah and her people would enter a new way of life this day, one that could prove fatal.

That evening, Puah and Hattush reclined on the rooftop discussing the day's events. For the first time, Pharaoh's inspection of the tomb seemed without obstacle. He had even paid a halfhearted compliment to Hattush on the most recent additions, and in that she took some comfort. One moment cold, the next hot, Khaneferre's severe mood swings only added to everyone's apprehension for the future. For now, at least, she could lay aside fears about Hattush's work.

Nothing seemed to ruffle Hattush. His incessant smile in the midst of adversity was sometimes irritating, but his strong faith was contagious, soon melting her sour moods and dispelling gnawing fears. He even carried himself differently. Indeed, whatever occurred in the tomb, heavenly messenger or not, her husband was transformed. Oh, that she too could have a measure of such medicine for the heart!

In private, Puah fought her own demons. Allowing Hattush to see her weak faith shamed her. She tried to bclicvc without question. Still, she could never rise to the same pinnacle, the same sureness he possessed. Whenever conversation shifted to Pharaoh's decree, Hattush would silence her, assuring their circumstance was as it should be.

"Stop worrying, love. It is in God's sure hands."

That was easy to say, but much harder to accomplish.

On the third night following the meeting at Heber's house, Anna knocked softly on the door of their sleeping chamber as she and Hattush were preparing for bed.

"Mistress!"

"Yes, Anna?"

"Mistress, the weaver's baby is coming. You must hurry. She failed to call earlier for fear of the soldiers, but now she's frightened and wants you."

Hattush rushed out to alert the others

who would watch the streets. Anna accompanied Puah to the woman's home, only two streets away. Once there, the examination revealed a baby whose arrival wouldn't wait.

"You've done strong work, Orah. Your baby will be here soon."

Beads of perspiration covered the young woman's face. Orah smiled wearily at the news. "Thanks be to God. I feared it would be much longer, and oh . . . I tell you true, I thought I couldn't bear anymore. Oh!"

Another pain peaked and Puah soothed the woman with comforting words as her body strained down, eager to bring new life into the world.

"Yes, push your baby out. Oh, Orah, I see lots of thick, dark hair!"

From the corner of the room, Orah's mother began weeping softly. Puah watched as the baby slowly followed the ancient path into the world.

LORD, protect us this night and watch over this little one.

There was nothing else to do but pray and continue the work to which she was called. Thinking too much wouldn't change anything, but only serve to upset her again. That wouldn't do. Orah might sense it and be hindered in her body's progress.

"Such a good job you're doing, Orah. That's it!" Puah's encouragement bolstered the young woman and she pushed all the harder.

More and more of the baby's head appeared. Puah massaged and eased its passage in the way Shiphrah taught her as a new apprentice. It seemed so long ago. Now, everything slowed as the baby emerged. It was always so.

In her hands Puah held life and death. She'd never fully comprehended the responsibility, the wonder of it. God had entrusted *her* with such a charge. She beheld her hands and wondered how they differed from others. She watched the baby appear and new awe swept through her. Would this be the last child she ever delivered? How precious it seemed now, when it might be whisked away as quickly as wind carrying chaff from the threshing floor.

"Easy now. Yes, that's it."

The baby rotated and slipped into her waiting arms. Quickly Puah dried the infant's mouth and smiled as it squirmed at her touch. A weak, raspy cough followed by a gurgling wail announced the arrival of new life to the world.

"You have a daughter, Orah. God is with you this night. She's beautiful. Look at those eyelashes, all that hair!"

From the corner Orah's mother wept with joy, openly relieved it wasn't a boy. To think of sending a tiny baby away to the wilderness by the hands of strangers was too much to imagine.

"Mama, it's fine. You mustn't cry so hard. Please, go tell Tobias all is well."

Orah sought Puah's eyes. "Thank you. We've all been praying for you. This must be a very difficult time for you."

The young mother's kindness brought a lump to Puah's throat.

"You're most welcome. It's always a joy to share a birth. Yes, it *has* been difficult. I do covet your prayers."

Puah soon had Orah settled, cleaned, and freshened. Then she set to caring for the baby. She bathed her in a basin of warm water, rubbing the body with salt before swaddling her tightly in clean, soft cotton. Finally she placed the infant at her mother's breast.

"God's blessings on your house, Orah. I pray your daughter will be a blessing to you and your family. I'll return in the morning to check on you." Puah bent down and brushed a wisp of downy hair creeping out from the swaddling on the newborn's forehead. A baby's soft skin and hair always amazed her, even after all these years of caring for them. Puah smiled at Orah. Understanding passed between them, shared only by women.

"Send for me if you have any problems. I'll leave some tea for your bleeding and cramping. Goodnight."

Puah glanced back at Orah's shining face, aglow with the joy of new motherhood. Her heart longed to know such rapture. Thus far there were no signs of pregnancy in her own body. Never had she thought a barren womb could be a blessing. Now she welcomed it with taciturn sadness. Perhaps someday she'd joyfully receive a child, but now it was far too dangerous.

Hattush met her in the gathering room, along with Tobias who offered a toast to his new daughter's birth. True joy rang in the laughter and celebration. The ever-present desire for a son seemed unimportant this night. A girl child had been born, whole and safe from Pharaoh.

"So, my flower, when shall you bless me with a child of our own?" Hattush teased as they walked through the gate of their home.

It brought a smile to her tense face. "Oh, my husband, wouldn't that be wonderful?" Hattush pulled her into his arms. Puah found herself looking up into his eyes, an oil lamp's golden glow reflecting there, threatening to burn a hole through her very soul.

"I pray our child has your lovely countenance." Hattush spoke softly, reverently.

"Husband, every time I think of you my heart grows warm. If I have my way, we'll someday have a household full of children, but they must all have your wonderful eyes."

Joyous laughter rang through the goldsmith's house, echoing in the evening's growing stillness. Soon the gaiety faded, replaced with the quiet cadence of night sounds. As Itj-tawy slept, Puah and Hattush comforted one another with the gift of their love.

Day followed day. Each new delivery now fell into a kind of numb drill. Since Pharaoh's decree, six tiny boys had been secreted to the back country of Goshen. Wet nurses or their own mothers accompanied them in the guise of a farmer's wife.

Hattush told Puah little of the smuggling. The less she knew, the safer she would be if questioned. She did learn a favorite device — the use of baskets in market carts. Surrounded by fabric containers, pottery, and other city-produced wares, it proved easy to hide a newborn.

The smuggling operation required much advanced planning. Immediately before transfer, each baby was nursed well, then given sips of an herbal infusion to induce sleep. Thus clean, dry, and swaddled, they snuggled down into a soft bed lining the basket. The lid allowed light and air to enter, so there was no fear of smothering. Most of the babies slept until well out of the city. There, traffic thinned and army patrols grew scarce. So far, the method worked well.

Truly God's all-seeing eyes and guiding hand kept them safe. Each new relocation raised hope, but at the same time, fear. Every passing day became critical in their willful defiance of Pharaoh's decree. Like gamblers at the market square who anted high stakes in games of chance, the risks of losing increased with each male baby's birth and rescue.

Thus far two homes had been raided, but only female children were found and the soldiers left in peace. Khaneferre's pride wouldn't allow things to continue this way much longer. The combination of his unbridled pride and mad fear of the Hebrews would demand success. Puah knew the soldiers wouldn't suffer the heat of Pharaoh's wrath for long without recourse, and for this she feared. They would soon increase the patrols, listening for babies' cries, making note of the homes where pregnant women lived.

Because of this, all women with child kept out of sight. Unless they searched each house, the soldiers wouldn't know where to begin their hunt. Even that would only work for a time. Then their haughty indifference would become brutal assaults on every home if necessary. It would continue until they produced the body of a newborn Hebrew male, an appeasement for the fiery wrath of their god-king.

The precarious security of these days drew Puah and Hattush closer. The intangible future colored their every thought and deed. Sleep became a thief of their time together. Every passing glimpse of Hattush seemed to capture Puah's soul. She tried to brand the image of his smiling face on her memory. They stopped leaving home unless necessary, giving in to the desire for time alone. As much as she loved her parents, the closeness she found with Hattush rivaled anything she'd ever imagined.

The amber-eyed goldsmith who captured her heart on Itj-tawy's streets now threatened to rob her of her very soul. Hattush's strength and determination to save the children, even at the cost of his own life, made him all the more precious.

And Hattush showered his bride with gifts, bringing her a single lotus blossom, a new scarf, or some delicate imported morsel from the ships.

He had not been this generous during their courtship. In all honesty, Puah was enjoying the game. Hattush took great pleasure from her reactions to his extravagances. Yet even as she glowed in the light of his thoughtfulness, a nagging sense something was missing wouldn't leave her. She longed to give her beloved a gift, a gift more precious than flowers, exotic fruits, or nuts from Nubia.

She'd not shared with him her budding suspicion. Since it was too soon to be certain, she kept the joy of the promise of a child hidden deep in the river of her heart. Soon enough she would know. For now, her reticence was for his peace of mind. From the very moment Hattush knew about the pregnancy, he'd worry more about her. With such distraction, he might heedlessly place himself in danger. At least for now, until certain she was with child, she'd spare her husband one more concern.

Puah daydreamed about the baby. Would it have Hattush's auburn hair, his amber eyes? The thoughts of a tiny, helpless likeness of her husband brought renewed determination to save every endangered child. Was she jeopardizing her own with the covert activities?

Carrying a baby under such stress could prove dangerous. When worries grew, pregnant women became susceptible to illness. And since this was her first pregnancy, the risks would be greater than at any other time. Would they be forced to flee when her condition became apparent?

Shiphrah couldn't handle both their workloads. Since Pharaoh's decree Puah had watched her friend age before her eyes. The elegant dark tresses, once glowing richly like henna, now boasted silver streaks. The grief Shiphrah carried seemed to sap her strength and the hope of living to see the Deliverer. Life's joy passed from her eyes too quickly. Puah felt helpless to do anything to stop it.

No, she couldn't run away to Goshen. But what of her work? Perhaps they could apprentice another midwife, but there was no time for that now. What was she to do when she could no longer conceal her condition? Disaster crept ever closer, and she was powerless to stop its dogged approach. She wished she had her husband's faith.

Faith? Perhaps it was only youthful idealism. But then, perchance, Hattush knew something no one else could understand.

"And so you stayed and delivered more babies?" Adam lingered at the tent door, acknowledging the end of the night's story, yet hungering for more.

Puah smiled and nodded. "I did, but as I said, each new dawn promised more danger. Pharaoh grew angrier with each passing day, raving with madness."

"Did you get caught?" a little girl asked, wiping sleep from her inquisitive eyes.

"We get ahead of ourselves, children. Tomorrow night."

Hannah followed Adam's lead, ushering the faithful listeners out. As the last child exited, Hannah turned to Puah.

"See the sky out there, Grandma'ma? I love you as big as the sky, even more," she said, spreading her arms wide.

For a moment Puah couldn't speak, her throat tight with emotion. When finally she regained control, she bid Hannah to her side with the wave of an arm.

Hannah rushed into her embrace. Yes, she'd been greatly blessed by God. What more could any woman want? Even the Promised Land didn't seem as much a treasure as before. It would happen as the Holy One promised, that she knew as surely as the sun rose each new day. Only one thing could make her life complete, and that would be to see her beloved husband once more. The long years hadn't dulled the ache in her soul, nor filled the emptiness.

XII

*He delivered me from my strong enemy,
from those who hated me; for they were
too strong for me. (II Samuel 22:18)*

"Everything looks fine, Yocheved. The baby's in position, low in the womb. I don't think we have long to wait now. Have you had any signs of labor?"

"Some mild cramping, but nothing that comes regularly. Do you think it will be within the week?"

"It's always hard to say," Puah said, "but I think perhaps we'll have a new one in the next few days. Try to be patient. The baby will come in its own time."

Puah assisted Yocheved into a sitting position, then sat on the rough woolen cover of the bed. It reminded her of her old room back home in Avaris.

"What are your plans if this is a boy?" The question was always uncomfortable, but necessary.

Yocheved's answer surprised her. "I'm

tired, Puah. Although I've enjoyed a healthy pregnancy, the worry has been almost too much to bear. With much prayer and thoughtful reflection, Amram and I have decided to do nothing for a time. I want to nurse the baby and gather my strength for the journey. When we leave, it will be forever. I don't want my children to grow up this way."

"Leave? But where will you go? Surely, you can't be talking of —"

"Canaan? Yes, that's exactly where we plan to go. With God's help, we will return to the land of our ancestors. If we don't make it, at least we'll not die wondering why we didn't try. This isn't a life here, Puah. Now our babies are to be murdered. No, it's too much." Yocheved paused and sighed deeply. "At least Aaron is safe in Avaris with my cousin. I couldn't bear for him to be here now." She wept softly as Puah hugged her tightly.

Yocheved's words were madness. Soldiers would surely hunt them down. Even if they escaped Pharaoh's wrath, how could she and a baby endure endless miles of harsh wilderness? Day after day of hot scorching sun would be too much for a nursing mother and infant. As menacing as it was under the daunting shadow of Pharaoh's palace, the desert was more so.

Perhaps Hattush could talk some sense into them. This wasn't a circumstance where she should interfere. Even with her respected role in the community, she was still a woman, and certain things were considered the realm of men only.

Puah patted Yocheved's hand. "Perhaps you'll change your mind when the time comes. Please think about the hardship of the wilderness. And how will you keep a baby quiet here in this city?"

"This child is peaceful. He rides quietly within and isn't easily irritated. I don't think it will be as difficult as it seems." Yocheved smiled reassuringly, but it did little to soothe Puah's troubled mind.

This disturbing news created another dilemma. If it turned out to be a boy child, the baby's presence would put everyone at grave risk. Of course, no one was in greater jeopardy than the child and its parents. For concealing the child they would be punished severely, if not killed. Already they had received chilling reports from other villages. Pharaoh's soldiers were purging the land of male Hebrew babies. Somewhere in Egypt families mourned the murder of their infant sons. *LORD, protect us!*

Puah remembered she'd sent word she

would visit Princess Batya this morning to check on the progress of her recovery. A messenger returned, confirming the princess expected her. Despite the trying circumstances, she had to focus on the present tasks and try to not think of things over which she had no power.

"I must be going, Yocheved. Send word if you need me. I remind you, *do not* send for me directly. Have Amram send a messenger to the carpenter's house. He'll have me summoned. Don't delay. It takes some time to organize lookouts and diversions, and I'm certain Amram has no plan to deliver the child himself." Her paltry sense of humor brought a soft smile to Yocheved's face.

Puah helped Yocheved stand. A bit shorter than Puah, she stood with a deep swayback, heavy with child. Pregnancy's blush had been replaced weeks ago with the drawn, tired expression of one anxiously awaiting delivery. Puah knew the look well. She'd seen it hundreds of times in her work.

Yocheved reached out and hugged Puah. "Thank you for not lecturing me about our decision. I just can't bear things as they are."

"It's not for me to judge, my friend. I

don't know what I'll do when I wear your sandals." With a pat on Yocheved's arm, Puah left.

As she walked toward the princess' palace, Puah thought about Yocheved's disquieting news. At this point, she couldn't see the wisdom in Amram's family staying in Itj-tawy with a male infant. She had spoken the truth. Having never worn Yocheved's sandals, she was in no position to judge. In the quandary created by Pharaoh, there were no clear answers. For Hebrews, all decisions were painful.

If Hattush's visitor was indeed sent by the LORD, she was destined to deliver the one promised to lead their people from bondage. *Why would God choose me?* Her vacillating faith shamed her — one moment sure and steadfast in the faith of her fathers, the next cold and doubting. Surely the LORD of All could find someone who trusted Him more completely for such a sacred task.

Could it be God would really use a simple, doubting girl to work His great miracle? A tingle of excitement coursed through Puah, her faith swelling at the thought. Hattush was convinced of his encounter. Time would tell. Meanwhile, if he was correct, then who carried this child?

Which baby was destined to grow up and lead their people to freedom?

At the palace walls a guard immediately ushered her into the courtyard. A young female servant led her through the maze of rooms, then through a wide door onto a covered porch. Princess Batya reclined on a couch no less opulent than her father's throne, the legs covered in gold leaf and shaped like lion paws. The saffron silk covering reflected morning light beneath the shaded awning, yet no such glow made its way to the princess' eyes.

Puah bowed low.

"My princess, I pray you are feeling well."

Batya wore an exquisite pleated gown of sheer linen, her eyes elaborately painted with kohl and malachite. Her lips glowed with the stain of crushed berries. Yet in spite of the adornment, none of it disguised her pain. Sadness echoed in her dark, almond eyes.

"I survive, Puah." With a snapped nod to the servants, they disappeared in haste. "I am glad for your visit. I think perhaps only you and Zayit know the pain in my heart. Sometimes I think I died with my child."

At Batya's beckoning, Puah moved forward and sat on a small stool near the lounge usually reserved for her closest servants and attendants. She perused the opulent porch. Fruits, cheeses, and wines covered a wide buffet nearby. Servants hovered in the wings, awaiting the slightest signal to do Batya's bidding.

"No, my princess, you didn't die, but a part of you passed to another place. It's natural for you to grieve. Do you feel this deep melancholy all the time? Do you ever have good days?"

Batya looked down, studying her slender, folded hands. "I do not sleep well. I have nightmares. My husband does not come to me anymore. He is afraid he will hurt me, yet I need his comfort more than ever." A silent tear rolled down Batya's cheek.

"Sometimes fathers feel the grief deeply, but don't know how to express it. Perhaps for him, seeing you is a reminder of his own loss."

"Perhaps . . . but now more than ever we need to console one another."

Puah couldn't deny this truth. "Sadly, that's not the way of men. Do you have work to keep you busy?"

Batya smiled, and for just a moment mirth entered her sad eyes. "Yes, I send one servant here and another there. Then I request a bath or massage. Sometimes I even dictate a message to a scribe." She sighed heavily. "It is a never-ending trial of work, ordering others to and fro," she said, laughing dryly. She looked into Puah's eyes, seeking understanding. "How I do envy you for your meaningful work, midwife."

"Don't envy me, my princess." She lowered her eyes, hoping Batya hadn't noticed the brimming tears. For a few moments nothing was said.

"You say much with your silence. I have heard of my father's decree. Despite the entreaties of his family and advisors, he refuses to retract the command. He is god-pharaoh. His will cannot be questioned. We can do nothing. He is not the same as before. I fear my father is not well. As always, I am the rebellious daughter. But I see him as father, not god. I know I speak blasphemy, but I have always spoken my mind. I suppose I always will."

"Then we share more than you can know, my princess," Puah said, regaining her composure. "I, too, was a rebellious daughter. Instead of marrying my parent's choice, I insisted on waiting for the love of my heart. It was during that time I became an apprentice to the midwife, Shiphrah. Four years later, I saw my beloved in the streets near the marketplace and fell instantly in love."

Interest sparkled in Batya's eyes. "And?"

The princess' quiet teasing made Puah laugh. "I married him as soon as I could after he asked for my hand."

This answer brought a full laugh from the princess, which soon turned to a more serious mask. "Oh, but I *do* envy you, Puah. I am the daughter of Pharaoh, but you have more freedom than I. It is true. So, tell me more about your husband."

"Ah, that subject is easy to talk about. He's tall and strong, yet gentle." As Puah thought of Hattush, she felt a warmth creep to her cheeks.

"Does the midwife blush? Oh, this is *too* delightful." Batya rose and walked over to Puah, then offered her arm. "Come, let us walk, midwife. You are good medicine for my broken soul. Honesty such as yours is a rare jewel."

As the sun trekked across the sky, Puah and Batya walked along the tiled path beside the river. Date palms heavy with fruit shaded their path. As they approached the princess' barge a heron took flight from the water's edge, its white plumage brilliant in the bright sunlight.

"Look! See how the sun falls on the distant hills? They shine like gold. They always remind me of my husband."

"Your husband?" Batya stopped and

peered at Puah with puzzlement.

"Yes, he is a goldsmith. He takes the raw ore and makes beautiful things with it. The golden hills remind me of him."

"Then am I to suppose papyrus reminds you of him also, for he is tall and slim?" The princess teased openly now.

Puah laughed aloud, pleased at Batya's lightheartedness. She followed the other woman's gaze to the surrounding beauty. A soft wind teased tall papyrus blades lining the bank, and the river's surface reflected the cloudless heavens. In the distance the hills' titian glow broke the vast blue of an endless sky.

Batya stared at the horizon, seemingly lost in thought. The kohl lining her eyes exaggerated the dark circles of her grief. Puah watched her, wishing she could read her thoughts. *Does she truly envy me, a young Hebrew woman, a slave?*

Even Pharaoh's abundant coffers couldn't buy peace and love. So much wealth and luxury, power and homage, yet this young, grieving woman of royalty seemed utterly alone. In Khaneferre's mighty kingdom, it seemed that no one cared for Batya's broken heart.

Batya turned to Puah and looked questioningly at her. "May I offer you some refreshment? I forget my manners these days. Please forgive me."

"No, thank you, my princess, I must be going. I only stopped to see about you. You've been on my mind."

Batya dropped her eyes and spoke in a soft voice, husky with emotion. "Sometimes I awaken at night and hear a baby crying, Puah. It frightens me. You do not think . . . could I be going mad like my father?"

Oh, LORD, how she must suffer! Please God, give me the right words to comfort her.

Puah turned, looking directly into Batya's drawn face. She took the princess' hands into her own, squeezing them tenderly. "No! You mustn't think that. You are grieving the loss of your child. It will feel like madness at times. One moment at the bottom of a well of despair, the next angry at the gods for your loss. Your spirit's healing will take time. Like your body, it must have sufficient time to recover. Please be gentle with yourself. If you need someone to talk to, I'll come. Promise you'll send for me."

Without warning, Batya embraced Puah. "You have my promise. Thank you for your comforting words. I hope you will come again soon." A deeply serious look covered her face. "Please, midwife, be careful."

Batya gave a quick nod. A servant appeared as silently as she'd disappeared. Padding in bare feet down the long tiled halls, she quietly escorted Puah to the palace gate.

As Puah walked home she tried to quell a rising sense of dread. The princess' warning hadn't fallen on deaf ears. Being circumspect in her dealings was imperative.

Hattush waited anxiously at the outer gate of their house.

"Where have you been?" he asked, a look of relief easing across his face. "I was worried."

"I visited Yocheved and Princess Batya. Let's eat on the roof and we'll talk."

Later, while settled over baked lamb and a cucumber salad with pungent goat cheese, Puah told Hattush of her day.

"Do you think you could persuade Amram otherwise? How can they hope to keep an infant quiet in the city? It's suicide!"

"I'll talk to Amram, my love, but don't expect any change of heart. You must understand, for some of our people to send a newborn child away is to doubt God's hand in their lives. *You* must trust God. He's in control."

How she adored him for his faith, even

before the encounter with the angel. She prayed he was right. She couldn't bear seeing his faith crushed. Eventually Pharaoh would grow tired of the lack of success in carrying out his decree. When the real trial came, would Hattush still hold such faith?

She knew her own faith was weak and temporal. It was always easy to give thanks to God when things ran smoothly. But in difficult times she often questioned God's presence in her life. No such doubt seemed evident in Hattush. Like a rock, solid and unmoving, he never wavered with the winds of trouble. And now more than ever, he glowed with a fervency that shamed her, making her own faltering convictions seem nonexistent.

She watched him eat. He chewed a bit of roasted lamb, its succulent juice clinging to the corner of his lips. She simply wanted to love him, tell him that their fond wish for a child might indeed be happening. By her calculations, it would arrive during the height of harvest.

Unable to resist, she reached over and wiped away the drop that threatened to fall from his mouth. Then she picked up a cube of cheese and offered it to him.

"Mmm." He grabbed Puah's hand and

spread kisses across her palm, slowly and leisurely, watching her reaction. "I believe . . . my wife . . . is worrying . . . too much."

Stifling a nervous giggle, Puah gave in to his teasing. Setting down her cup, she stretched out on the pillows and lay her head in his lap. "I agree. I think, as my husband, you have a duty to help me forget my worries. Now, I order you to assist me."

Mischief played in Hattush's expression. "Duty? Order? My, have we not come far since the shy midwife who couldn't speak on the night we met!"

"Indeed, my husband. I was in such awe of your beauty my heart galloped away when I saw you. Now, I suppose I should tell you my secret."

"Secret? My bride keeps secrets?"

"I do. It's a very private secret."

"Then by all means, please share it with me."

Puah twisted around in a half-sitting position, looking Hattush squarely in the eyes. He was indeed handsome, and she loved just looking at him. "I saw you on the street walking to the palace on the day we met. You didn't see me, but I saw you. I fell in love that very moment."

Hattush smiled broadly. "And how did I miss you? That's difficult to believe. Surely

I would've remembered such a beautiful face." He reached over, outlining her lips with a finger.

"I hid behind a corner and watched you. I think I knew then you were the one for me."

"Why didn't you tell me this before?"

"I've told no one but God. I had many conversations with Him about it. I desired a husband who made my heart sing. He sent you." Her confession brought a touch of embarrassment. Perhaps it was the vulnerability of telling all, even to her beloved. Instead of a teasing laugh, Hattush's next words caused her chest to tighten.

"Do you know how blessed we are, my wife? Do you realize how few ever experience what we've shared these past months? Many live a lifetime and never know what we share *every day.* Some haven't felt this special love, even for one moment. Truly, God's strong hand brought us together."

He pulled her close and they clung tightly, perfect and whole in each other's embrace. The world outside with all its woes receded. For this one night there was no Pharaoh, no work, no problems. For one perfect, tender evening there was only a man and wife joined in body, heart, and spirit.

"Did you ever go to Goshen?" asked

Ariel, one of Hannah's closest friends.

Puah smiled wearily. "All your questions will be answered soon. Patience, children, patience. Sometimes we have to wait for things a long time, including the answers to our questions. You'll not have to wait nearly as long as I to discover who the Deliverer was. So, let us rest and we'll meet back here tomorrow evening. Agreed?"

"Agreed!" The shout rang out and the children left, leaving Puah alone in the tent.

She started to rise, but a deep pain stabbed her chest. Quickly she grabbed the earthen vessel holding her herbal infusion and took a generous gulp while concentrating on her breathing. After a time the pain subsided. Using a scrap of soft cotton, she wiped perspiration from her face.

With great effort she settled back to rest. Someone would check on her soon, bringing water. The reality of her condition didn't frighten her. When Moses wrought his first miracle before Pharaoh's throne, she knew God had everything under control. Whatever He had planned for her would be fine. She would just watch and wait. A soft chuckle escaped her powder-dry mouth. At ninety-eight years of age, what else was one to do?

XIII

For He remembered His holy promise, and Abraham His servant. (Psalm 105:42)

News of Yocheved's labor came soon after Hattush returned from the foundry, just as they settled down for the evening meal. According to the messenger, her labor came with little warning, the pains strong and close together.

Now they waited behind the gate for word that it was safe to leave. "Lookouts are in place," Hattush reminded her. "You must be careful, and don't leave until I come for you. Patrols are doubled tonight."

Puah's leather sandals clicked briskly on the stone tile as she paced the courtyard's narrow walkway. She always felt an urgency to get to deliveries. For some reason this particular report of labor caused her to feel unduly anxious. Was it Yocheved's decision to stay in Itj-tawy that made her so nervous? No, that wasn't the reason for this feeling of restless unease. It seemed almost a protective drive to get to the delivery, to see it through. Puah sensed this delivery was different, significant in some way. She dared not miss it.

"Your pacing will only wear out the stones," Hattush said, grinning as he turned to take another peek at the dark street through a crack in the gate.

"Are they dull witted?" Puah snapped impatiently. "Don't they know a baby won't wait?"

"Sweet, the lookouts cannot control the soldiers. They only watch for patrols and send word when the streets are clear. What good will it do if you're caught? The soldiers will follow you. Is that what you want?"

Puah took a deep breath and allowed some of the tension to ebb away, then settled onto the stone bench near the gate. Hattush was right, of course. Lookouts were even now on housetops throughout the Hebrew district watching for soldiers. By using oil lamps to signal one another, they could observe the streets and warn anyone in the area when soldiers were near.

They would just have to wait. Silence meant it was unsafe. To rush the process now would only risk innocent lives. If the baby came, then it came. There was nothing she could do about it. Rushing out and being discovered would be disastrous.

"You're right," Puah admitted. "I'm just exceptionally anxious. Pharaoh's lunacy is unsettling."

"I know you're nervous, my love, but don't forget who is in charge."

There it was again, his seemingly endless belief that all was well. Sometimes it made her want to scream!

Pharaoh was losing face. No male babies had been reported killed in Itj-tawy, either by the soldiers or the midwives. Rumor had it that other villages had not fared so well. Sennerfer's visit to the foundry brought a warning to Hattush to be on guard for anything. Khaneferre was inconsolable on this issue. His decree to destroy all Hebrew males had been a near failure. Now he would have to find a way to show his power and authority, a way to salvage his image as god-king. Whatever the outcome, it would be grave.

Sennerfer had confided to Hattush that he didn't believe Pharaoh's next move would come immediately. The royal family would leave for Luxor within days for the Feast of Opet. The royal procession began in Thebes where the statue of Amun would be carried from Karnak to Luxor, accompanied by boats also carrying the graven images of Mut and Khonsu. There was to be a great festival and the royal family would attend to glorify Amun. Officials from all over Upper and Lower Egypt would gather there. Khaneferre and his entourage were to be gone for many weeks. At least for now, preparation for the trip kept Pharaoh distracted.

Someone rapped sharply on the gate. "Hattush, it's clear. The soldiers are eating. Go with God!" Soft footsteps faded into the night.

Puah and Hattush hurried through the streets. Amram answered their knock, anxiety in his eyes. His young daughter, Miriam, sat quietly near the door of the sleeping chamber. She smiled with relief when she saw Puah. From beyond the wall of the room, a muffled cry resonated. With every new sound Amram clenched his fists and his brow knitted deep furrows. Sweat glistened across his forehead.

"Mama needs you." Miriam's simple, innocent statement drew the midwife's attention. Little girls were often fearful of birth sounds. Nothing Puah could say would comfort her; only a good outcome would soothe her fears.

"Miriam, is there plenty of water? I'll

need water and salt. Can you get that for me?"

"Yes, I can do that. Water, right away!" Miriam dashed off, happy to have something helpful to do.

"I'll go to the roof with Amram and watch for soldiers," Hattush said, planting a gentle kiss on Puah's cheek. "If you need us, send Miriam." He led Amram to the roof.

Puah found Yocheved lying on a thick pile of bedding. Her mother, Yovela, stood nearby holding her hand. As Puah walked into the room, another pain seized Yocheved. She bit down on a soft cloth, quieting her moans.

"How long has she been like this?"

"Since the evening meal," Yovela said. "It started quickly."

"Has there been a gush of water?"

Yovela started to answer, but the contraction ended. Yocheved pulled the cloth from her mouth and said hoarsely, "No water, not yet."

"Perhaps we're close." Puah set down her bag of supplies just as Miriam entered with a bowl and pitcher of water.

"Thank you, Miriam. Your mother and father must be very proud to have such a helpful daughter." The girl's shy smile was endearing but short lived. Another pain gripped Yocheved and Miriam's eyes widened in alarm.

"It's only hard work, Miriam," Puah said to calm the girl, "yet the hardest work a woman will ever perform. You'll see. Now, go relax. You'll not be getting much rest in this house with a new brother or sister." Puah's teasing brought a happy grin to Miriam's face as she scurried out.

Puah wiped Yocheved's brow, offering encouragement in a gentle, singsong rhythm, reminding her to breathe easily. A small reprieve from the pains signaled the next stage of labor might be near. She dared not give Yocheved false hope, so she said nothing as the woman rested quietly.

A new pain took Yocheved by surprise and she arched her back, reaching out for Puah's hand. As it peaked, Puah heard the unmistakable sound of Yocheved's bearing down.

"I think we are near. When this pain is over, I'm going to examine you."

"Yes, I think it will be soon," Yocheved panted. "This baby is in a hurry. He pushes down now with each pain."

"He? You're sure this is a son?" Puah teased.

"Yes, I think it's a boy."

"We'll soon see." Puah spoke as she examined Yocheved. "Oh, yes, it *will* be soon."

This welcome news brought a smile to Yocheved and her mother.

"With the next pain, give me a strong, steady push. Listen to what your body tells you to do. Would you like to rest on your side or use the birthing chair?"

Yocheved chose the chair. They assisted her into position. With each new contraction, evidence of impending birth became more evident. Puah watched as a bulging bag of fore-water appeared.

"It comes with the caul in place," Puah said. "Ancient ones say this is a sign of those who see the spiritual world." With Puah's gentle guidance, the shoulders and body soon followed. As the baby arrived, the opaque bag of water broke.

"It's a boy!" Puah exclaimed. "You have a new son!"

She placed the newborn on a clean fold of cotton provided by Yocheved's mother, cleared his mouth and dried his wet, glistening body. Pale, flexed arms and legs straightened in angry protest, then with a gasp the baby sucked in a breath and let out a lusty wail. The bluish tint turned to ruddy red. Then, as quickly as the baby began crying, he stopped and gazed around his new environment.

Puah watched in wonder as the infant's dark, unfocused eyes tracked around the room, as if searching for someone or something. Undaunted by his new surroundings, he seemed to assess his new world with great wonder.

A strange emotion billowed through Puah. Never had she seen such peace in a new baby. A seed of question formed in her mind as she recalled Hattush's account of the heavenly messenger. She quickly dismissed the idea.

Nonsense. These are ordinary people. Surely God wouldn't send the Deliverer from such a humble home, would He?

Shaking off the disquieting thought, she turned her attention once more to her patient. "He's a healthy boy, Yocheved, and a mighty curious one, it appears."

Soft sobs of joy flowed from Yocheved. Puah severed the cord, washed the baby, rubbed him with salt, and swaddled him tightly in clean soft cloths.

"Let mother hold him, Puah," Yocheved whispered, exhausted from her labor.

Puah smiled and handed the bundle to his grandmother who clucked and cooed over him in the universal language of babies. Turning back to her work, Puah soon had Yocheved clean and refreshed.

229

"Mama, I'm ready to hold my new son now."

Yovela gently placed the infant in his mother's arms. A priceless moment of wonder followed as mother and son gazed at one another, as if memorizing every detail for all eternity. Yocheved's weary face softened into the joyous blush of new motherhood.

"Thank you, Puah. Isn't he a goodly child?" She beamed a tired smile.

"Indeed, he's a fine boy. I pray he'll be a blessing to the tribe of Levi and a joy to your home. I'm going to leave you alone for a time with your new son so he can nurse. Would you like me to get Amram?"

"Oh, yes! Won't he be excited to have another son? And please tell Miriam we're both fine and I'll send for her in a moment."

On the roof Puah found Hattush and the new father seated in deep conversation. When Amram realized her presence, he jumped to his feet, the unanswered question written all over his face.

"The baby? Is it here? And Yocheved?"

"Relax, Amram," Puah said with a smile. "They're fine. You may go see them now."

It never ceased to amaze her. Strong, self-sufficient men turned to uncertain little boys at the occasion of birth. The look of anxious worry turned to uncertainty on Amram's face. He glanced at Hattush as if to say, "What should I do?" Hattush chuckled and patted him firmly on the back.

"Go! Your wife and child are waiting for you."

That was all Amram needed. As soon as the words left Hattush's mouth he darted for the ladder.

Puah watched Hattush as Amram hurried to his wife and new son. A spark of longing shone in his eyes. Puah caught her breath. She must tell him of her suspicions soon. Worry or not, it would make him happy. Who was she to deny him such joy?

"You envy Amram?"

Hattush turned and folded Puah's hands into his own. He gave an embarrassed grin, but a serious look occupied his eyes.

"Is it wrong for a man to want a child?"

Puah stretched up and planted a kiss on his lips. She wanted to wrap herself in his arms at this moment and whisper her secret to him. She refrained. When she told him, she wanted it to be special, a celebration, and very private.

"No, it's not wrong. I have to admit, with each new delivery I leave with a sense of longing. Soon, my husband. God will bless us soon. Aren't you the one always telling me to have faith?"

Hattush laughed at her playful scolding.

"Indeed. You put me in my place, dear wife. I'll trust the LORD for that blessing."

There was stirring in the room below. "I must check on my patient," Puah said. She turned toward the ladder and started down. At the bottom, Miriam stood anxiously awaiting news, her small hands twisting nervously in the folds of her thick woolen sheath.

"My mother?"

Puah smiled warmly. "Your mother and the baby are fine. I'm going to check on them now. I'm sure your mother is eager to introduce you to your new baby —"

"Baby what? Sister or brother?"

"That's not for *me* to announce. You'll know soon enough." Puah brushed stray hairs from Miriam's pouting face. "Only a few moments more and the great mystery will be over. Can you wait that long?"

"If I must. Could you hurry, though? I think if I have to wait any longer, I'll burst like a ripe melon."

Puah laughed. "I'll hurry, child. Why don't you heat some water? I'll prepare some herbal tea for your mother. It won't be long."

Miriam nodded and rushed out to the cooking alcove.

In the sleeping chamber, Amram knelt at his wife's side and stared in wonder at his new son nursing contentedly. His eyes beamed with joy as Puah entered.

"A son . . . I have another son!"

"Indeed, and a fine one, too. Even now as we speak his sister is biting at the bit to see him. If you're ready to tell her the news, I'll check your wife's recovery while you're gone."

"Oh, how could we have forgotten?" Yocheved said as she placed the baby on her shoulder and patted him. "Yes, Amram, please go tell Miriam, then bring her here. She's been fretting like an old woman for weeks now."

Amram hurried from the room as the baby emitted a tiny burp.

Quickly Puah examined Yocheved. "Everything's normal here. Are you hungry?"

"Famished!"

Yovela hurried to prepare her daughter something to eat. Then Miriam eased into the room, her hands tucked shyly behind her back, dark eyes never leaving the swaddled bundle in her mother's arms.

"Father says I have a new baby brother."

Yocheved smiled gently at her daughter. "Yes, you have a new brother. Come, he's been wondering where you are." Yocheved patted the bedding at her side. "Sit. He wants his big sister to hold him."

"Me? But Mama, he's *so tiny.* I might hurt him." Even as she spoke Miriam sat, her gaze still locked on her brother's tiny form.

Yocheved settled the baby into Miriam's hands, showing her where to place her arms. Once Miriam had the baby firmly in her grasp, Yocheved lay back, smiling at her daughter's look of wonder.

"He's so perfect, Mama. Why, he has the tiniest lashes I've ever seen. And his mouth, it's like a tiny bow of scarlet." Tears glistened in the girl's eyes.

"He *is* beautiful," Yocheved said. "He reminds me of you when you were born." The statement surprised Miriam, and she looked at her mother questionably.

"Yes, you were once that tiny *and* just as beautiful!" Yocheved's voice cracked with emotion. "And you're still as beautiful today. You see, all your fears were unfounded. God's hand is strong. Our baby is here and safe, thanks to the LORD's mercy and Puah's fine care."

Puah's stomach knotted at the reminder. This baby was indeed in the hands of the LORD. With his parent's decision to keep him under Pharaoh's shadow, he would surely need God to protect him.

"My hands are guided by God, thus it is the LORD that insures each safe arrival."

"Puah is too modest, Miriam."

Amram and Yovela returned and the conversation ended. Yovela brought a bowl of warm soup.

"You're doing fine now," Puah said, gathering her things. "I'll return in the morning. Drink plenty of liquids, and be sure to drink the tea each time the baby awakens and nurses."

She turned to Miriam, who hummed quietly to the sleeping baby. "Congratulations on such a fine baby brother. I know you'll be a good helper for your mother. I pray God's blessings on this house and your new brother."

Yovela rushed over and hugged Puah, her eyes full of grateful tears. "God bless you, child."

"Thank you, all of you, for allowing me to share in the miracle of your baby's arrival. Goodnight."

Amram led them into the main room, delaying their departure, insisting Hattush join him in a glass of wine.

"To your new son. May he be a delight to the LORD and a blessing to your house."

Hattush's hearty toast brought a laugh

from Amram's usually serious face. "And pray heaven that he's not as rowdy as I in boyhood!" They all shared a laugh as they toasted the newest son of Abraham.

After a final goodnight, Puah and Hattush stepped out onto the deserted street beneath a blanket of sparkling stars. Puah pulled her scarf over her head, blocking an unusually cool breeze. Or was it just a chill racing through her? They hurried along as lookouts waved oil lamps from rooftops at each successive post, signaling a clear path.

After awhile they relaxed into a pleasant stroll, enjoying the night air. Caught up in the excitement of the evening's events and feeling thankful for a good outcome, they almost failed to notice the warning ahead. A lamp moved rapidly up and down from a roof a few houses away. The pounding of many horses' hooves clattered on a nearby street, drawing ever closer.

Panic tightened Puah's throat and she fought to stifle a cry of alarm. Hattush squeezed her hand.

"Follow my lead!"

The harshly whispered command left no room for argument. He pulled her arm around his back and began stumbling along as if drunk, laughing and babbling nonsense

236

at the top of his lungs.

No sooner had his first bellow of song erupted into the night air, than a single mounted soldier rounded the corner. The rider drew the snorting steed to a halt before them. Hattush staggered back in a delayed reaction and looked up at the soldier.

"What business have you here?" the soldier barked, addressing Puah.

"We shared dinner at the home of my uncle," she said, fighting to keep her voice from trembling. "I fear my husband has had too much wine."

The soldier leaned forward, staring hard at Hattush. "I know you," he said, pointing. "Are you not the goldsmith who works on Pharaoh's tomb?"

Swaying back and forth, Hattush looked up, grinning foolishly and mumbled something unintelligible.

Without warning the soldier slid from his horse to the ground and in two brisk strides came face to face with Hattush. The silly grin spread wider across Hattush's face as he stared back at the soldier in mock stupor.

"Indeed, he smells of cheap Hebrew wine. Get him home and off the streets. Tell him when his head clears that it will not sit well with Pharaoh if he learns one of his goldsmiths is a wine bibber."

"I will, thank you. Goodnight."

Wasting no time, Puah pulled Hattush along, praying silently. He continued to sway and sing loudly. From a nearby courtyard a dog howled in accompaniment to her husband's caterwauling. She dared not look back at the soldier. As they finally turned the corner Puah heard the sharp order of the patrol's leader and horses galloping away.

Only when she could see an oil lamp swaying from a rooftop signaling safety, did she allow herself to breathe deeply.

"You were wonderful!" the suddenly sober Hattush said, hugging Puah close. "You're shaking."

"Of course I'm shaking! Don't you realize how close we came to being caught? It could've meant death for all of us!"

Hattush squeezed her even tighter. "But as you see, my love, God kept us safe once again. Let's get home."

Safe inside their courtyard gate, Puah threw herself into Hattush's arms, clinging tightly until the trembling subsided. *How close indeed! How long will Yocheved be able to hide her baby's cry?* Puah didn't want to think about it tonight. She wanted only to wrap herself in Hattush's loving embrace. For this night she wished to forget where she was and what she'd done. She was a criminal by Egyptian law, guilty of a crime punishable by death. But facing death at the hands of a mad king was not nearly as foreboding as acing the judgment of her own conscience and God's all-seeing eyes.

She'd done the best she could, given the circumstances. Now it truly was in God's hands.

"Did they find the baby boy?"

The question hung in the hushed air. The children in Puah's tent sat quietly, wanting to know about the baby's outcome. Puah tried to hide the smile playing at the corners of her mouth.

"Almost. They came very, very close. Since we stopped early this evening, perhaps you might like to hear some more?"

"Yes!" a united chorus rang out.

"Very well." Puah took a sip of the warm goat's milk Daphne had brought moments ago.

"Then I must tell you the next thing that happened. For you see, even in the midst of great trial God can bring wonderful blessings and unexpected help. He is truly our helper in times of trouble."

239

XIV

*I will give you the treasures of darkness
and hidden riches of secret places, that
you may know that I, the LORD, who call
you by your name, am the God of Israel.
(Isaiah 45:3)*

Puah planned the dinner for the next full
moon. With Anna's help she prepared a feast
of baked fish, salad with leeks and cucumbers, as well as Anna's special date bread.
Grape leaves stuffed with delicate herbed rice
rounded out her surprise dinner for Hattush.
Finally she added nutty sweet cakes dripping
with honey for dessert.

The previous month had been peaceful.
With Pharaoh's court away, the patrols
made only cursory watches. Two more male
babies and six girls were born, the boys
smuggled safely away to the countryside. It
seemed that even heaven was watching over
them, sending more female children than
males.

Without constant pressure from the

palace Hattush seemed less tense, his work moving forward to his satisfaction. He worked long days, rarely complaining. Even when exhausted, he took time to talk with Puah about her work. The testing of previous weeks had brought them closer than ever, but one secret remained between them.

That would end tonight.

Puah was now certain she was with child. Although too soon for movement, all the signs were present. Her waist had thickened slightly, but only enough that she noticed. The bouts of nausea were still present, but not as bad as in previous weeks. Anna now watched her with knowing smiles, but Puah refused to utter the words to anyone until she'd shared this miracle from God with her beloved husband.

She practiced the words, but after spending days rehearsing she still didn't know exactly how to tell Hattush. She only knew it should come as a great surprise. The mere thought made her nervous as a new bride.

Puah dressed with special care this night. After bathing she massaged oil scented with myrrh into her skin. With Anna's help she wove her hair in several braids, then wound them together at the nape of her neck. Anna added a coil of lapis beads to the arrangement. Finally she donned a soft linen sheath, its pleats falling softly from one shoulder.

Excitement surged through her as she thought of the night ahead. She sneaked into the cooking area, knowing full well how Anna would react.

"No, mistress! You'll stain your dress. Go wait for your husband. I'll finish the preparations. When he arrives I'll send him up and serve dinner."

Anna's firm command left no room for argument. Puah felt a girlish grin erupt and couldn't find it in her heart to disagree. "You know, Anna, this is a special night for Hattush. I want it to be perfect."

"It will be. Now go. Clear your mind. The wrinkles on your forehead make you look like an old woman. Go!"

Puah scooted up the stairs laughing, then settled onto the soft cushions under the awning. It was indeed perfect. Fragrant lotus blossoms floated in a bowl of water on the low table near the cushions. Shadows from an oil lamp danced along the roof's low perimeter wall. The boisterous noise of late afternoon activity was gone, replaced by evening's quietude.

Puah scanned the clear sky and sighed

contentedly when she found the object of her search. A full moon's glow now hung suspended over the horizon. If she watched closely enough, she could see it climb in its slow arc across the heavens.

In six more moons I'll be holding my own baby! Unconsciously Puah's hands traveled to her belly and caressed the soft rounding she found there. Hattush would laugh when she told him she was already beginning to feel plump. It was true. She'd heard patients say the same thing hundreds of times, but until she felt the puffy evidence of her own body's changes, she'd not believed.

It would be at least two more moons before she felt movement. *What will it feel like? Is it true it feels like the flutter of butterflies?* She wished it would hurry, but in the same breath she wanted it to wait. She wanted to cherish every moment of this miracle, savor every change and event. *Will Hattush think me fat and ugly as I grow cumbersome?* Puah shook off the thought. No, he was too kind and loving. Even if he thought such things, he'd never let her know.

The sudden rustle of clothing and soft treading of leather sandals announced his arrival. For an instant Hattush froze at the opening of the roof and stared at his wife, a

243

mischievous gleam lighting his eyes.

"Welcome home, my husband. Come, have a seat. Let me help you wash. Our dinner will be served presently." Puah smiled impishly and patted the cushions beside her.

Hattush walked over and sat. He leaned closer, inhaling deeply. He grinned. She refused the bait, gently pushing him into a reclining position. With a soft cloth dipped in citrus-scented water, she began wiping the day's grime from his face and hands. He gave in, closed his eyes and sighed his approval.

"You'll spoil me, my wife. I'll turn into a demanding master and expect this every day."

"Perhaps, but you're worth it, my lord."

"Something smells delicious. What is it?"

"Ah, that would be your dinner. Let's see, we're having —"

"No, you're quite wrong. I smelled it earlier." Hattush rose and sniffed the nape of Puah's throat. He inhaled again, then exhaled with studied slowness. "That exquisite fragrance is my wife, who smells of heaven on earth. Forget dinner." He took the bowl of water from her hands and set it aside, then pulled her into his arms.

"You grow more beautiful with each

passing day. If you continue, I'll be forced to hide you away from the prying eyes of Itj-tawy." He rained soft kisses over her face.

Puah could only sigh for the wonder of it. His love left her breathless. How had she been so lucky? Luck? No, blessed. Truly, Hattush was a gift to her from the LORD.

Approaching footsteps broke the spell and they sat up like young lovers caught in a stolen kiss. Anna bore a tray laden with the evening meal. She placed it on the low table and bowed softly.

"Master Hattush, mistress requested your favorite dishes. I trust you'll find everything you need here. With your permission, I'd like to visit my mother. Will there be anything else this evening?"

As always, Hattush said just the right words. "It looks and smells delicious, Anna. Thank you for such a delightful feast. You may go. Enjoy your visit."

After Anna's departure, Puah served the meal. They ate in comfortable silence, interrupted only by sparse conversation, mostly about Hattush's day. He ate heartily and soon put the last morsel of bread into his mouth. With a deep sigh he reclined against the cushions, smiling contentedly.

"I don't think a man could ask for more. A beautiful loving wife, an excellent meal, and a full moon to light the way."

Puah wiped her mouth, then reposed next to him, resting her head on his broad shoulder. "Is there *nothing* else you'd want if God granted your request?" she asked playfully.

"Not this night. I can think of nothing."

Puah took a deep breath, then turned to face her husband. She looked deeply into his eyes and could only smile at the love reflected there. Before she could speak, Hattush pulled her to him and kissed her. When the kiss ended, only pleasing sighs and distant night sounds competed in the near silence. Puah searched his eyes a moment before speaking.

"Hattush, son of Abraham, we're going to have a baby."

A quick blink and slight turn of the head was his first reaction. Then comprehension leapt into his mind. "A baby?"

Puah reveled in the glow of joy which shone in his eyes. "Yes, my husband, we are going to be parents!" She guided his hand, placing it on her abdomen. "Your child grows here."

Puah didn't know what to expect, but what she saw moved her in a way she could never have dreamed. Hattush half rose and bent down, nuzzling his face in the folds of her dress where her hands had placed his just moments before. She felt his shoulders shake and when he lifted his head to look at her, his eyes welled with ears.

"I adore you, my wife, my heart. I've known more joy in our short time together than most men know in a lifetime. I thank the One True God for you, and I thank Him now this night for our child." Unashamedly, tears slid down his cheeks. He pulled her into his strong arms and embraced her tightly.

As the moon rose over Itj-tawy, a celebration began. As ancient as time itself, Puah and Hattush rejoiced in the gift of life they'd been given. The moon was past its apex before they slept. As Puah drifted into a pleasant slumber, the last thing she saw was a boyish smile on her husband's sleeping face. Truly, God *was* good to Israel.

Hattush's initial response to her pregnancy was amusing. Puah soon laid to rest his insistence that she lay abed and eat. She reminded him of countless women who worked until the day of their delivery and did well. Finally Hattush capitulated. He agreed she could continue working if she agreed to take a nap every day and to never forget a meal.

"You win. I promise. A nap every day and three meals. There. Are you satisfied?"

"Perhaps, but if I find you're not being compliant, I'll be forced to become a harsh taskmaster."

"I'll be a good girl. I promise I won't do anything to endanger our child. On this you must trust *me*."

Her promise seemed to satisfy his concerns and he let the matter drop. Still, in subtle ways he continued pampering the mother-to-be. An extra bite of bread or bit of meat or fruit would find its way onto her dish. With eyes that dared her to refuse, Hattush would indicate what he expected. *Eat, feed my child!* they commanded.

Laughing even as she ate, Puah would scold, "You'll make me fat, Hattush!" She dared not let him know she was indeed very hungry these days. She seemed to stay famished, even rising during the night for a nibble of bread or sip of cultured milk.

"I doubt that will happen, mother of my child, but if you do grow plump, I'll love you all the more."

His declaration reaffirmed what she already knew — Hattush loved her unconditionally.

The peaceful lull ended six days later. Pharaoh's court returned to Itj-tawy. The

Feast of Opet sent Khaneferre into a religious frenzy, fueling his mad drive to finish his burial chamber. One by one, artisans faced Pharaoh's cruel mocking and threats if new work he ordered could not be completed to his maniacal expectations. He seemed to take pleasure in the impossibility of his excessive demands. Consequently, Hattush arrived home later and more exhausted with each passing day.

The toll of the king's renewed fervor was apparent. Dark circles appeared under Hattush's eyes, and he lost weight. Puah knew he already fretted about her too much. How could he not? The strain of hiding babies had been great before. Now, with her delicate condition, his worry only increased.

Many days Puah was tempted to go to the foundry in the evenings and bring Hattush home, feed him a hearty meal and insist he go to bed and sleep through the next day. But she knew such an effort would prove futile. Pharaoh must not be given any further incentive to exercise his wrath.

This couldn't go on much longer. Sooner or later their good fortune would run out and the soldiers would discover a baby. Puah shuddered at the thought, for she knew they would make public example of those caught disobeying Pharaoh's command. Only God could stop this madness. *God must intervene!*

"Thank you for coming, my friend," Sennerfer greeted Hattush. "I arranged this meeting so we could talk privately. No offer ears must hear what I have to say."

The vizier had summoned Hattush to meet him at a secluded park along the bank of the Nile. Hattush was both surprised and troubled. It required he leave the foundry during a vital step in the molding of an inlay for Khaneferre's sarcophagus. Sennerfer's message left no room to decline. It was a royal command. Now that he was here, he dreaded the next words from the aged man's mouth. Since Pharaoh's return the streets rumbled with rumors of his tantrums. Some were said to have occurred in the presence of foreign dignitaries and envoys. His next decree might prove even more hideous than the last.

They followed a narrow trail along the shore of the vast river. Monkeys chattered high in the fronds of palms lining the pathway. To their right a thick growth of papyrus created a hedge between them and the river's edge. Sennerfer's servants waited behind, far beyond the sound of their voices. When they reached a natural break in the reeds, Sennerfer bade Hattush to sit in the shade of a tall palm.

"I will not waste words. Pharaoh's trip to the feast only fed his madness. He is more determined than ever to serve Amun and destroy any who do not bow to him. For now, I have persuaded him from sending troops into the villages and plundering for evidence of disobedience. He suspects that babies are being born and hidden, but the soldiers have not offered any proof. This enrages him further. He is like a frothing mad dog, pacing and ranting between prayers to Amun."

Sennerfer stared across the river. Great sadness filled his eyes, and when he again looked at Hattush, moisture glistened in them.

"Hattush, you have a friend in me. I have thought long of what I could do to earn your trust. After much prayer, I have decided that I should tell you something no other living person knows. I beseech you to keep these words hidden in your heart. Do not even tell your wife."

"I'll tell no one, Sennerfer." What else could he say? The second most powerful man in all of Upper and Lower Egypt was asking for his trust. Perhaps it might someday help his people.

"I was adopted shortly after being born. My birth mother was of Benjamin's tribe . . ."

Hattush hardly heard the next words. *The vizier is of the Hebrew people? How can this be?*

His attention snapped back to Sennerfer's story. Amazement and admiration grew with each utterance.

"I have been forced to walk a narrow line. Through the years I have tried to protect my mother's people, indeed, your people. Now I find my hands tied. My counsel is being overshadowed by Khaneferre's madness. May God forgive us, but we can only pray for his death or a change of heart. The latter is not likely."

"What do you think will happen?" Hattush dreaded the answer, but this was no time to hide his head in the sand. His people must prepare. He dare not admit any wrongdoing to the vizier. *Could this be a trap?*

"It is difficult to say. Pharaoh has been meeting secretly with the soldiers. I have not been allowed in the meetings." Sennerfer sighed deeply and stared wistfully across the broad expanse of the river. "I fear they may soon be ordered to sweep through the villages. Who can know?" He looked earnestly into Hattush's eyes. "You must tell your people to prepare. Any male infants hidden in the city should be removed at once."

"What if they don't find any babies?" Hattush whispered, his throat tight with fear at what they discussed. Hadn't the messenger assured him the soldiers would be blinded?

"It will only enrage Pharaoh more. I say to you truly, Hattush, God's hand must move or there will be a massacre. Your wife is in great danger."

An invisible fist slammed into Hattush's bowels at the mention of Puah. Now she carried their child. *I should've taken her to the country. I should've prevented her part in this madness!* Yet it was his unyielding faith that kept her involved in the work. If anything happened to her or their child . . . he couldn't bear to think of it.

"Sennerfer, I have never asked anything of you. Now I must ask something. I pray you'll help me." His voice broke. All he could see were Puah's trusting eyes staring up at him as he related the story to her of God's messenger at the tomb.

The old vizier studied the water as it danced under a sudden gust. Then he reached out and placed a hand on the goldsmith's shoulder. "I will do anything I can to help you, my son. Had I been blessed with a child of my own, I pray he would have been like you."

Hattush continued. "My wife . . . I want you to do everything in your power to keep her safe. She has done nothing wrong. I'm sure Pharaoh believes she's involved in wrongdoing, but again I assure you, she is doing nothing improper. If ever there is *any* doubt about her guilt or innocence, I want you to place the blame on me. Please, don't let any harm come to her. I beg this of you."

It was the truth. Before the Living God, his wife was doing nothing amiss. If saving innocent babies was wrong, then they were all doomed. He didn't want to mislead Sennerfer, but he couldn't trust him enough to tell him the whole truth.

"You have my word, my friend. Before the One True God, you have my solemn oath. I will do everything I can to protect your wife. I believe she is a heroine of the Hebrew people."

Without waiting for comment, Sennerfer signaled an end to the meeting. Gently, Hattush assisted him to his feet. They walked slowly back to Sennerfer's litter. Hattush helped him to his seat. As the bearers lifted the litter, Sennerfer glanced down at Hattush.

"I keep my word, Hattush. I am an old man and I have lived a full life. Death does not frighten me." Slowly the old man dropped the gossamer curtain. A tap on the side of the litter signaled his bearers.

Hattush watched as the vizier's entourage grew small in the distance. A brisk wind blew from the north. It whipped the glassy surface of the river into small angry waves, the foamy tips breaking and splashing among the reeds. A deep, haunting shiver ran through him. No words would come to comfort his heart. No plan could form to soothe his worries.

Like a frightened child he fell to his knees, crying out his heart to heaven. Only God could stop the nightmare threatening to descend upon his people.

"So you see children, you never know from where the LORD will send a helper. He can be someone you least expect. Don't ever forget this. Keep your eyes open for the one who will be there at just the right moment to help you."

The children filed out silently, as if pondering the truth about Sennerfer's past.

Hannah trimmed Puah's lamp, then

hugged her Grandma'ma and bid her good-night before securing the tent flap.

Puah sipped the last of the warm milk and reflected on the night's story. She was amazed that after all these many years re-telling the story seemed to make the details even more clear, as if the events had oc-curred only yesterday. Perhaps it was the keen emotional depth that leaving Egypt had wrought. She and her little ones were witnessing the fulfillment of a promise made centuries before.

She nodded and slipped into a deep, restful sleep, content at how her life had un-folded. Yes, it had been a good life. In spite of many trials and moments when her faith seemed nonexistent, she had managed to stumble along through the trying years, unseen hands always supporting her.

XV

Let those be put to shame and brought to dishonor who seek after my life; let those be turned back and brought to confusion who plot my hurt. (Psalm 35:4)

"What! When? Where did you hear this?" Puah couldn't accept the words Shiphrah brought with her precipitate morning visit.

"A friend who works in the palace overheard soldiers talking. They plan a raid of the Hebrew district this very day. She didn't hear when, but it's for certain. They were laughing about all the fun they will have. Pharaoh has ordered them to produce some Hebrew male infants or he promises someone will die for failure to obey his order."

Puah's mind raced. Would they have time to warn Yocheved? And if so, where would she and the baby go? "When did your friend hear this?"

"Shortly after the priests conducted their

morning prayers."

"Do you think there's time to get Yocheved's baby out of the city?"

"No." Shiphrah paced the room, her brow knit in deep thought. "The soldiers have been ordered to seal the city. No one can leave or enter. They're determined to find a male infant." She stopped pacing and wrung her hands in nervous despair. "Think, Puah, think! There must be a way!"

"We must go to Yocheved and warn her," Puah said. "There's no time to lose!" A sudden wave of nausea swept through her. For a moment she feared her meal would come up. *Not now!* She took a deep breath, concentrating, trying to remain calm.

"Puah, child? Are you all right?" Shiphrah grabbed Puah's elbow and led her to a seat. "You're pale as death."

"I'm fine," Puah said, attempting to rise. "We must warn Yocheved!" She swooned, nearly falling to the floor. Shiphrah caught her and eased her back to the seat.

"You're not fine and you're going nowhere until your color returns," the older midwife scolded. "How long have you felt this way?"

Puah attempted a weak smile. "About three moons now. Oh, Shiphrah, I'm ashamed for not telling you sooner. Hattush and I are expecting a baby."

Tears misted Shiphrah's eyes. She kneeled and hugged Puah tightly. "I expected so much, my sweet child. I'm so happy for you, but, oh, Puah, it is so unfair. You shouldn't be faced with Pharaoh's madness at such a time."

Briefly, they clung together in silence, tears of joy and sorrow mingling. Finally Puah pushed away, wiping her eyes with a sleeve. "I'll be fine in a moment. It usually passes quickly. I've really been blessed. In fact, I already feel much better. We must get to Yocheved."

Shiphrah placed a firm hand on Puah's shoulder. "No, you must rest awhile. Come when you're feeling better. I'll go now and warn them. I won't take 'no' for an answer. Your mother would beat me if I allowed you to make yourself sick."

"Truly, I'm fine. I just needed to let it pass."

"No, child!" Shiphrah said sharply. "Hattush would also be livid if I let you leave when you're this pale. No, you wait here. Better yet, wait until Hattush arrives. I sent word for him to return home immediately. He should be here soon."

Puah wanted to scream in frustration. Of all times for her body to rebel! Now — when

Yocheved needed her most.

Yocheved! She must be warned. Already too much precious time had slipped away because of her selfish stubbornness.

"Very well. Go now, and hurry! I'll wait here and try to think of a way to hide the baby. When Hattush arrives, we'll leave at once to join you."

Shiphrah departed in haste, leaving Puah with her own demons to wrestle. *There must be a way!* If the soldiers sealed the city, they would have to find a way to hide the baby within the city walls. *How? Where?* The questions plagued her. *I cannot let harm come to this child. Please God, help us!*

Puah chewed on mint leaves and soon felt the comforting effect as the nausea subsided. There was no time for sickness now. She choked down a wedge of dry bread while her mind whirled.

"I'll need my heavy cloak and a veil. I must be ready when Hattush arrives," she said aloud, trying to stem the panic descending upon her. "Also, my bag of herbs and a small vial of strong wine. We'll need to sedate the baby to keep him quiet."

By the time she'd gathered her supplies she felt better, almost normal. She washed her face in cool water and rinsed her mouth, then chewed a juniper berry to freshen her breath.

Sandals clicking rapidly on tile announced Hattush's arrival. He hurried down the hall into their sleeping chamber.

"Have you heard?" Even as the words gushed from her mouth, the stricken look on his face told the story.

"Today. They plan an attack today. Where is Shiphrah?"

"With Yocheved. We must go there. We have to form a plan to hide the baby."

They hurried through the nearly deserted streets. No traffic clogged the crossroads. The daily vendors were nowhere in sight. The usual boisterous groups of children playing games in the dusty streets were absent. No women walked with baskets of laundry from the river. An eerie quietness reigned throughout the city.

The silent streets proclaimed the message — the children of Abraham already knew their fate. Even now as she and Hattush rushed to Yocheved's aid, families were gathering, praying for deliverance from the wrath of Pharaoh.

The main room of Amram's home hosted more than family. Several elders of the community gathered there, talking earnestly with Amram, trying to devise a plan to protect his new son.

"Where is Yocheved?" Puah's sharp question was answered with a motion of Amram's head toward the sleeping chamber.

There she found Yocheved rocking back and forth, nursing her son. Shiphrah sat in a corner talking quietly with Yovela. Miriam sat near her mother and baby brother, watching everyone intently with wide, anxious eyes.

"You were right, Puah," Yocheved said, her eyes brimming with tears. "We should've sent him to the countryside. What are we going to do now?"

"We'll think of something," Puah said, placing her bag on a small table near the bed. "For now, you must stay calm. If you allow yourself to become upset, your baby will sense it. This isn't the time to have a crying baby."

Puah rummaged in the soft bag of supplies. "Miriam, I need hot water for an infusion." When she glanced up, she saw Miriam's haunted face. One silvery tear sat on the girl's cheek and she bit her lips together to halt their trembling.

"Are the soldiers going to get my baby brother?"

Puah's heart jolted at the girl's pitiful

question. She voiced the fear no adult could bear to speak. Somehow, not saying it made the thought less troubling. Unless they found a way to hide the infant, he would surely die this day. A shudder raced up her spine, stone coldness almost caused her heart to stop at the horror of it.

"Oh, Miriam!" She dropped the bag and gathered the girl in her arms. "No, we'll find a way to protect him. With God's help we'll find a way." She wiped the girl's tears and kissed her damp cheek, then pushed a few stray hairs from her eyes.

"You must be strong, Miriam, because I need your help," Puah whispered in her ear. "We need to give some calming herbs to your mother and your baby brother. Would you bring me some hot water and some mixing utensils?"

Her confidence in Miriam seemed to calm the girl. A tremulous smile appeared on her still quivering lips as she rushed out.

"Do we have a plan yet?" With Miriam out of hearing range, Puah could speak freely to Shiphrah.

"As I feared, the city is already sealed. We cannot get him out. When the raiding begins, there'll be too much confusion to move him safely from one part of the city to another. The only other choice is to find a hiding place in someone's home. Some place where the soldiers won't think to look."

"Where will we find such a place?" said Puah. Her home had no such sanctuary.

Shiphrah rose and began pacing across the room, her face pinched. Suddenly she stopped and snapped her fingers. "I know a place! My garden. Near the pool there's a secret room beneath the tile floor. I had it constructed many years ago to store food in case of another famine, or worse. It's cool and well ventilated, but more importantly, it's a place where any sounds a baby might make will be muted."

"Is it near the fountain?" Puah asked.

"Yes, just below where the cistern feeds from the fountain. If soldiers do indeed search there, their ears will be stopped by the bubbling water. There are also the many birds which feed and roost in the garden, and other sounds floating over the area from the streets. Yocheved and the child could hide there in safety. What do you think?"

Puah was amazed. In the four years she lived with Shiphrah she never suspected a hidden chamber lay underfoot. It *did* sound safe. Soldiers would not likely spend much time searching the house of a woman Shiphrah's age.

Then the doubts began. Shiphrah was a midwife, charged by Pharaoh to kill all newborn Hebrew males. And there had been none reported in Itj-tawy. Undoubtedly, she would be suspected more than other Hebrews for usurping Pharaoh's cursed decree. What if soldiers took up residence there, refused to leave? Yocheved and the baby would surely be discovered, or else perish from the lack of nourishment.

"I don't know. It sounds like a good hiding place under most circumstances, but I have concerns about it being your house. You and I are not among Pharaoh's favorite Hebrews right now."

Puah dared not utter the thought of her heart, that she and Shiphrah might be summoned at any moment to answer Pharaoh for their failure to carry out his evil edict. Her eyes locked with the older midwife's. Despite their dilemma, quiet courage stared back. It calmed her. *God must prevail!*

"It's the only option we have at the moment," Shiphrah said.

Miriam returned, interrupting the discussion. Puah quickly set to work making an infusion for Yocheved. When the baby finished nursing, Yocheved drank the brew, then spooned drops of the mixture into the baby's mouth. Afterwards, Miriam helped her grandmother freshen his clothing and bundle him snugly.

"Let's ask the men what they think," Puah whispered to Shiphrah.

The midwives entered the main room where a hushed discussion continued among the men.

"Hattush, Shiphrah has an idea."

The men were attentive as Shiphrah described the secret room and explained her plan. While Hattush discussed the matter with Amram and the elders, Shiphrah motioned Puah aside.

"We've never talked of what we'll say if called before Pharaoh. Have you discussed this with Hattush?"

Puah didn't want to talk about this. It meant talking about the threat of death, about her beloved being in danger because of her. But she knew she must discuss it with Shiphrah. They were in this together, yet each held different perils. Somehow, Puah sensed Shiphrah did not fear death as she. Perhaps she longed to see her husband once more. Perhaps death didn't seem so frightening to one her age. Puah's heart almost stood still in her chest to think of leaving Hattush behind, or worse, losing him.

"Yes, we've discussed it. We have vowed silence. We will neither affirm nor deny any knowledge of the other's dealings in this matter. It's the only way. To do otherwise would endanger many."

"Then I join you in your vow." Shiphrah drew her young friend to her. Puah was shocked to hear the midwife praying, "God, please grant us Your strength when needed. Help us be strong in Your work and to trust Your judgment."

Hearing the simple prayer acknowledging their weakness gave Puah new strength and assurance. It reminded her of Hattush's strong conviction that the LORD saw, heard, and cared for them and their trials. No matter what the outcome, the Creator who framed the universe knew all things and would not forsake them.

"I need His strength, Shiphrah. I don't think I could live if anything happened to Hattush."

"My dear, I've learned through the years one thing about trial. The LORD provides the strength you need when you need it, seemingly at that very instant. I once felt the way you do. Having lived through such a loss, I know one does not succumb to a broken heart. You may pray to die to escape the pain, but you'll not die."

"I cannot think of such loss," Puah said with a quivering voice.

"Indeed, we'll not think of such things now. Be strong. We have a baby to hide. Amram approaches. It seems the men have reached a decision."

Amram stood before them. Deep emotion shone in his black eyes. "We will proceed with your idea, Shiphrah. I can only thank you for your generosity. You place yourself at great risk."

"I could do nothing less, my friend. Come, Puah, let's help Yocheved get the baby ready."

The women packed necessities for Yocheved and the baby. It would be difficult to say how long they might be required to hide. They would need bedding, clean clothing, and food.

As Puah stooped to roll up some bedding, a loud commotion sounded in the front room. Men's voices rang out in loud whispers, sharp with alarm. She froze. Had soldiers come already?

Puah glanced around the room. No one moved. Yocheved stared wide-eyed at the doorway. Puah watched her eyes track to the tiny form of her son asleep in the cradle. They stared at the door in silent terror, barely breathing.

The noise increased. Men's voices grew louder. Amram and Hattush rushed into the room, their ashen faces etched with alarm.

"Soldiers are on the street! There's no way to get the baby to Shiphrah's now." Hattush ran his fingers through his hair as if trying to sift an answer there. "The riverfront is the only way of escape."

"I'll flee with him!" Yocheved said with determination.

"No!" Hattush said firmly. "They'll see you. We must create a diversion. Puah, get a sturdy basket with a lid and place the baby inside. When you receive word, I want Miriam to take the baby and hurry to the thick reeds near the princess' palace."

Hattush's calm voice quieted the others. He seemed sure of his plan, but how did he intend to get them safely out of the reeds? They couldn't hide there indefinitely. And what of the crocodiles? Still, to stay here frozen with fear would mean certain death for the baby.

"Miriam, do you have such a basket?"

The girl stood clutching her mother's skirt. She nodded mutely to Puah.

"Then get it now!" The urgent order snapped her to action. She ran through the door and reappeared quickly with a large basket, the bottom and sides coated with pitch.

"It's Mama's laundry basket. She floats it

nearby when washing our clothes. She says it saves her tired back from moving in and out of the water."

"It will do." Without waiting, Puah rushed to the crib. Taking a deep breath and uttering a silent prayer, she reached down and gently scooped up the sleeping baby. When she turned, animal panic coiled in Yocheved's eyes. The mother seemed near hysteria.

"Kiss him, Yocheved," Puah ordered. "He is the LORD's. I'll guard him with my life. Help the men with the diversion." Once more, her terse command brought the desired result.

Yocheved placed a tender kiss on her newborn son's cheek. "I love you, my lamb."

Hattush reappeared in the doorway. "Everyone, everyone to the streets! Wail. Rend your garments. Make a great noise of grieving!"

He turned to the girl. "When I motion to you, Miriam, I want you to hurry down the alley to the street that will lead you to the rushes near the princess' palace. Can you do that?"

"I'll do anything to protect my baby brother."

"That's my brave girl," Hattush praised

her. "Puah, watch for my signal and then get her on her way. There's no time to lose!"

Time slowed as in a dream. People poured into the street from many houses. Pharaoh's soldiers guarded the intersections at each end. Screams and shouts erupted from other houses now under inspection further down the lane. A burly soldier seized a frail old woman and flung her into the street as others ransacked her home, tearing apart anything that might possibly hide a baby. Puah cringed at the crack of a whip lashing the woman's husband who tried vainly to reason with the soldiers. His agonizing cries almost forced a scream from her own lips. She bit hard to stifle the wail, tasting salt as she drew blood.

At the doorway, Puah's hand rested on Miriam's shoulder, the basket hidden just inside the opening, lid in place. Thus far the baby slept despite the deafening noise. Crowds swarmed the streets. Women screamed. Others rocked back and forth, wailing with grief, ripping their clothes. Men prayed aloud, swaying in religious fervor. Older children scampered among the throngs, whimpering and crying for their parents. The soldiers in the streets stared at one another in abject astonishment. What were they to do with such nonresistant mourners?

At the height of the confusion Hattush saw a window of opportunity. He turned and nodded to Puah.

"Go! Go now, Miriam. I'll be with you shortly!"

Without hesitation, Miriam snatched up the basket and hurried out the door and away from the soldiers as fast as she could walk. Puah watched until she disappeared around the corner of the house.

Miriam hurried down the alleyway that led to another street which would take her to the river.

With the girl safely out of sight, Puah turned back to see if any of the soldiers had noticed Miriam's flight. Their eyes remained fixed on the wailing masses.

A moment of lightheadedness swept through the young midwife, and a glimmer of hope swelled in her breast. When Hattush found her eyes, she nodded, the smallest smile on her lips. His reassuring look braced her hope.

Hattush's story of the strange visitor at the tomb came flying back into her mind. Hadn't the messenger promised that God would blind the eyes of the soldiers? Had He not just done that very thing? Perhaps, but they still had to get the baby to safety.

Miriam couldn't stay with him in the bulrushes forever. Yet something about Hattush's victorious look and confidence bolstered Puah's precarious faith. *He truly believed every word of the messenger's announcement!* His strong yet childlike faith made her feel small. *Oh, that I could believe with such conviction!*

Puah looked up as three soldiers made their way toward Yocheved's house. As they entered, one shoved Puah aside, sending her reeling into the doorpost. She leaned there, catching her breath and praying silently when another reappeared from Yocheved's sleeping chamber carrying the empty cradle.

"Where is the child?" he demanded, eyes dark with fury.

"He's dead. He was born dead into my own hands. God did your Pharaoh's work for you!" She veritably spat the words at the young soldier. She'd never felt such rage. Such a bold lie, and to blame God for the fabricated story of a stillbirth! Yet she couldn't allow suspicion to fall on Yocheved.

The soldier struck suddenly, his large hand slapping hard across her cheek. Puah's head snapped back, pain shooting through her jaws. She tasted blood.

Behind her came scuffling and shouting. Hattush struggled as several men restrained him. Rage filled his eyes. If he could get to the soldier, the man would surely die. Raw fury contorted her beloved's face. Puah caught his eye and shook her head in warning.

She turned back to the soldier, her head bowed humbly before him. "I'm sorry. This is very difficult."

"We will see about this, midwife. For now you may go, but I will report your insolence to my superiors." He marched off, still holding the empty cradle. Puah's knees would have given way except for the strong arms of her husband surrounding her.

"Oh, Hattush, you frightened me. You would've been killed had you struck the soldier." She cried softly against his chest.

"I wasn't thinking, my love. I couldn't bear it when that beast slapped you."

"Promise you'll never do anything so foolish again," she sobbed. "You must *never* go against Pharaoh's men. Never! Promise me!"

"You were magnificent, my beautiful, courageous wife." Hattush smiled at her in adoration, wiping blood from her mouth with his tunic.

Puah's heart thumped as the aftershock of

fear hit her. She turned and buried her face in Hattush's robe, clinging to him, wishing the whole matter gone before she let go.

Nearby, Yocheved wept openly. Puah's selfish thoughts rebuffed her. Yocheved's baby's life hung by a thread and she stood gathering comfort from others. *She* should be the one comforting. She turned to Yocheved and hugged her tightly.

"You saved our family, Puah. May God bless you. You are the bravest woman I've ever known."

Puah pulled back and stared at Yocheved. No, she wasn't brave. She'd just uttered a horrible lie. "But I lied. I blamed God."

"My dear friend, is it a sin to lie to protect God's children?"

"Yocheved is right, my brave one," said Hattush. "God sees our hearts. He smiles at your courage in protecting the baby." Such assurance lay in his words that Puah almost believed.

She looked out into the street. Soldiers continued to mill about in disorder, running here and there with their raiding. Perhaps Hattush and Yocheved were right. Still, her heart was troubled. How did God feel about the lie?

From childhood she'd been taught the great value of truth, no matter the cost. Was there ever a time when an untruth was just and acceptable before the LORD? There were too many things she didn't understand. Though weak of faith, she still wanted to please God. Would He forgive her? For the first time in her life, her place in God's family came into question. Was her lie weakness or strength? Sin or obedience?

"Oh, Grandma´ma, you *were* very brave! You stopped the soldiers from looking for the baby, didn't you?" Hannah's wide-eyed excitement seemed contagious. The other children sat quietly, mouths agape, waiting with bated breath for the rest of the story.

"No, child, I didn't completely stop their search, only misled them for a time. It took me many years to understand my lie. It was as if the words were placed there without thinking. I regretted the lie, but didn't regret telling it, as you will see tomorrow night. For now, we must rest. With dwindling water supplies we must save our strength. We have a long march before we reach Canaan."

"But what about the baby?" Ariel asked. "Did the soldiers find him in the reeds? Did . . . did he get eaten by a crocodile?"

Puah cackled and clapped her hands at the child's innocent concern. "No, my dear, the baby didn't fall prey to the crocodile. But you must wait until tomorrow to find out just what did happen to him. Now, out, all of you! This old woman must rest her weary bones."

With disappointed reluctance the children filed out, their clothes still thick with dust from the day's march. Their journey was hard, yet in her heart Puah felt no pity for them. She knew the trial would bring them greater faith, deeper character.

This night she welcomed her blankets and the warmth she found there. She didn't know how many more days she would be able to continue the strenuous march. Heat, thirst, and her weakening heart were taking their toll. Perhaps she wouldn't live to see Canaan. However, the alternative would be to see Paradise and her beloved Hattush. The latter no longer frightened her as it once had. In fact, she welcomed it.

XVI

The LORD is my rock and my fortress and my deliverer; my God, my strength, in whom I will trust; my shield and the horn of my salvation, my stronghold. I will call upon the LORD, who is worthy to be praised; so shall I be saved from my enemies. (Psalm 18:2–3)

As soldiers continued plundering houses along other streets, the sounds of chaos receded. Occasional screams echoed across the distance, with the deep bark of harsh orders. Activity slowly resumed along the narrow road. Shocked dismay gave way to tempered relief. No male infants had been discovered.

People hovered about in small groups, murmuring quietly. In bewildered silence, women and young girls retrieved personal effects or their remains from the street. Small children clung fearfully to their parents.

Several women eyed Puah with singular

interest. What were they thinking? Did they blame her for this? Perhaps if she'd left the city immediately after Pharaoh's decree, this would never have happened. *No, that was wrong.* If she'd left the city, the babies might have fallen into the soldiers' hands. Everyone had been in agreement. No, she mustn't blame herself for this. She wouldn't!

"Hattush — Miriam! I must go to her. I promised I'd follow. We must find her and the baby. They're still in danger!"

"No! I won't allow you to put yourself in any more danger." Hattush grasped her shoulders. His eyes blazed into hers with fierce determination. "I'll find them and bring them here. When things are quiet, we'll hide them at Shiphrah's."

"No, I'll go. I'm the only one who can. If I'm seen, I can use a visit to the princess as a ruse." Puah's eyes stared pleadingly at her husband. "You know I'm right. Anyone else would be suspect."

Hattush loosened his grip. With a shrug of resignation he dropped his head in acquiescence. By now he recognized that tone, he knew her resolute determination. He drew her closer into his arms. "It doesn't make it any easier each time you leave my sight. I have two of you to protect now. I couldn't live with myself if I allowed something to happen to you or our child."

Puah pulled back and searched his eyes, trying to brand his visage on her heart. "I promise I'll be careful. If there's any reason for concern, I'll go directly to the palace. No one would dare accost me while visiting the princess. Batya wouldn't allow it."

"Then go with God," Hattush whispered, releasing her from his grasp.

Puah gave him a bright smile and quickly turned to go lest he see any evidence of her racing heart or shaking hands. Just before rounding the corner she glanced back. Hattush gazed longingly after her. The love she saw took her breath away.

"I love you, my wife." The words formed silently on his lips.

"I love you, too, my husband," she whispered, then turned and walked as rapidly as she dared. If she didn't go now, she feared she would run back into his arms, the only safe haven in her perilous world.

Winding through the narrow streets, Puah approached the river's bank. Thick papyrus rushes hid the water from view. She slowed, listening, watching for signs of movement. Where were Miriam and the baby? She swallowed the knot in her throat, praying under her breath.

"Miriam!" She whispered as loudly as she dared, easing along the shoreline. Again and again she called for the girl. Nothing. Puah's panic grew. *LORD of All, please don't let this be!* She turned around, fighting the urge to thrash through the sedges looking for the children.

As she neared the walls of the palace an urgent whisper came in answer. "Here!" It was Miriam.

"Where are you? Keep whispering to me!" Puah worked her way toward the voice. She pushed and struggled through tall, thick bulrushes which caught the edges of her sandals. She removed them. A few steps more and she found herself in thick, muddy water. Several cubits later, Puah broke through the tall thicket. Miriam was there, stooped over the basket.

Miriam signaled for Puah to keep quiet. She pointed beyond the reeds toward the palace. Once at her side, the girl finally whispered, "I heard voices nearby." Again she pointed in the direction of the palace. "Women, perhaps the princess' maidens. Puah, what about my parents? What happened?"

"They're fine, child. And the baby, he sleeps?"

"Yes, like an angel. Not one whimper.

How long will your herbs help him rest?"

"Not much longer. His empty belly will soon awaken him. We need to get back to the elders and decide on a plan to get him out of —"

The rumble of galloping horses broke her words. The pounding grew closer and closer.

Puah froze. Miriam's eyes widened, her small hands clutching the basket tightly. Like a frightened animal ready to bolt, she rose. Puah pushed her back down, shaking her head, signaling her to remain quiet.

The heavy thunder of many hooves drew near the reeds, but instead of continuing past, the soldiers halted. Clattering sounds of dismounting and horses' lathered breathing were only cubits away!

Silently, she motioned for Miriam to follow. Puah's heart was in her throat, her pulse pounding in her ears. Quietly they worked their way deeper into the reeds, away from the riders.

A deep commanding voice rang out. "Search the reeds. Comb the bank. Leave no hiding places unchecked!"

Now nothing else mattered but to get the baby as far away from the soldiers as possible. As quietly as they could manage, Puah and Miriam forced their way further into the thick growth. The water level rose to Puah's waist. A shudder rushed through her as she envisioned the jaws of crocodiles known to hide in the bulrushes waiting for prey. Puah's hand clenched the basket's side until her knuckles turned white.

Suddenly they could go no further. They stopped as light broke through the reeds. A few women walked along the shore behind Batya's palace, just cubits from where she and Miriam cowered with the sleeping infant. How long would he remain quiet? Surely the herbs must be wearing off. *LORD, don't let him awaken now! Please, God, don't let him cry!*

Several maidens and servants sat beside the tiled walk at the water's edge. In the midst of them, Batya rested on her lounge while a slave girl fanned her with a huge plumed fan of bright colors. Another anointed her freshly washed skin with oil. Carefree chatter and laughter carried on the light breeze, but it was impossible to determine what they were saying.

Behind them the soldiers loomed ever closer. Water splashed nearby, and reeds swayed in frantic patterns all around them. The soldiers talked in loud voices, and heavy breathing could be heard a short distance away. Puah squatted beside Miriam and grabbed her small, trembling hand. Hers were no steadier. She fought back the scream forming in her throat. *Please God, don't let them find this baby!*

They were trapped! What were they to do? If the soldiers found the baby, he would surely be killed. They would proudly present their trophy to Pharaoh at the end of a spear. Frantically Puah searched her mind for a way out.

Suddenly her eyes locked on the princess. Batya! What would she do if she found the baby? Surely the child would stand a chance in her protection!

Discovery loomed closer by the moment. There was no recourse. Without another thought, Puah made her decision. Signaling for Miriam to remain quiet, she leaned and whispered into the girl's ear.

"Trust me, Miriam. Trust me and pray."

Miriam gasped as Puah tore the basket from her grasp and shoved it through the reeds into open water toward the bank where Batya lounged. An eternity passed as the basket stalled, swaying back and forth in gentle rhythm on the river's soft ripples. For a moment Puah feared she might have to retrieve the basket, then a stiff breeze arose. The basket tipped and wobbled as it caught the growing current. Like an earthbound cloud the tiny ark drifted toward the bank and Batya.

Puah held her breath. Soldiers thrashed among the reeds, but it didn't seem important anymore. The basket — that was all that mattered. If this tiny one had a prayer, a chance to live, it would be in Batya's protection. This truth rang more clearly in Puah's heart than anything she'd ever known.

The snapping of reeds and voices grew sharper. The soldiers worked their way through the stands of papyrus toward them. Puah signaled to Miriam and they sank lower into the water. In a growing sense of wonder, Puah couldn't take her eyes from the basket. She watched in amazement as the small ark drifted lazily toward safety as though God's hand guided the baby from danger.

"There is nothing here, Captain. Nothing!" The sudden shout came from behind a clump of rushes a hand's breadth from Puah's face. She could see muddied water dripping from the soldier's bare calf.

"Back to the horses! We return to the palace. We have been at this long enough. It is useless."

The splashing of tramping feet and clinking of equipment grew fainter as the soldiers returned to their horses. "Mount!"

At the command, the soldiers climbed their steeds. In unison the horses sprang into action and were gone, leaving a cloud of dust rising above the tops of the reeds. Soon the rumble of hooves receded and an uneasy silence prevailed. Miriam shuddered, tears streamed down her face. Her small, wet body still quaked with the terror of near discovery.

Puah's heart went out to Miriam. What courage she'd displayed this day! Love for her brother sent her willingly into imminent danger without thought for her own life. Tears welled in Puah's eyes. Love drove the girl, nothing less.

Excited voices shifted Puah's attention back to the basket, now resting on the muddy bank. On the tiled walk above, Batya stood with her servants and guests. They stared curiously at the covered basket.

Dear God, Your hand has delivered him this far. Please, keep him safe!

Batya spoke to one of the slave girls. Bowing, the girl slid off the raised walkway onto damp mud and walked hesitantly toward the covered hamper. She crept closer, superstitious fear in her eyes, occasionally glancing back at her mistress for reassurance. Finally Batya's patience dissolved.

"Get the basket, girl! Bring it to me!"

The sharp order sent the girl scurrying. She grabbed it and scrambled awkwardly up the bank, depositing it on the tiled walkway at Batya's feet.

With a nod of her head the princess signaled the slave to open the hamper. Puah held her breath. *LORD, please let mercy be found in Batya's heart.* Hesitantly, the girl lifted the lid. As the late morning sun glared down into the opened basket, a lusty cry rang forth, echoing around the stone walls of the palace compound. Astonishment covered the gaping faces of Batya and her entourage.

Puah held her breath as she studied Batya's expression. Slowly the haughty, emotionless demeanor of a princess of Pharaoh's house disappeared. The proud, high turn of her head dropped and a tender smile appeared. A ruler's mask softened into the face of a woman. All Puah had hoped for, all she'd prayed for, was coming to pass!

Closer, I must get closer! She eased through the reeds as near to the women as she dared, waiting in breathless anticipation.

"It's a baby!" the slave girl exclaimed.

"Is it a *Hebrew* baby? See the rough blanket, the coarse weave?" another declared.

Batya remained silent. Her almond eyes, filled with emotion as old as time, gazed upon the gift of life at her feet. With royal grace she leaned and gently drew the crying babe into her arms. Oblivious to her attendants' astonished stares, she began humming, swaying gently, soothing the bawling infant.

Puah watched in silent wonder. Soon the baby's raspy cries gave way to softer whimpers of protest. Then he quieted, soothed by Batya's gentle song and rocking. As his last whimper fell on the morning breeze, a triumphant Batya smiled radiantly.

"Mistress, this could be one of the Hebrew children. Shall we summon the soldiers?"

"No! This child is under my protection," Batya hissed. "You will summon no one!"

The daughter of Amid, chief priest of Amun in Itj-tawy, spoke with haughty petulance. "Surely you do not plan to keep this child. It *could* be Hebrew."

Batya's icy glare silenced her. When the princess finally spoke, it was with the voice of royalty, secure in her position as favored daughter of Pharaoh, god-king of Upper and Lower Egypt.

"Not only do I plan to *keep* this child, I intend to *adopt* it. It shall be mine, raised in the house of Pharaoh. Amun has heard my prayers and delivered this baby to me. I will accept the charge to which I have been entrusted."

Batya turned to her personal maid. "Go! Find a wet nurse for my new —" Suddenly realizing she didn't know the gender of her new child, Batya pulled back the heavy blanket. A smile lit her face. "— son. Find a wet nurse for my new son!"

No one dared further challenge the princess. A soft chorus of female chatter ensued as they examined the child from head to toe, giggling and admiring him.

Like the purest bubbling spring, wonder flowed through Puah's soul. With His great and powerful hand God had delivered this baby from all danger, placing him in the empty arms of a grieving princess. Instinct assured her that Batya would cherish the child and protect him from all harm, even her father's vicious decree. Batya's spirit was pure. As surely as the sun would rise tomorrow, the princess would allow the baby to fill the aching void left in her heart by the loss of her own child.

Puah smiled, her heart at peace. Hadn't Hattush said as much? Truly, the visitor at the tomb *had* been a heavenly messenger. The only Hebrew boy she'd failed to smuggle out of Itj-tawy now lay contentedly in the arms of Pharaoh's daughter, protected and loved.

Miriam tugged at Puah's sleeve, a worried frown on her face.

"He is safe, Miriam. I know the princess well. She will love him as her own child." Tenderly, she hugged the girl, trying to suppress the overwhelming sense of joy she felt.

"Now, you must follow the shore to the palace." Puah gently directed Miriam toward the muddy bank. "Approach the princess and inquire about the child. Tell Batya you know of a wet nurse. Don't be afraid. The God of Abraham is with us."

Miriam glanced back, wide-eyed, unsure.

"You have nothing to fear, child. I know Pharaoh's daughter. She has a good heart. Go! God has opened the door, but we must walk through it. Go and help your brother!"

Mention of her baby brother sent Miriam into action. The reeds rustled as she made her way out of them, moving toward the palace. Moments later she appeared on the muddy bank, ambling hesitantly toward the princess and her entourage. Puah strained to hear.

"Yes?" Batya's maid addressed Miriam as she stood staring blankly at the princess.

"Is . . . is that a baby?"

"Yes. What business brings you here?" the maid snapped, stepping quickly between the girl and the princess.

Puah prayed silently. *LORD, don't let her run off now.*

Batya smiled down at the trembling girl who stood dripping with river water, her feet and legs muddy. "Yes, child, it is a baby. Amun sent him to me in this basket. I have taken him as my own." Batya paused, speaking softly and rocking the hungry baby who began crying again, "I have need of a wet nurse. Would you happen to know of one among your people?"

"Yes," Miriam said shyly. She wrung her hands, scuffling mud with her bare feet. "My . . . my mother. She is with milk. We lost our baby."

"Go, then. Bring her to me. Tell the guards at the gate when you return. They will be expecting you."

"Yes, princess." Needing no further encouragement, Miriam bowed her head, then turned and hurried away.

She nearly ran headlong into Puah where she waited. Fevered excitement mixed with fear covered the girl's face. "She wants Mama for her wet nurse!" Miriam gasped for breath.

Puah pulled Miriam to her and hugged

her tightly. "I heard. You did well."

Dark thoughts dampened Puah's euphoria. Something might yet go wrong. Her optimism could be for naught. She tried to hide her doubts from Miriam. "Come, let's get your mother. Didn't you hear, child? The princess needs a wet nurse for her new son. Your brother is safe!"

Later, the group listened in stunned silence as Puah and Miriam told their harrowing story. Yocheved wept quietly as Puah recounted the baby's discovery in the floating basket. She observed Hattush's reaction, not surprised to see peaceful acceptance in his handsome face.

Amram gathered his young daughter into his arms, ignoring her wet muddy clothing, his thick frame trembling with emotion. "We must get you out of these wet clothes, my child. You might catch a chill."

The ever-practical Shiphrah reminded Puah of her own soaked clothing. Her sandals were saturated, the once fine leather now dark with mud.

"I'll take her home and make sure she gets clean and dry," Hattush said, wasting no time in agreeing with the older midwife.

Puah grabbed his arm. "No, I can't. I must go to the palace! We must get Yocheved there before the princess finds another wet nurse. Batya will trust my recommendation."

At first Hattush balked at the idea, but he soon saw the wisdom of Puah's endorsement. He agreed and the women sprang into action.

"Come, Puah," Yocheved said, "I'll let you wear my things. I'm sure I have something suitable that will fit. Let's get you cleaned and dressed."

Yocheved and Shiphrah herded Puah and Miriam into the sleeping chamber where they peeled away the wet, heavy clothes. A short time later Puah stood before them, refreshed, dry, and presentable. After a hurried goodbye, Puah, Yocheved, and Miriam hurried toward the palace.

"What if she's already engaged a wet nurse?" Yocheved asked fearfully.

That was certainly a possibility. Perhaps the princess would have pity on Yocheved. Batya might be curious about Yocheved's dead baby. If questioned, Yocheved would have to tell the same story as before. A stillbirth. Once again Puah felt a tinge of guilt. She hated to lie to the princess who'd shown such kindness.

"We will deal with that when and *if* it happens," Puah answered quietly.

At the palace gates the heavily armed

guards ordered them to wait. Time slowed to a tortoise's crawl. It was all Puah could do to contain her impatience. Finally they were ushered inside. Zayit met them in the great hall.

"I won't mince words," Puah said to the aged nurse. "This girl said the princess is looking for a wet nurse. I've brought one."

The old woman looked from Puah to Yocheved. Knowing light shone in her eyes. Without hesitation she said, "Follow me."

They drew closer to the private wing of Batya's quarters. A baby's cry rose louder as they neared the princess' sleeping chamber. Puah glanced at Yocheved. She was near tears. With a firm shake of her head, Puah warned she must show no emotion.

"Don't speak unless Batya addresses you directly. I'll speak for you," Puah whispered as they approached the arched doorway leading to the chamber. The wailing grew more insistent.

Batya paced back and forth, talking softly to the infant, her brow furrowed with worry.

"Princess." Puah waited at the entrance for Batya to acknowledge her presence.

"Puah! This is a surprise. Please, come in." The princess spoke loudly, trying to be heard over the child's cries.

"I've brought a wet nurse, and it seems

none too soon." She smiled and motioned to the loudly protesting bundle in Batya's arms.

"How did you hear?"

Puah glanced down at Miriam. "Word travels fast in the streets these days. This girl came to me. Her mother recently lost a baby. She was afraid to come alone, but she knew her mother could provide good milk for the baby."

Empathy filled Batya's eyes as she looked at Yocheved, who stood with head bowed, staring quietly at the floor. "Once again you have done well, midwife." She turned to Miriam and smiled warmly. "And your young friend, also. I thank you both."

Without another word, Batya approached Yocheved and lay the squalling babe in her arms. "His name is Moses. It seemed appropriate. I found him floating in a basket on the water and drew him out."

Yocheved searched Puah's face with questioning eyes.

Puah smiled, wanting to cry out in relief. "Feed the child. I believe you have the job."

Color filled Yocheved's face, her countenance glowing. Needing no further encouragement, she hurried to a corner and sat. Soon the baby quieted, settled, and calmed in the familiar cradle of his mother's arms.

He nursed greedily. Relief relaxed Batya's anxious face and she smiled at the happy sight.

"It seems they agree. Again I thank you, Puah. Come, sit with me. Allow me to tell you the amazing story of how I found my new son."

With Batya's clap, a maid came running.

"Go find lengths of fine linen for the midwife and her young friend. I want to reward them for finding my son such a pleasing wet nurse." The maid nodded in compliance and hurried away.

Puah followed Batya to a soft divan. While Moses nursed at the breast of his own mother, the princess told her the story of how Amun sent her a baby.

"He is a most comely child. You will see. When he sleeps he rests with the peace of the gods."

"He is a favored son to have found you, my princess," Puah said. "Surely, God is looking out for him."

Batya turned, watching Yocheved as she nursed the baby. Even from across the large room unmistakable peace could be seen on Yocheved's face. The princess sighed. "My heart goes out to my son's new nurse. It seems this child will fill empty places in two hearts instead of one."

"Indeed. He is a fortunate child," the young midwife agreed.

Now Puah faced the greatest hurdle of all. She must somehow convince Batya to allow Yocheved to return home to her family.

"There *is* one problem with this nurse, my princess. She has a family and the responsibility of her household. Would it be possible for her to care for the child in her home until he is weaned?"

Batya looked pensive. She reached for a bowl of fruit nearby and plucked a succulent grape from a cluster. "I had not thought of such a complication. Perhaps if she stayed here during the day and returned home at night, it would be acceptable." She placed the grape in her mouth, chewing thoughtfully.

"I want to be near Moses as much as possible. My heart already tightens to think of him not being near." Batya stared openly at Puah. "Of course, I will provide protection for him and Yocheved's family. I would not risk my father's soldiers mistaking him for a Hebrew baby."

"Yocheved will comply with any request. She is shy and soft-spoken. I know she wants to be with her husband and children. Her loss has been difficult." Puah sat quietly after speaking, allowing her words to rest on the princess' heart.

For a time Batya studied Yocheved and the baby. She observed the smooth, confident way the wet nurse removed the baby from feeding, placing him on her shoulder. Missing nothing, Batya watched as Yocheved offered Moses her other breast.

Is it too obvious that Yocheved belongs with Moses? Could Batya see the untroubled manner in which his mother held him, the self-assured way she met his needs? *Perhaps not.* For a princess whose only training in womanly arts was presenting herself at court, maternal skills would not easily be recognized.

Turning her attention once again to the midwife, the princess spoke. "Your idea seems a reasonable solution. The wet nurse will remain with me during the day, and may return home at night with the child to care for her family. If *you* trust her, midwife, then I shall not worry."

Puah felt like shouting to the heavens. Somehow, out of the chaos brought about by Khaneferre's madness, God had brought order to an impossible situation. He'd created a solution that revealed His power *and* protected the child. Surely this Moses must be special to warrant God's ardent attention.

Could it be? Could this be the child of whom the messenger spoke? Was this tiny baby, this Moses now nursing at his mother's breast, the Promised One? She *had* delivered him. He'd certainly known God's protecting hand. How close they'd come to being discovered by the soldiers today!

Puah shuddered at the possibility. She couldn't wait to tell Hattush every detail of the day's events. Would he give her one of his knowing 'I told you so' looks, or would he also be amazed at the turn of events? If Moses was indeed the Deliverer, then God must surely be watching things as closely as Hattush reported.

She smoothed the woolen folds covering the soft rounding where her own baby grew. Certainly time would tell. But the Hebrew's troubles were not over. What would Pharaoh do now that no babies had been discovered? Would he allow Batya to keep a child who was obviously Hebrew?

Puah surveyed Miriam from the corner of her eye. The young girl watched her mother's care of Moses with keen interest. A soft smile played on the child's lips, revealing no worry beyond the moment. If only one could return to the carefree days of childhood's innocence!

But that could not happen. Puah was a woman now, and she would have to face the consequences of her actions, whatever they might bring. She knew someone would be held accountable for the midwives' and soldiers' failure. Someone would have to explain why no male babies were found in Itjtawy. Reason told her it would not be Pharaoh's troops. That left but one offering for Pharaoh's wrath — the midwives.

Wonder filled the children's eyes. After a long, grueling day, they squirmed more than usual. Dust, thirst, and fatigue warred with their curiosity about Puah's story.

"And the princess never knew that Yocheved was Moses' real mother?" Ariel asked.

Puah shook her head. "No, child, I don't think she ever knew. I believe Batya's nurse, Zayit, suspected, but she would never have told. For Moses, the trouble was over. But don't forget, Pharaoh's decree was still in effect. This man who thought himself a god didn't take kindly to being defied."

XVII

Yet for all that, when they are in the land of their enemies, I will not cast them away, nor shall I abhor them, to utterly destroy them and break My covenant with them; for I am the LORD their God. (Leviticus 26:44)

The princess escorted the women to the palace gates. A guard waited, ready to accompany them to ensure no harm came to Moses. Several slaves stood ready with supplies for the infant. Baskets of fine linen, cotton, and other bedding and clothing fit for a small prince filled the arms of slaves, as well as an abundance of foods to enhance his wet nurse's milk.

Moses slept peacefully in Yocheved's arms, and at the gate Batya leaned down and softly kissed his cherubic cheek.

"My son is beautiful, is he not? Look at those long eyelashes," Batya said to Yocheved with all the pride of a new mother.

Yocheved gazed down at the sleeping infant as if trying to memorize every detail of his face before answering.

"He is indeed beautiful. It will be a great joy to care for him. Thank you for allowing me that privilege."

Later, inside the safe confines of their home, Amram stood in stunned silence at their tale. "It's an abomination!" he ranted when he found his tongue. "I won't have my son raised in the house of Pharaoh!"

Troubled silence followed.

"Would you rather him dead?" Yocheved said, barely above a whisper.

Amram spun around to face her, and when he saw the pain in her face his anger melted. His shoulders sagged and he shook his head, resigned to their fate.

"He'll be safe from Pharaoh," Yocheved adjured, "and raised as a prince. Could we do more for him? He'll stay in this house until he is weaned. By then he'll know who we are, and the One True God. He'll never feel the lash of a taskmaster's whip!"

Amram's concern fled under the rational argument his wife presented. What could he say? The alternative was unspeakable. Gently he lifted his son and kissed him. A tear trailed down his bearded cheek. "God has delivered you from Pharaoh's wrath and made you a son of his household. Who can know the ways of the LORD? So be it."

Hattush and Puah escorted Shiphrah to her gate, then continued home. Puah felt as though she'd lived a lifetime in one day. Her legs and back ached from stooping while hiding from the soldiers. Her head throbbed. She hadn't eaten since early morning and felt she could sleep for a week.

After a light meal, Hattush insisted she rest. Puah offered no argument. He led her to the sleeping chamber and plumped the pillows and bedding. After she was comfortable, he removed her sandals and began massaging her feet with fragrant oil.

Slowly, tension lost its grip on her muscles. Puah sank deeper into the bedding, her eyelids growing heavy. "Please, lie with me, my husband. I want to fall asleep in your embrace."

Hattush snuggled against her and cradled her lovingly in his arms. "I adore you, my beloved wife. Your courage sustains me."

She reveled in his love, and for a time the day's worries were lost in the balm of his attention. The rising moon found them sleeping peacefully, Puah's head resting on Hattush's broad shoulder. As the moon traversed the clear night sky, no dreams found their way to disturb her rest. No concerns plagued her slumber, just the haven of her husband's arms and the memory of a miracle.

Anna ladled thick vegetable stew into serving bowls, then wiped beads of perspiration from her brow. The noonday heat lay heavy in the house, broken only by an occasional waft of equally warm air.

"Mmm, it smells delicious," Puah said, nibbling on a piece of flat bread. "Let's eat on the roof. Here, let me help you —"

Hard pounding on the outer gate echoed through the hallway and into the cooking alcove.

Anna swallowed hard. She placed the platter on the stone shelf with shaking hands. "It's probably only a baby in a hurry to be born," she said hopefully, rushing to answer the door.

The pounding resounded louder, sending cold dread to Puah's heart.

Within moments a deep voice boomed through the house, "Step aside, Hebrew trash!"

"Please, my lord, don't —"

A loud slap stung Puah's ears, followed by Anna's cry.

Suddenly a tall soldier stood before Puah,

the same captain she confronted yesterday over Moses' cradle. Anna cowered behind him, holding a reddened cheek, tears streaming down her face.

Puah's knees buckled. She grabbed the edge of the stone shelf to steady herself.

The soldier's black eyes bore through Puah with the steel glint of cruelty. A tight smirk played on his lips. "I, Nebhotep, Captain of the Royal Guard, appear before you in the name of your Lord, Khaneferre Sobekhotep IV, Pharaoh of Upper and Lower Egypt. Pharaoh commands your immediate presence. I am to escort you to the palace at once."

What Puah had feared was finally here. The foreboding of this dreaded moment had occupied her thoughts for many weeks, yet with the joy of the coming baby and the business of living, she'd managed to suppress the worry. Now it was here, like a ravenous jackal, to strip away the short-lived peace she'd found.

What would she say? Did she dare lie to Pharaoh? Despite her fear, she silently thanked God that Hattush was away at the foundry, glad he wasn't here to see the captain's vengeful countenance.

She dared not incite this one, especially considering their previous encounter. Only blind wrath had allowed her to speak to him in such a manner. Now, fear prevented any anger from taking root.

Looking down at her bare feet, Puah asked, "May I get my sandals?"

"Quickly!"

Anna ran to get them and returned without delay, placing the sandals on Puah's feet and fastening them with trembling hands. Tense silence followed. Anna's silent prayers for her mistress were evident in her frightened eyes.

"Come."

With a guard on either side, Puah hurried to keep up with the arrogant stride of the captain who led their march through the streets. There was no delay at the palace gates, for they stood open and waiting. For the second time in her life, Puah entered Pharaoh's daunting palace. She followed the Captain of the Guard through winding halls and echoing corridors, their sandals pounding like the drums of a death march on the pink granite floor. Too soon they stood in the antechamber outside the throne room.

Tall Nubian sentries guarded the door, their obsidian bodies glistening with oil, imposing figures daring any to pass without invitation. The soldiers departed, their footsteps fading gradually, leaving her with silence, fear, and the statuesque presence of the guards.

An eternity passed, then more footsteps growing ever closer. Puah was afraid to turn her head to look. Suddenly Shiphrah stood at her side. A ragged sob escaped Puah's mouth. They locked trembling hands, holding tightly to one another, finding a small measure of courage in each other's touch. Thus they stood until a guard opened the door.

"Enter!" he boomed.

"Remember your vow," Shiphrah whispered. "Be strong."

A degree of strength seeped into Puah. She straightened her shoulders as they began the torturous trek to the foot of the dais where Pharaoh sat in cold silence.

This time no crowd of nameless faces stood about the throne room. Khaneferre Sobekhotep sat haughtily on the raised platform. Sennerfer stood at his preferred place below, his face etched with trepidation. A scribe sat quietly to the left of the vizier. His tools lay idle. He avoided making eye contact with anyone. Did even the king's own scribe fear him?

At each corner of the dais guards stood at attention like stone statues, strong hands clutching upright spears. Other sentries were positioned at every door of the vast room. As the midwives fell prone in obeisance, another soldier entered the room, walked to Pharaoh's side and whispered into his ear. Pharaoh nodded.

Puah kept her face pressed to the floor, not daring to look right or left. She sensed Pharaoh's macabre loathing, chilling as the bitterest desert wind. *Please, God, hear my prayer! Give me words, Your words. My heart fails me.* Her prayer echoed in her ears. What would she say? She knew the truth, the most important truth. She'd done nothing wrong. On that she would stand.

"Rise!" Khaneferre roared.

Puah's knees quaked as she found her feet. Rising slowly, she focused her eyes on the likeness of a date palm painted on the wall near the edge of the dais. Looking at Khaneferre in all his madness would be her downfall. Like a small rodent hypnotized by the stare of a cobra, she knew his evil eyes would reduce her to a terrified prey. She mustn't allow that to happen.

"I commanded the midwives to exterminate *all* male Hebrew babies born in *all* of Upper and Lower Egypt. When that did not seem to be happening in Itj-tawy, I commanded my soldiers to look for the mysteriously absent births." He spoke with deadly calm, then rose and walked down the steps toward Puah and Shiphrah. He stopped before Puah.

Like an odious cloud, the evil issuing forth enveloped her. She felt the heat of his breath as he stood glaring down. Though she couldn't see his eyes, the young midwife felt Pharaoh's deep malevolence. She tightened her jaw, stifling a scream.

Without warning Pharaoh howled like a rabid beast, so loudly Puah's ears rang. She recoiled from the vehemence spewed forth.

"But no babies have been delivered! Can you explain this, *midwife?*" He spat her title as if she were filth on the streets of the Egyptian quarters.

Puah concentrated harder on the wall, trying to slow her pounding heart and calm her raspy breathing. At any moment he might strike her, so great was his unbridled fury.

She cleared her throat and licked her lips. *Oh, God, be with me now.* From the depths of her bowels, words came, clear, strong, and worthy of confidence. The strength and calmness of her voice surprised her as she responded. "My lord, as you know, the Hebrew women are lively. They birth easily. Since your decree, they give birth before I arrive. It's beyond my power to know the time of each delivery."

Pharaoh spun on his heels and marched back to the dais. He sat, glaring down at her like a cunning predator, waiting for a sign of weakness, anything that would betray her tale.

"So, when you arrive at these homes, where are the babies?"

"There are no male babies to be found, my lord. Only female children have been born alive."

"You expect me to believe this fantasy? You would have me believe that since my decree only *girl* children have been born?" The icy control of his voice frightened her more than his previous ranting.

"I don't know what to tell you, only that I've done nothing wrong. I serve Egypt. I serve you, my lord. My failure to please you saddens me deeply. Even your soldiers have been unable to find any boy infants."

For several moments Pharaoh sat silently. Then with a nod, he stood and signaled to Sennerfer. The old vizier followed Khaneferre from the throne room, leaving the midwives standing silently in the presence of guards and the scribe. Puah stole a glance at Shiphrah. The older midwife nodded approval of her young protégé's encounter with Pharaoh.

But deep in her heart, Puah felt something onerous. Somehow she knew the confrontation wasn't over. Nothing good would come of this, nothing at all. . . .

How long Hattush had been in the darkened room he didn't know. At first the stinging of the lash had only sharpened his wits, helping him ignore the pain. Over and over the burly soldier uttered the same questions.

"Where are the Hebrew boys? Does your wife know? Why do you defy Pharaoh?"

After each question, the same answer found its way to Hattush's mouth. "I've done nothing wrong. My wife has done nothing wrong."

Again and again the whip lashed out. Still Hattush held his tongue. Then the beatings commenced, the pummeling growing more brutal each time. Finally, blessed darkness enveloped him.

When he awakened, he was alone in the darkness. Sharp barbs of pain burned his back and shoulders. His couldn't see out of his left eye. Gingerly, he felt the orb. Beneath the sticky surface of coagulating blood, it swelled hideously. His mouth throbbed and when he moved his hand up to assess the damage, he couldn't feel his lips. They were swollen as thick as large grapes.

How long had he been here? *Puah!* Dear God, what had they done with his wife? And Shiphrah? When he struggled to rise, an anguished cry escaped his throat, his legs failing him. He was weak, his head and jaw throbbed with excruciating pain. Sharp, stabbing agony shot through his ribs with each attempted movement. His lungs rattled wetly, it was difficult to take more than the shallowest breath. He fell back and cried out once more as his back made contact with the unforgiving floor. He was helpless to get up, to find his wife. Tears stung his remaining eye.

Hattush lay on the cold stone, trying to clear the fog from his mind, to recall what had happened. He couldn't remember saying anything to condemn them. Had he? After the blows to his head began, everything turned fuzzy. *Holy LORD! Don't let me have betrayed my wife. Keep her safe!*

The thought of Puah wounded and hurting wrenched his heart. He gave in to his helplessness, listening to his own sobs echoing in the bare room. A thousand doubts plagued him. He should've sent her to Goshen immediately. What had stopped him?

The LORD's messenger — that's who had stopped him. The messenger took away his fear, leading him down the road to this place. Everything had come to pass as predicted. Somewhere in this land the Deliverer now grew and thrived. And Puah had delivered the Promised One with her own hands. Hadn't the soldiers' eyes been blinded just yesterday to Miriam's retreat with the baby?

Yet the messenger hadn't warned him of *this*. What was it he said, that things would not turn out as you planned? A knot grew in Hattush's throat at the thought. Would it cost him his wife?

Oh, LORD, not that! Not my bride, my love. And my child! LORD, I cannot give that much! I'm not that strong. Please take me! Don't allow her to suffer for her own goodness and brave heart.

Once again helpless cries wracked him. When he could weep no more, he waited. For how long he did not know. He wanted to sleep, he yearned to sink into the approaching blackness, to escape this nightmare.

Someone was coming! The heavy wooden latch lifted. Were the guards coming to

313

finish him off? *Dear God, let it be swift!* His heart beat wildly in his chest.

"Leave us," a vaguely familiar voice said. The door slammed shut. Silence filled the room.

"Oh, my son, what have they done to you?" Sennerfer's voice broke with emotion. The rustle of fine silk drew nearer. The aged vizier knelt by Hattush's head. Hattush tried once more to lift himself, but the whirling dizziness wouldn't allow it. A shroud of darkness enveloped him. He gave in and fell back.

"Puah . . . Shiphrah . . . where?" The words were thick on his tongue and swollen lips.

"They are in the throne room. So far, they fare well. Pharaoh has questioned your wife. She denies any wrongdoing."

"And Shiphrah?"

"Thus far Pharaoh has questioned only Puah. He realizes Shiphrah has nothing to hold her to this earth. Therefore, he will try to make your wife confess."

"Does Puah know I'm here?"

"No, but she will soon. Khaneferre plans to use you to loosen her tongue."

"If she talks . . . we'll both die, won't we?"

"Yes, that is Pharaoh's way."

Hattush reached out and caught the

corner of Sennerfer's sleeve, using his remaining strength to lift himself slightly. He stared up at the vizier. Pain-filled eyes gazed down at him.

"I . . . I'll confess. It's the . . . only way to . . . save Puah."

"She will cry out to save you," Sennerfer countered, fighting back tears. "What then?"

With certainty Puah would rally to defend him, but he must be convincing to save her from Khaneferre's wrath.

"I will declare . . . she is lying . . . to save me." Hattush coughed against the blood and spittle filling his throat. "Everyone knows of our love . . . for one another." He coughed again and swallowed. The taste of blood lay heavy on his palate. "Sennerfer, please help me do this!"

The vizier began to rise, but Hattush pulled him back. Summoning every ounce of strength left in him, he beseeched Sennerfer, "Support my story! Declare Puah a liar if she tries to confess any wrongdoing. Please, if God be with you . . . you must!"

Hattush struggled, pulling in a ragged, painful breath, "I beg you. I'm dying. Please . . . grant me this one request. You promised . . . at the river." He rasped, struggling to clear his throat. "I beg you, keep my wife safe. She carries . . . our child." Weakness claimed Hattush and no more words would come. He tried to study Sennerfer's face, but his eye wouldn't focus.

The vizier reached down and squeezed Hattush's hand. "You have my word, my son. With all that is in me, I will keep her safe." The old man's voice broke, his trembling hand gripping tighter.

"I must take you before Pharaoh now. May the LORD our God keep you in His mighty hand."

As Sennerfer left, two guards entered. Lifting Hattush to his feet, they half-dragged, half-carried him to the throne room. He passed out once, but a jarring step jolted him back to consciousness. They neared the place where Hattush knew he would see his beloved Puah. With each step closer, renewed strength surged through him. A pleasant warmth spread over him and the pain receded. For the first time since the beatings, he could think and see clearly.

Then he saw Puah. She stood before Khaneferre's dais, as lovely as ever. His precious bride, his friend, and lover. To her right, Shiphrah stood in quiet dignity.

No one seemed to notice the figure

standing behind the midwives, the same heavenly being who'd visited Hattush in the tomb. In silence he stood, fierce judgment cloaking him like a robe, his sword drawn, eyes fixed on Pharaoh.

Don't they see him? Why would the soldiers allow him to stand before their king in such a threatening manner?

Hattush smiled. The pain grew numb, like the effects of poppy juice. His heart was warm and filled with unspeakable joy, even as Puah turned to behold him; even as he watched a horrified scream form on her lips; even as her eyes widened in abhorrence at his mangled visage — jubilation flooded his soul.

His spirit soared as the guards restrained Puah while Sennerfer renounced him as traitor to the throne. His heart knew joyous laughter as Puah's outraged shriek filled the great room.

Pharaoh rose and stood defiantly, a cruel sneer curling his lips. "Hear me!" he declared, his voice filled with venom. "From this day forth, all male Hebrew infants shall be cast into the Nile!"

The heavenly warrior turned to Hattush and said, "Fear not, Hattush, son of Abraham. God has answered your prayers. Be still now, and see the power of the

LORD, the Holy One of Israel."

With long, purposeful steps the heavenly warrior strode toward the dais. He passed through Puah and the royal guards who constrained her, both unaware of his presence. Puah's eyes were locked on her battered husband and tears streamed down her cheeks. She screamed Hattush's name as the holy warrior ascended the dais. With outstretched hands she sought her beloved in vain, while the dazzling heavenly sword sliced through the air, striking Pharaoh. She cried Hattush's name again and again as Pharaoh clutched his head and crumpled to the floor.

The throne room receded as Hattush found himself traveling like a bird in flight toward the pulsating warmth. The messenger traveled beside him, transformed into a being of light, an angel of the Most High. Hattush sensed the source of the light, so pure he couldn't look upon it, but drawn to it by all his being. He only knew he wanted to be near it. He yearned to glory in the presence of the Creator, his LORD.

"Did Pharaoh die that day?"

Other than the one question, a stunned silence filled the tent. Tears ran freely, including Puah's own. Even now, more than eighty years later, she remembered the help-lessness she felt, the utter despair watching her beautiful husband die, unable to hold him or comfort him. Time dulled the memory by tiny increments, but then, how did you ever fully dull a sword that cut right through one's very heart and soul?

"No, Pharaoh didn't die that day, but God's judgment on him changed the course of events and ultimately opened the door for us to be here this very night."

Confusion filled the children's eyes, and Puah felt a smile break past the pain of her memories.

"You will soon understand, my children, but not tonight."

Later, as the aged midwife lay on her bed listening to pleasant night sounds, the pain of Hattush's death resurfaced as sharp as if it were only yesterday. Bittersweet, the memory wrenched her heart, tempered only with the knowledge that she would soon see her beloved husband once more.

XVIII

The joy of our heart has ceased; our dance has turned into mourning. (Lamentations 5:15)

The dreams would not go away. They came night after torturous night, so frequent and haunting Puah finally decided the reality of waking was less painful than the horror of sleeping. Awake, at least, she could control the stream of family and friends by refusing to leave her room. She could simply close her pained eyes and rest.

Sometimes the nightmares came shortly after falling into a fatigued slumber. Other times, their absence would lull her into a period of rest, then crush the short-lived respite she'd found. They marched across the netherworld of sleep in bold, disturbing color, refusing to leave no matter how hard she willed them to go.

The dreams were always the same. Hattush appeared before her, mangled and broken, drowning in ragged breath frothy with blood. Sennerfer stood at his side, pointing a long gnarled finger at her, accusing her of murder. Pharaoh hovered on the other side, howling with laughter, his kohl-painted eyes glazed with madness driven by pure evil.

"I love you. I did it for you!" Hattush cried night after night. Through his pain she could see the love in his eyes.

The words incited Sennerfer and Khaneferre and their taunting began anew. She was unable to move, paralyzed by some unseen force. Her throat sealed, making it impossible to cry out. Her hands couldn't reach out and comfort Hattush. Like the graven images of Egyptian gods, she stood stiff, unmoving, helpless to aid her husband.

The dreams always ended the same, Hattush fading away like a cloud of smoke dissipating into a clear sky. Further and further he retreated, his form becoming more and more transparent. As she vainly tried to scream his name, he evanesced until she could no longer see him.

Then her accusers would begin once more, but this time she screamed, her cries full of rage and helplessness. She spewed her fury at them, wishing them dead for taking Hattush from her. Sometimes her screams awakened her, but most of the time it would be Anna or her mother wiping her brow. They spoke softly in soothing voices as she awakened to once again find her world utterly empty.

After countless days and nights of the haunting nightmares, Puah felt herself slipping into madness. She decided not to sleep at all, but even awake the voices still came. One night her mother discovered her trying to leave the house, and Shiphrah was called. The older midwife administered the bitter juice of the poppy. The medicine carried Puah where dreams could not enter, voices could not disturb, and pain floated blissfully away. Mercifully, time ceased to exist.

It was her father's voice that finally pulled her back from this stuporous realm. "My dove. Please wake up, drink something for me."

It wasn't his words that pulled her away from the place of dreamless sleep; it was his sobs. He wept at her side, crying and praying, begging God to bring her back to him and her mother. Puah knew that pain; she knew the sound of loss. It was the same cry her heart now made without ceasing. She wouldn't allow the sounds to come from her mouth, for if she did, they would never stop.

The lethargy brought by the elixir made

her eyelids heavy. Opening her eyes was difficult. "Please, don't cry," she mumbled, her voice hollow, distant. "I don't like to hear you cry, Father." She slurred like a drunkard.

Amiel's voice broke. "Then drink something for me, Puah. *Please, for me.*"

Puah forced her eyes open slightly, expecting bright, blinding light. The dimness surprised her. Soft shadows swayed on the wall from an oil lamp's flickering flame. Her father crouched beside the bed. *How long have I slept?*

Amiel offered a cup but her stomach revolted at the odor of the goat milk, setting off deep heaves. Behira appeared, wiping the waves of nausea from her daughter with a cool, moist cloth. Finally, when the queasiness passed, Puah lay back exhausted. Her lips were dry, her throat parched.

"Water, please," she rasped.

Her father held the cup while she took a tentative sip. She swirled it around her mouth, wetting the dry, parched tissue. It felt wonderful as she swallowed. She took another sip, then another.

"That's it, my lamb. Drink slowly. That's right." Emotion deepened her father's voice. Puah prayed he wouldn't start weeping again.

Her eyes slowly adjusted to the light. When she met her father's eyes, the anguish there stunned her. Had she caused her father such pain?

Still groggy, forming words took complete concentration. "How . . . long? How long have I slept?"

"After Shiphrah gave you the sleeping potion, you slept for two days," Amiel said, the worry on his face beginning to ease. "Tonight would have been the third day. I praise God you've decided to awaken."

Puah's father reached down, brushing hair from her eyes. He gazed at her in the same way he had all her life, with eyes full of love and adoration. Yet this time something else tinged his expression. Fear? Grief? His hair seemed grayer than she remembered, but then they'd not seen each other much since the wedding. She regretted it now. His familiar, comforting touch reminded her of how much she loved her parents.

"Mama?"

"I'm here, love." Behira leaned down and placed the cool, moist cloth on Puah's forehead. "Won't you please try to eat something for me? You must eat for your child."

The baby! So imprisoned in the abyss of pain, she'd forgotten. Hattush's baby. His child grew within her. She slid her hand down, caressing the soft mound of her belly.

She'd been truly lost. Her pain had buried her, covered her as surely as dust now covered her precious Hattush. How could she go on without him? How would she face each day without his gentle smile to light her way? Their child would never know its father's tender, loving touch.

She looked into Amiel's troubled eyes. How blessed she'd been knowing the secure love of two caring parents. More importantly, they loved God, conducting themselves in such a manner that they glowed with God's love. She reached up, touching her father's bearded cheek. His curly beard tickled her palm and she felt herself smile as she remembered her childhood and the many times she'd giggled at the sensation.

At her touch Amiel's eyes welled with tears. That was Puah's undoing. Her throat grew tight and her own eyes filled with tears, blinding her.

"Oh, Father, I miss him so! How do I stop missing him? How can I go on knowing it's my fault that he's dead?"

Amiel pulled his grieving daughter into his arms, holding her with a fierceness that almost frightened her.

"No! You must never say that again, Puah! Hattush is dead because of Pharaoh's madness. His silence saved your life. You were powerless to change anything. It was God's will. Somehow you'll find a way to accept that truth. In time you'll be able to see things clearly."

"But they lied! Sennerfer lied. He told Pharaoh that Hattush confessed to all wrongdoing. I know Hattush would never have done that!"

The memories of that morning were branded into her mind. She could still hear Sennerfer's cold response when Pharaoh demanded Hattush speak. . . .

"He is beyond the ability to speak, my lord. There is no need. The goldsmith confessed all to me. *He* is the guilty one. His wife knows nothing. The midwives are innocent of any wrongdoing. *He* is the mastermind of the Hebrews' plan to smuggle the male infants out of Itj-tawy."

Had Hattush in his tortured state actually said such a thing? She tried not to think of how he'd looked in the throne room. At first she hadn't realized he was near. She heard activity behind her, but dared not turn. Pharaoh's rage immobilized her. Then she heard the rattle of labored breathing.

She'd heard that sound often before, when fever had done its worst. When fluid filled lungs and the patient no longer responded to treatment, she'd listened to the horrid sound of death's approach. Slowly she turned her head, following her ears.

Even then she didn't immediately recognize Hattush. A hideously mutilated remnant of humanity sagged there, held up by two brawny eunuch guards. Only when her eyes caught the glint of auburn on an area of hair not darkened with matted blood did recognition stir. She sought his eyes. One was too swollen to tell, but the other, unmistakable. Rich amber stared back at her. Dear God — it *was* Hattush!

Had he smiled? Was it peace she somehow detected on his battered face? She couldn't tell with all the bruising, cuts, and swelling.

Then she'd screamed and tried to reach him, but guards held her back. Everyone focused on Pharaoh. He declared that all male Hebrew infants were to be thrown into the Nile. As the last word of his new murderous order left his lips, he collapsed to the floor. All Puah could remember then was the sound of her own screaming. She couldn't stop. After that, she remembered nothing. . . .

"The lie saved your life, daughter!" Amiel

exclaimed. "Think. By taking all the blame, Hattush saved your life. What good would your death have done anyone?"

What good? It would have ended her pain. She would be with her husband. Couldn't they see that? No one could understand what she felt. Her parents had been married more than thirty years. Besides the harshness of life in captivity, all they'd known was joy and peace.

"I would be with my husband now. How can I go on without him?"

"I don't know, daughter, but you will. You will go on for yourself, for your child. Your child will need you now more than ever. You must find the strength to continue, to tell your child of his father's valor for our people."

"I want to die, Father. I want to be with Hattush." She spoke blasphemy but didn't care. It was the truth. She *did* want to die, want the pain to end. Life without Hattush wasn't life. Never would she see his smiling face as he swung their child through the air for the pure joy of hearing childish laughter. How could she get through the endless nights? Death would be so easy.

Amiel cupped her face in his hands. "You may want to die, but you won't. No, Puah, you're stronger than you know. You'll rise from this bed and make a life for yourself *and* your child. Your mother and I are here as long as you need us. For now though, you must eat."

Behira entered with a steaming bowl of soup. It smelled delicious and Puah's stomach growled with hunger. How long had she gone without food? Could she have hurt the baby? Guilt washed over her at the thought of her own selfishness. She would *have* to eat. To do less would make her no better than Pharaoh — a baby killer.

"I've brought your favorite. Your father slew a lamb this morning, just for you. He's been near ill himself worrying over you. Now, I want you to sit up while I feed you."

Puah managed a small smile as Amiel rolled his eyes in humor at Behira's bossy ways.

"Yes, Mama."

With her father's help, Puah sat up while Behira placed pillows to support her back. Her weakness surprised her, and for a moment she felt dizzy. It took some effort to remain upright.

Over the next moments Behira spooned thick, hearty soup into Puah's mouth. When she could hold no more, she pushed the bowl away. Her mother clucked disapproval but didn't argue. Feeling somewhat better, Puah sank against the cushions, trying to shut out the longing that filled her heart.

Any moment now Hattush should walk through the door, tired and dusty from a long day at the foundry. He'd gleam down at her, his smile full of love. Bending down, he'd plant a kiss on her forehead as tender as a baby's sigh. Then he'd gather her into his arms, so strong and yet gentle. He would tell her he loved her. They would talk of growing old together and filling the house with laughing children.

No! No matter how much she longed for him, no matter how deep the pain, he wouldn't be coming through the door, not this day nor any other. Her beloved husband was in the bosom of Abraham. She wouldn't see him again in this life.

Oh, to God that Hattush's words were true! If only the Deliverer would come and lead their people out of Egypt. Did she dare believe she would live to see the Deliverer? Or was she fated to die in captivity as her ancestors?

Behira's voice interrupted her thoughts.

"I want you to drink the sleeping potion one more night so you will sleep without the dreams. Tomorrow you are getting out of this bed. I won't stand by and allow you to do this to yourself. I want to see my grandchild!" Her mother's voice broke as she turned and quickly left the room.

Fresh tears sprang into Puah's own eyes. How she must have vexed her parents with her selfish grief. Worry lines etched both their faces. No, she mustn't hurt them, too. She'd already caused enough pain to others. *Had I not been so selfish and headstrong, had I not become a midwife, Hattush would still be alive.*

"You look pale, my friend."

Shiphrah sat beside Puah where they reclined under the rooftop awning. The elder midwife had arrived shortly after the household began stirring for the day. Shiphrah and Behira pulled Puah from bed, bathed her, anointed her body with fragrant oil, and dressed her. Then, despite her protests, Shiphrah combed Puah's matted, tangled hair and wound it into a neat coil atop her head. Only when both older women nodded their approval did they stop pestering her.

It *did* feel good to be clean and fresh. She wouldn't have been able to summon the strength herself for such grooming. Her arms and legs felt like iron. It seemed all the power within her was gone, as surely as Hattush.

Puah reached out, taking Shiphrah's hand. Since Hattush's death, Shiphrah had assumed her share of the workload. The toll on her older friend was obvious. Dark circles shadowed the older midwife's eyes, a mask of fatigue covered her face.

"The babies, Shiphrah . . . please, I must know. What has become of them?"

Shiphrah smiled and touched Puah's cheek. "Our work continues as before. Two more boys have been safely transported to Goshen. God is with us, Puah. Since Pharaoh was struck down, the soldiers seem to have lost heart for the hunt. Perhaps they fear the power which felled their king. Who can say? They give little effort to carrying out Pharaoh's decree."

Puah sighed deeply at this most welcome news. "Thank you for everything, Shiphrah. You're truly a dear friend. But you look tired. Are you getting much sleep?"

Shiphrah squeezed her hand. "Enough. These old bones don't leap out of bed as quickly as in the early days, but I arrive at most deliveries in time." She smiled wanly. "I've worried about you."

"You mustn't worry about me. Mother and Father are taking good care of me, although I admit I've not taken very good care of myself lately." Puah bit her lip to halt the trembling and hoped the tears wouldn't start again. "I can't seem to mount the strength to leave my bed."

"Your loss has caused some of my own memories to resurface," Shiphrah said, gazing out across rooftops to the expanse of golden hills beyond. "I remember your pain, Puah. I, too, wanted to die."

How could Shiphrah know how she felt? Had her father been talking to her? Guiltily, she remembered. Hadn't Shiphrah's own husband died all too soon? She recalled their long talks, remembered hearing of Shiphrah's devastation when her Nathan died.

"I don't think I'll ever feel again."

"As soon as you allow yourself to feel the pain without fleeing from it, when you face your new life and try to find the good things in it, you will begin recovering. Whether you accept it or not, Hattush's death was God's will. He would be very saddened if he could see you in such a state, Puah. Somehow, in the weeks and months to come, you must find the strength within yourself to go on living, not only for yourself and your child, but for everyone that loves you and needs you."

Needs her? She had never thought about others needing her. How could she possibly go back to her work? No, that wouldn't do. She would never find herself before that devil king's throne again! *Never!* "I don't think I'll ever be able to go back to my old life, Shiphrah. I cannot."

"I'll pray for you, child. Grief is a lonely valley, I know." She paused, gently touching Puah's cheek. "When you find yourself at the other side, you will have some answers. You may never know exactly why Hattush died, but you must accept it as God's will. To our understanding, there is no answer."

Puah looked at Shiphrah. She loved and admired her so very much. She was stronger in character than many men she'd known. With great patience, she'd taught Puah the skills needed to become an accomplished midwife. Many late night walks after an exhausting vigil attending a birth had sealed their bond, made them lasting friends despite the difference in age. Now, tragically, they shared yet another bond.

"How did you do it?" Puah hesitated. "I mean, how did you continue after your husband's death?"

A bittersweet smile lit Shiphrah's face as she again stared out at the distant countryside. A lone falcon soared high above, circling slowly on the rising thermal. She watched it climb for a moment, then turned to face Puah. Soft lines gathered around her sparkling eyes.

"I went back to work. Without joy or even any degree of motivation, I forced myself to go through the motions. Then one day I realized I was enjoying it again. Time passed. I realized that I'd found joy in the simple acts of each new day."

Deep in thought, Shiphrah shifted her gaze beyond the rooftops. When she spoke, she looked directly at Puah with eyes that seemed to sear into the young midwife's very soul.

"When I learned to look back at the wonderful memories my husband and I shared, when it no longer brought me great pain, I knew I was healed. The memories became like a warm blanket I could wrap around myself, shielding me from the coldness of life without my beloved Nathan. You *will* reach that place, Puah. I know right now you feel as if you'll never stop crying inside, but you will."

Suddenly without warning, memories flooded Puah's mind. Like stampeding horses they crashed into the present. She could see Hattush as she'd seen him the first day on the streets of Itj-tawy, so tall, handsome, magnificent. She remembered how her breath grew short and her heart fluttered. Then, in Shiphrah's garden, when he declared his love and announced his intent of offering a bride's price for her. She could see the dark brooding passion in his eyes on their wedding night, just before he'd drawn her into his arms. She saw his joyous smile when she'd announced her pregnancy. Then the images merged into one sorrowful remembrance as Hattush sank to his knees at the foot of Pharaoh's throne.

Puah shuddered, recalling the moment when life's light left Hattush's eye, leaving only a battered shell where her beloved once dwelled. Yet there was something more. It was as if a mantle of peace and joy had covered his wounded visage. Truly, he'd seen something no one else in the great throne room noticed.

Puah sought Shiphrah's eyes, and the love and understanding there released the floodgates of her grief. She wept openly as Shiphrah gathered her into her arms. Would the painful memories never cease?

"Why, Shiphrah? Why my Hattush? He'll never see our child. Has God forsaken me? Am I that bad? Is my faith such that God doesn't hear my prayers any longer?" Puah wailed. Deep sobs rent her. Again and again she cried out to the LORD in anger and desolation. In the safety of Shiphrah's embrace the pain she'd held back in a hidden, dark cavern rushed forth. As she mourned, the flowing tears washed some of grief's poison from her.

When blessed numbness came, Puah lay spent against Shiphrah's soft bosom. Shiphrah smoothed Puah's brow, rocking her like a child and humming a cradlesong. Like an injured child, Puah lay there, allowing healing warmth from her dearest friend to seep into her pummeled soul. In the arms of one who'd known like pain, Puah took her first step along the rocky path back to life. Somehow she would find the strength to brush away the weight of her despair and begin the rest of life's journey.

"So you see, little ones, a friend is indeed a great treasure," Puah instructed.

The day's journey had been arduous for the aged midwife. Every word was an effort, but she was determined to finish her story for the children.

"When you find a true friend, you've truly found a wonderful thing," she continued. "They'll be there with you in the valley *and* on the mountaintop."

Later, when the others were gone. Hannah stayed by the tent door. She faced

Puah, playing nervously with the front of her cloak.

"Grandma′ma?" Hannah's forehead wrinkled in innocent worry. Puah sensed the precocious child would ask a question of deep importance.

"Yes?"

"I've never seen you cry for Father Hattush. Did you stop missing him that day?"

Puah's heart lurched at Hannah's guileless question.

"Sweet child, I've cried silently for him every day of my life. I miss him today as much as I did the day he died. He was my heart, my soul, and my dearest friend."

"Oh, Grandma′ma!" Hannah launched herself into Puah's arms and clung to her. "I'm sorry."

Puah caressed the child's dark curls, soft as silk against her own dry, wrinkled skin, relishing the moment. She lifted Hannah's chin and looked into her eyes. Tears dampened the child's long, silky lashes.

"Hannah, I *will* see my beloved again. When I leave this life, I shall join him and be with him always."

"But that means you'll leave *me!*" Hannah's anguished look caused Puah's chest to hurt.

"Only for a short time, my child." Puah took Hannah's hand and led her to the tent door. "Look around you, my love. All of this is temporary. Eternity is more vast than the grains of sand in this endless wilderness, or the stars which inhabit the heavens. For every instant of this life, we'll have ten thousand times ten thousand years to enjoy being with our loved ones and our God. Death is not to fear, for you *or* me."

Too wise for her own good, Hannah turned and looked deeply into Puah's eyes.

"Will you find a way to say hello to me from Paradise?"

Puah threw back her head and cackled. "Indeed, child! Every time you hear a nightingale's sweet song, think of me. When you hear a new baby's cry, think of me. When your feet stand on the far bank of the Jordan, looking upon your new home in Canaan, think of me. Most of all, whenever joy fills your heart, know that I am there with you, even as I am there in spirit when you are sad."

"May I sleep here with you tonight, Grandma´ma?" Hannah asked, hugging Puah once more.

Puah couldn't refuse her. In truth, she wanted the child's company this night.

Soon the waning moon rose, peeking

softly into the tent. Hannah's breathing deepened as she fell asleep in Puah's arms. Puah sighed, reveling in the preciousness of the moment. When her back began to ache, she slid Hannah onto the blankets, then curled up beside her.

"Grandmother?" Daphne slipped into the tent sometime later. "I'm here to get Hannah. The poor angel is worn out, I see."

"Let her sleep here with me, child," Puah demanded softly. "You go. Get a good night's rest. Tomorrow's journey will take its toll on all of us."

Without argument, Daphne planted a kiss on Puah's forehead and slipped out into the night.

A gentle desert wind blew in rhythm with Hannah's soft breathing. Puah extinguished the oil lamp, then curled up beside the child. Her joints ached a little more deeply than usual after the day's long trek. The pain in her chest abided as she relaxed deep into the bedding. Soon, sleep overtook her too, leaving only the whisper of the night breeze playing at the tent walls.

XIX

Go and cry out to the gods which you have chosen; let them deliver you in your time of distress. (Judges 10:14)

"Do you think he will die?" Batya whispered to Sennerfer. They stood over Pharaoh's still, pale form. Since his collapse some days ago, he clung precariously to life with no signs of awakening from the deep coma. Family came and went, including Pharaoh's only son, Amunhotpe, heir to the throne.

The nine-year-old boy looked much like Khaneferre, though he still possessed the round cheeks of childhood. He'd been frail from birth, and his mother chafed over his slight size and fragile nature. As a result, she'd coddled him, shielding him from Khaneferre's wide mood swings, especially the rages. She insisted his lessons be held near her chambers so she could watch over him and ensure his physical needs were met.

Because of his safeguarded existence, Batya rarely saw her younger half-brother.

She was shocked but pleased when her father allowed her to marry the husband of her choice. She had fully expected Khaneferre to insist she marry Amunhotpe. Perhaps Pharaoh had seen the results of close family marriages once too often. If the frail Amunhotpe could not assume the throne, then Batya's sons would some day rule with a strong hand.

Now Pharaoh's two oldest heirs stood over him. Incense filled the air of the royal sleeping chamber with thick, acrid smoke, so sickeningly sweet it threatened to drive them away. The high priest to Amun chanted a prayer for Khaneferre's healing. Pharaoh lay still as death, his breathing shallow and irregular.

Sennerfer moved back a few steps from the stricken king and motioned for Batya to follow. Khaneferre's son remained at his side, aware only that his father rested soundly.

"It is hard to say, Princess. He is gravely ill. Notice the sagging of his mouth. I have seen this kind of sickness before. It is most serious. Even if he awakens, I fear he will not be in control of all his faculties. Since you are the eldest, it would be wise for you to become co-regent until Amunhotpe is old enough to assume the throne. If your father recovers, he will need your help for some time."

Sennerfer watched Batya's face, smiling inwardly at the flash of excitement he saw in her dark almond eyes. Did she harbor illusions of gaining the throne? There *were* recorded incidents of females ruling until a suitable male heir could be crowned. What problems would this independent young woman bring? Or, what victories?

Batya drew her shoulders back, straightening her graceful carriage even more. With a nod of her head, she indicated Amunhotpe.

"Bring the boy and his mother to my quarters for dinner. We will discuss the matter. You are right, vizier. We cannot stand idly by at Pharaoh's bedside. The work of Egypt must move forward."

That evening Sennerfer smiled as he rode in his curtained litter from Batya's quarters back to the palace. The meeting had progressed as he'd hoped. After a succulent feast of roasted duck, Sennerfer and Batya discussed Egypt's immediate future with Mayati, the young prince's mother. Delighted by her son's imminence to the throne, she seemed happy to comply with most anything Sennerfer suggested. Persuading her that Batya should assume the responsibilities of the throne until her son was more prepared proved almost too easy. The offer of larger apartments and other gifts of opulence didn't hurt the vizier's and princess' cause.

Upon hearing of the gravity of his father's illness, Amunhotpe's immediate response was to run to his mother's side and bury his face in the folds of her silk gown.

"Amunhotpe looks tired. Perhaps you should get him to bed." Batya's dry observance did not escape Sennerfer. The princess tired of her brother's whining. Nothing further could be accomplished with the prince and his mother here. Indeed, the boy's complaining stretched Sennerfer's own nerves as thin as a papyrus scroll.

Batya clapped her hands and a servant girl scurried forward, the gold chain on her girdle jingling, creating a musical echo in the vast dining hall of Batya's palace.

"Have the prince's litter brought to the courtyard. He and his mother will be leaving momentarily." With a nod, the slave hurried away.

Sennerfer rose with effort, offering Mayati his arm. Soon, he and Batya sat alone. After a servant refilled their cups with wine, the serious business of state began.

"I understand you have adopted a child."

Sennerfer observed Batya's face and was rewarded to see it brighten at the mention of Moses.

"Yes! He is a beautiful and bright child. Amun knew my heart and provided a child to fill my emptiness."

"Is it true the child is Hebrew?" the vizier asked quietly, moving imaginary breadcrumbs across the dining table's glossy surface.

"Why is *that* important?" Batya's icy, defensive tone told Sennerfer what he wanted to hear.

"It is inconsequential to me, my princess. However, your father ordered all Hebrew infant males killed. If someone in the palace, say the high priest, decides to follow Pharaoh's orders, your son could be in danger." Sennerfer paused, taking a sip of wine from his golden goblet. "Perhaps," he continued with a hint of a smile, "while you are co-regent, you should rescind the decree, announce the purging a success. That would save face for Pharaoh and bring peace to our inner gates. It would also allow us to concentrate our efforts more clearly on defeating the Hittites. They mount yet another campaign on the eastern front. They must be stopped with all haste, or else all Egypt is in great peril."

Batya searched the wise old vizier's eyes, discerning the wisdom she found there. "Very well. Let it be done. Have the scribes prepare the order immediately. I shall issue it at morning court in my father's name. We must move decisively on matters. With Pharaoh ill, the throne is at risk unless someone assumes his role and does it swiftly. It *must* be me."

Sennerfer hid the joy he felt at Batya's pronouncement. He admired this young woman, seeing much of her father in her. Not the man of recent years, edging ever closer to madness, but the young king whom Sennerfer watched ascend the throne. Young Khaneferre had seized command of the mightiest nation on earth with decisive and evenhanded control.

Yes, Batya would do well, perhaps even overshadow her weaker brother. The young prince's mother would most likely remain amenable as long as the luxuries and recognition of state were maintained. For the first time in recent years, Sennerfer wished for more days to live. He longed to see how all this played out, hoping his assessment of Batya's heart and strength was accurate. Egypt would need a ruler with a firm hand. The Hebrew slaves' morale had suffered greatly under Khaneferre's murderous decree. It might never heal. Without rational leadership, the days to come could prove tumultuous.

Gossip of Pharaoh's sickness swept through the streets of Itj-tawy like a desert sirocco. Behind closed doors of Hebrew homes, speculation about the future dominated conversation.

"I hear he has the fever," Uncle Namir announced. The family lingered over hot, strong tea following a meal at Puah's home.

Her parents remained at her side. Depression's fog receded a bit more with each new day. At least now she could rise mornings and dress herself. She still couldn't bring herself to return to work.

"I hear he's near death," Amiel responded.

The paltry amount of food she'd eaten knotted in her belly. Did they have to talk of Pharaoh? She didn't want to hear of him, *ever!*

Puah wiped her mouth and offered her mother a weak smile, then rose and ascended the stairs. At least on the roof it was quiet. The peace there eased her pain a bit. Alone with her memories, she faced her grief, remembering Hattush. On the roof she wasn't hampered with such trivial matters as politics.

It did no good to discuss such things anyway. The royal family would do whatever they chose. Nothing would ever change that. Aside from God's intervention, the royal family was all-powerful. Their words stood, and no one could strike them down.

The cool night air refreshed her sagging spirit. Herb-scented smoke wafted from a nearby cooking fire. It smelled wonderful. The fish and barley she'd eaten for dinner had actually tasted good. Since her talk with Shiphrah, Puah's appetite was returning, little by little.

The baby grew inside her. She could feel the gentle rise of her womb. When she'd surfaced from her deep grief, she prayed each day that God would keep His gentle hand on her baby, her only tangible link to Hattush. Now an ache filled her, one that would be eased only by holding their child.

Puah's parents would stay with her until after the birth. Her brothers-in-law could manage the flocks for a season while they awaited the baby's arrival. Afterwards, the family would decide her future.

Perhaps she *would* heal as everyone maintained. Still, aching emptiness followed her at each turn. When she began her day it was there, and when she lay on her pillow at night it was there. At least the taunting nightmares no longer awakened her. She now realized she wasn't responsible for Hattush's death, but still the accusations the dreams had invoked felt like a knife twisting in her breast. She'd relived the previous months a thousand times in her mind, finding nothing different she would've done. She would still fight to save the babies. Yet, always the question lurked in the back of her mind. What might she have done to save Hattush?

The night sky melded with the hazy outline of the eastern horizon. Overhead, wondrous stars twinkled back at her, just as they had the night of Hattush's proposal. The words he'd spoken in Shiphrah's garden had brought such joy to her heart! Fresh pain stabbed Puah at the memories. She gulped and fought back tears.

The sound of someone ascending the stairs broke her reverie. Puah drew her mind back to the present and wiped away a tear.

Amiel's head and shoulders appeared in the opening. Soon he stood beside her. The concern on his face caused her heart to lurch. Something was wrong!

"Daughter, you have a visitor. We spoke at length. He realizes you'll be angry and upset to see him, but he insists that you hear him out."

"Who is it, Father?"

Amiel hesitated, his feet pacing nervously in place. Noisily he cleared his throat. "Sennerfer."

Puah recoiled at the mention of the vizier's name. Bilious rage threatened to spew from her mouth. *How dare he come to my home! The liar!* She could clearly picture his wrinkled face full of cold indifference in the throne room. He'd condemned her husband to death with his declaration to Pharaoh. What could he possibly want with her?

Puah rose and walked briskly to the edge of the roof, pretending to look across the vast eastern wilderness. The Nile lay somewhere in the darkness beyond. "I have nothing to say to that vile man!"

"I believe you'll want to hear what he has to say, my dove. He comes in peace."

"No!" The cry tore from her throat, its vehemence shocking her. Gasping, she spun around and looked at her father. She'd never spoken to him so.

"Puah, I've forced you to do very few things in your life. I've always been soft in my heart with you. But this time, as elder of our family, I insist. Trust me. I love you and want only what's best for you. I'll help him up the stairs. Do not shame this house."

Amiel's harshness deflated Puah's prepared retort. He turned and left, not giving her time to answer his command. Even her father didn't understand the depths of her feelings on this matter. How could he? He'd not been present when Sennerfer pointed the accusing finger and announced Hattush's guilt before Pharaoh, condemning him to death. Only God in His boundless mercy spared her husband further suffering, taking him before the executioner's blade could fall.

Her uncle and father appeared at the top of the stairs, Sennerfer between them. They led him to the cushioned seats and assisted him as he sat. Puah watched without concealing the hatred she felt. How dare he befoul her home with his presence?

The frail old man adjusted his robes, then looked up into her eyes, his own filled with deep, unreadable emotion.

"Puah, I have come to tell you of your husband's last wishes. I talked to him before he entered the throne room on that fateful day. I know you detest me and do not trust me. You have no reason to trust me. Still, I came to love your husband as a son. Please, hear me."

Is this some kind of obscene trick? Her

stomach pitched and rolled. Why wouldn't they just leave her alone with her grief? She would hear what he had to say, but it would change nothing. Her beloved's body lay cold in his grave because of Sennerfer's words to Pharaoh.

"I'll listen," she spat coldly. "Tell me what you've come to say."

"That is all I ask of you. Please, come sit." Sennerfer patted the cushions.

"No, I'll stand." The thought of coming near this man made her skin crawl. He could be here for nothing good. Did he desire to punish her more? She turned to face the distant horizon, blinking back tears.

"I understand."

Something about Sennerfer's subdued answer bothered her. Was it sincerity she detected in his tone? Either he was a master of lies, or he indeed must perceive her pain.

"I told your husband something that I have never revealed to another living soul. He took that secret to his death, having asked something of me in return." Sennerfer's quavering voice was thick with emotion.

"I honored his request. Puah, child, Hattush loved you as much as any man could love his wife. In his last words to me, he made me vow to do whatever necessary to keep you and his child safe."

Doubt stirred within Puah. *Could he be telling the truth?* She turned from the railing and faced the old vizier, wanting to see the light of truth in the eyes of his soul. He met her gaze solidly.

"What secret, Sennerfer? Tell me what secret won my husband's trust into the confidence of Pharaoh's vizier, his sycophant." Puah spewed the accusation, her fury spilling over the dam of her heart. This man and his god-king had destroyed her joy, her hope, indeed her life.

"Sit, woman. Your anger will only upset your child," Sennerfer commanded sternly like a reproving grandfather. No judgment, perhaps even understanding, abided in his words.

Slowly, Puah walked toward him and sat stiffly nearby. He didn't seem so powerful here. *Why, he's just an old man who shakes with palsy.* She noted the thin skin of his gnarled hands and the curve of his ancient back. But the clarity of his eyes startled her. Warm light abided there, and she sensed something familiar, yet indefinable.

"I'm listening. If you can tell me anything that will ease the pain in my heart, I will be grateful."

With gentle words the aged vizier spoke.

"Very well. What I say is true." Sennerfer turned his head until their eyes met. "My mother was Hebrew, my father, an Egyptian taskmaster. She took her own life when I was but an infant."

Puah gasped. Sennerfer ignored her shock and continued. "A childless Egyptian couple of great means took me in and raised me as their own. They kept my secret, but told me of my mother's people. I vowed that one day I would avenge her death. You see, she took her own life because the shame of my birth was too great. I rose through the hierarchy of the palace with but one goal — to help my mother's people."

Puah froze. What kind of story was this? The second most powerful man in Egypt, a Hebrew? Was this a ruse to entrap her? "Surely, you don't expect me to believe this . . . this *fable?*" She didn't try to keep the acid from her question.

"My dear, whatever you choose to believe is between you and our God."

Sennerfer smiled at the shock he saw in her eyes. "Yes, child, *our* God, the Holy One of Israel. He is also *my* God. You may stand in judgment of me, but it has been *my* influence in the past years that have saved our people many times. Khaneferre is mad. He truly thinks *he* is god."

"But what does this have to do with my husband?"

"Hattush and I shared a common goal — to keep our people safe from Pharaoh. It proved increasingly difficult as Khaneferre's madness waxed ever worse. You must understand, had I ever revealed my true alliance I would have been killed immediately. Only by holding this secret do I have any chance of effecting a good outcome for our people."

The old man sighed wistfully. "It has not been an easy path. How I have yearned to join my mother's people, to worship the One True God openly and without fear. As it is, I have been a man belonging to no one."

Puah was stunned, unable for the moment to comment on this remarkable confession. From a distant garden crickets chirped and a nightingale serenaded the rising moon. The night air grew cooler. Puah shivered and pulled her cloak closer about her shoulders.

Sennerfer shifted his position and winced. Pains of old age had not escaped his bones. "Several weeks before Hattush's death, he asked one thing of me. He implored that I do whatever necessary to keep you safe. Then, on that terrible day as he lay dying in my arms, moments before soldiers dragged him into the throne room . . ." Sennerfer's voice broke, choking with emotion. It took a moment for him to compose himself before continuing.

"He asked me once again to protect you. He implored me to do whatever necessary, even lie, to save you." Sennerfer's lips quivered as he neared tears. "Puah, Hattush's last thoughts were only of you and his child."

A cry escaped Puah's throat and she could only draw up her knees, hugging them tightly as she rocked away the pain. *Hattush sacrificed himself to save me?* He'd taken a fatal beating for her, for their child? It was more love than she could imagine. Yet, she knew she would have done the same. His sacrifice truly saved not only her and their baby, but many others.

"Puah, God never blessed me with children, but if I had been given a son, I would have been proud to have had one like Hattush. He was a most godly man, a faithful husband. You can be sure of that. I know my days on this earth grow short. I look forward to seeing him once more in Paradise."

Suddenly Puah couldn't stop the sobs. They tore from her aching throat as the magnitude of her husband's love filled her. As pain poured forth, a gentle warmth grew, filling her with the beauty of his unselfish devotion. What greater love could a person have than to give the ultimate sacrifice to save others?

Hattush's prophetic words rang in her ears. *"My wife, we have known more love in our short time together than most people know in a lifetime."*

A gnarled hand patted her clenched fists. When Puah turned to face Sennerfer, a river of tears coursed down his wrinkled cheeks, testament to the truth of his words. He'd condemned Hattush for one purpose — to save her and her unborn child. Too late to help Hattush, Sennerfer honored her husband's dying request. How much he must have suffered under the guilt!

Unable to bear the sadness she felt for Sennerfer's lonely position, Puah reached out and hugged him to her. Her action released Sennerfer's own grief. His frail body shook as he wept in her embrace. God in His infinite wisdom had placed an ally for her people near Pharaoh's throne. Sennerfer had carried his lonely secret like a heavy yoke these many years. Truly he'd loved and trusted Hattush, else he would never have risked sharing his secret. And now that same trust had been placed in her own hands. *May God grant me the strength to carry it faithfully!*

Sennerfer drew back, seeking Puah's watery eyes. "Pharaoh is gravely ill. It is doubtful he will recover. Princess Batya is now co-regent, standing in for her brother. She has rescinded Khaneferre's ungodly decree. You may safely go about your calling and work without fear."

The old vizier smiled, his face shining with the peace that passes all understanding. "The one who now rules Egypt is our friend, *and,* is raising what would appear to be a Hebrew child as her own. The God of Abraham, Isaac, Jacob, and Joseph still reigns from above, even in this godless land. God be praised!"

First disbelief, then relief, swept through Puah. As Sennerfer's words settled into her being, she felt the unmistakable music of joyous laughter begin to well. A huge smile broke forth on the vizier's seasoned face and soon they were laughing together as healing tears rolled down their faces.

Her mother and father and Uncle Namir appeared at the top of the stairs, bewilderment in their eyes. Seeing their look of astonishment, Puah and Sennerfer laughed all the harder.

She'd reached a turning point in her life's journey. Her path was destined to follow a trail that only God could foresee. For now, she would stand and begin walking as best she could. If she stumbled, she would get up and try again. For the first time in a long while, hope blossomed in the trampled garden of her heart. Even as she gazed up at the stars, recalling Hattush's gentle smile, the impression was clear. She was now climbing the wall of her own dark valley, and the light just over the hilltop was beginning to shine on her broken heart.

"Daphne, sit with me awhile. You work much too hard. You're going to drop if you don't relax and give your back a rest."

"Oh, Grandmother, I'm fine, really." Even as she spoke, Daphne sank wearily to the pillows beside Puah. They rested silently under the awning outside Puah's tent, watching the waning moon rise over the distant horizon in the fading daylight.

"Is Hannah already asleep?" Puah asked.

"Yes, like a rock. Between the long walks, heat, and dust, she's exhausted. But mind you, never too exhausted to hear her Grandma'ma's famous stories. What *have* you been telling these children that draws them back here each night like moths to a flame?"

"Only the story of our people."

"Ah, now I see. I'm surprised there aren't more adults listening outside your tent each evening. Many have never heard. Most are too young to know about your life and Pharaoh's decree of death."

"Well, I think the parents use the time to rest." Puah shifted to face Daphne. "I want to talk to you about something that has been weighing on my mind for some time."

"Yes?" Daphne sat up and directed her full attention to her great-grandmother.

Puah sighed. "I'm not well, child. The herbs for my heart no longer work very well. I know my time on this earth grows short."

"No, Grandmother, don't say that!"

"Shush, my love. It's true, and it's not a bad thing. I've lived a long and rewarding life. I'm ready for the rest to come.

"I want to speak to you of Hannah. I don't have to tell you that she has stolen my heart."

"She *is* special, isn't she?"

"Indeed, she's like a lotus blooming in this arid wilderness. I want to give you this." Puah pushed her medicine bag toward Daphne. "It's for Hannah, when the time comes. Soon I'll have no need of it. I sense

Hannah will need it someday. It is hers."

Tears filled Daphne's eyes. "Oh, Grandmother. It's like you're saying goodbye."

"Not yet, my dear, but soon. Since I don't know when that will be, I wanted you to take these and put them safely away for Hannah. She has a special place in my heart. She has the healer's touch, you know."

"Yes, I know. Did you know she gives me back rubs at night?" Daphne's warm eyes grew misty with the talk of her daughter.

Puah threw back her head and laughed. "Yes, that's my girl. I suspect you'll have quite a time getting her married. She may give you a test as I did my parents, insisting on her own way."

"Grandmother, if she follows in your footsteps, it will be a great honor to our house."

Daphne pulled Puah close and hugged her gently.

"You're a good girl, Daphne. I'm so proud of you. I pray God gives you a son this time."

"That would be nice, but if all girls are as special as Hannah, then it doesn't matter to me.

"I should get back to my baking." Daphne rose, reached down for the package and walked slowly to the edge of the shelter.

"I'm going to miss you, Grandmother."

"And I shall miss you too, dear child. Just take good care of yourself and your children. Promise me."

"You have my word," Daphne said, near tears. "Goodnight." She turned and walked away, looking back once to meet Puah's eyes with clear understanding of what had transpired.

Puah waited until Daphne disappeared behind her tent, then let tears of goodbye flow.

XX

You have turned for me my mourning into dancing; You have put off my sackcloth and clothed me with gladness. (Psalm 30:11)

"How can I turn my back on the women? They need my help. Shiphrah is much too weary to take on all of the responsibility. Besides, we need to train a new midwife soon."

"Daughter, how do you plan to care for your baby *and* work such long days caring for others?" Behira asked.

Puah sat on a small stool in the cooking area with the other women. Anna vigorously kneaded bread, minding her own business during this intense family discussion. Puah's mother prepared a leg of lamb for the spit, rubbing it with fragrant herbs. Aunt Etana nursed her baby squirming restlessly in her lap.

"Teething?" Puah watched the baby pull at the soft fabric of Etana's shift, kicking her legs occasionally in angry protest of the discomfort she felt. Her aunt nodded.

Behira stopped rubbing the meat and looked at Puah. "Well?" She tapped a foot at Puah's disregard of her most serious question.

"Oh, Mama, it's too soon to answer such a question. I don't know what I'll do. Part of me wants only to mother my child and watch it grow; the other part needs to continue my work, though my joy is diminished."

"Well, you should be thinking about that and other things. Your baby will be here all too soon. You only have a short while to decide."

"I do little else but think of my baby. The thought of a child has been the one thing that's kept me from going insane since . . . without Hattush." Puah felt her throat tighten. It still stung her heart to speak his name. He was gone. Each new day confirmed the painful reality of living without him. Her family stayed closer than ever, but that couldn't fill the gaping hole his death created.

"I'm sorry, Puah. I know you must think about these things a great deal. It's just that I worry about you. I want you to be happy, but I also want you and the baby to be safe." Behira rubbed her hands together to clean them of the seasonings. "Of course, if I had my way, you'd return to Avaris with your father and me."

"I know, Mama. I know how much you and Father love me. When the time comes, I'll consider everything you've said."

Her mother was right. She would soon have to make a decision. If she continued her work, she'd need a wet nurse to help with the baby. If she decided to stay home, she sensed she'd never fully be satisfied. Midwifery was too much a part of her.

There was nothing as exciting or reverent as delivering a new life into the world. In that sacred instant it seemed all creation paused, waiting for the newborn to take its first deep breath, cry out its first beautiful wail. God had truly blessed her with such a joyous vocation. Did she have the right to refuse her calling because of fear? But could she leave her baby while she spent interminable time ministering to laboring women?

Puah sighed deeply. Trying to figure it all out made her head swim. Besides, there was still time to think things through. Perhaps she would discuss it soon with Shiphrah.

Later, after a meal shared with Aunt Etana, Uncle Namir, and the children, they retired to the roof. The women rested while the men and older children played senet.

Puah fought drowsiness for most of the evening, her full stomach and the quiet drone of happy, familiar voices lulling her like music of the harp. She was almost asleep when a gentle tap on the shoulder stirred her from the comfortable spot on the cushions.

"Puah, go to bed, child."

Puah opened her eyes to see Aunt Etana stooping over her. "Your body is telling you something. Listen to it."

Yawning, Puah stretched and smiled at her aunt. "Yes, I think I will. I'm tired."

After bidding everyone goodnight, Puah retired to her sleeping chamber. This was always the worst part of her day. Facing the empty bed, knowing Hattush wouldn't be there beside her in the cozy confines of the covers. No more alluring aroma of his manly scent. Her heart ached to feel his tender embrace, to share her deepest secrets and dreams for their future.

Puah sighed, then set to the task of preparing for sleep. After washing her face and hands, she slipped into a soft linen gown and knelt beside her bed.

"LORD, keep me and my child in Your tender care. Thank You for Your goodness and love. Show me Your plan for my life and help me hear Your voice. Forgive my weaknesses."

A light breeze wafted through the chamber. Puah settled back onto the soft bed, hands resting behind her head, listening to muffled night sounds. Beyond the window a myriad of crickets chorused in the darkness. From the rooftop, muted noises of her family's lively discussions and laughter drifted down through the long tiled hallway.

Never had Puah felt so alone. Tears burned her eyes. How could she go on when part of her own body and soul had been ripped from her? Would she ever face the quiet of day's end and not ache to the very marrow of her being?

She lay there, allowing pain to flow out through her tears. Suddenly a soft flutter in her belly stopped her cold. *What was that?*

Puah slid her hand down and rested it on the soft mound. Firm resistance told her the baby was indeed growing. She lay smiling in the darkness, thinking of her child. Then a soft kick thumped her palm.

"Oh!"

Once . . . twice . . . three times the baby fluttered against the pressure of her hand as if to say, *"I am here."*

There really *was* a baby in there! She knew it in her mind. She'd watched countless babies grow, but could never imagine the feel of her own baby moving inside her. Hattush's child lived — *within her!*

A soft, assuring voice whispered into the deepest chamber of her heart, *"You see, Puah, I do love you."*

Suddenly she saw it all with sharp clarity. God loved her. Yes, her! She sobbed aloud, repentant for her doubtful heart. The LORD had blessed her in so many ways. Had He not sent Hattush into her life? God could have sealed her womb, left her barren. So many things could've been withheld from her. But God, in His immeasurable mercy, reached down and gave abundantly from His provisions. According to the heavenly messenger's words, her own hands would welcome the promised Deliverer into the world. Perhaps they already had! And now, the seed of her beloved grew within her, healthy and strong, a new miracle waiting to make its appearance.

Truly, the LORD loved her. And at this miraculous moment Puah knew without a doubt that all would be well. Life would go on. She would find fulfillment as she journeyed toward eternity and her beloved Hattush's arms once more.

In the deep recesses of Puah's heart a new song flowered — just a mere refrain — but a new song nonetheless.

Puah sat on a cushioned chair opposite Batya at the royal riverside palace. A courier had delivered Batya's summons early that morning, worded carefully to allay Puah's fears.

Princess Batya, most grateful patient of the midwife, Puah, requests her company for noon meal refreshment at the royal princess' palace.

For a fleeting moment alarm gripped Puah's heart, but reason soon soothed her concerns. Had Batya not quickly gathered young Moses into her arms, knowing full well he was of the house of Israel? Had she not rescinded the accursed decree? No, there was nothing to fear from the princess.

They dined in an open courtyard bordered by a beautiful flowering garden. The fragrance of lotus blossoms from a nearby pool wafted on the gentle breeze. A brilliant sunbird feasted on honeysuckle, its indigo plumage radiant in the dappled sunlight.

"I had you meet me here, rather than at the king's palace," Batya said. She nibbled at a wedge of cheese and searched Puah's face through kohl-painted eyes. "I felt it would be too frightening for you to return there. The palace teems with physicians and magicians. I grow weary of it. Besides, your last summons there was, well . . . oh, Puah, I am truly sorry for your loss."

"Thank you for your thoughtfulness, my princess. I'm not sure I would've been able to gather enough courage to go to Pharaoh's palace." Puah shuddered inwardly at the thought. "Indeed, that was the saddest day of my life."

"You loved your husband very much. I see deep sadness in your eyes."

Did it still show so easily? Did she wear her grief like a cloak? "Yes, I loved him very much. He made my heart sing each day we were together. I'm slowly learning to live again. There are days I feel I cannot continue, but still I survive."

"It is true we heal," Batya said, reaching out and touching Puah's hand. "Just as you told me when I lost my baby. I still wonder what my baby would look like. There is an empty place in my heart, but I have accepted the loss. Now my days are filled with the joy of Moses."

Batya pointed to Moses, who lay across Yocheved's knees as she massaged his back with fragrant oil. His chubby legs pumped in rhythm with his mother's stimulating caress. He cooed happily.

"Look. See how he springs up like a reed?" Batya boasted.

"He's a beautiful and blessed child to have you for a mother, my princess."

Batya returned her attention to her guest. "And you, Puah, what are your plans?" Her dark, almond eyes drilled deeply into Puah's own.

Puah took a sip of citrus water from an ornate cup. "I'm not sure. I'm expecting a child during the harvest. My parents want me to return to Avaris, but my heart finds it difficult to forego my work. I miss it."

"A baby!" Batya beamed at Puah's news. "How excited you must be!"

"The child will fill a large void in my heart."

"What would you require to continue your work and still care for your child?"

"Well, I . . ." Puah paused, contemplating Batya's question. "I really haven't thought much about what it would require. I have been so consumed in my grief that practical matters have been neglected."

"Well, certainly you would need a wet nurse during the times you are away," the princess said, lifting her eyes in thought. "You would need more servants to care for your household while you are working, and to care for the child while you sleep. You cannot expect to stay up all night and care for the baby by yourself."

"Well, yes, I'd need a wet nurse to supplement the child, but I hadn't thought of extra help. I cannot afford more servants. It's out of the question."

Batya sat up regally and locked Puah in her gaze. "Nothing is out of the question, midwife. I hereby order you to the king's palace at mid afternoon. I will be holding court. Your presence is mandatory, but do not be afraid. I assure you, there is nothing for you to fear."

"But, I'm not —"

Batya's raised hand stopped Puah's protest. "I would never do anything to hurt you, Puah. Trust me. Now, be there, and bring Shiphrah with you. Bring *all* your family."

Without further discourse, Batya excused herself. She had the king's business sitting heavily on her shoulders now.

Puah sat in confused silence for a few moments, wondering what lay behind Batya's mysterious summons. What could the princess possibly want that she couldn't talk about here and now? She was certain Batya meant her no harm, but the idea of going to Khaneferre's palace sent cold dread through her.

As quickly as her fear arose, it subsided. She watched Yocheved draw a fretting

Moses to her breast, and the joyous smile that lit her face soothed away the last vestige of Puah's anxiety. God's hand remained faithful and powerful. He'd saved this tiny baby, blinding the soldiers' eyes and stopping their ears. He'd opened the heart of an Egyptian princess. Even in the trial of fire the LORD had been merciful. Hattush's child grew and thrived. No, she needn't walk in fear. God loved her and would keep her. Puah returned Yocheved's smile and bid her goodbye. She needed to hurry home. She must tell everyone of Batya's summons.

Puah, her parents, and Shiphrah followed a royal escort through the vast hallways of Khaneferre's palace. Batya's influence was already in evidence. Massive urns of fragrant flowers filled the corridors. Light flooded rooms from high, previously closed windows. Pharaoh's oppressive rule was noticeably absent as they drew nearer the throne room.

Behind Puah and Shiphrah, Behira whispered excitedly to Amiel. She would talk for years of this experience within the walls of Pharaoh's domain. Puah suppressed a smile, remembering her own awe at first witnessing how extravagantly the royal family lived, her own amazement at the vast amounts of gold and other treasures in the palace.

A sentry announced their arrival, and Nubian guards pulled open the huge cedar doors. Puah heard her mother gasp in wonderment as they entered the great hall.

The atmosphere inside the throne room was vastly different from Puah's previous visits. Halcyon contentment filled the room, more family reunion than royal court. Yocheved sat on the dais behind the throne, holding Moses while watching with amused interest. From a padded couch, Sennerfer flashed a furtive smile as they entered. Gone was the tight-lipped expression he'd worn on previous visits. His eyes reflected one at peace, and his comportment reminded Puah more of Hebrew elder than royal vizier.

Upon the throne, Batya reigned in regal elegance. She wore a pleated sheath of the finest linen, exquisite gold embroidery embellishing the sleeves and skirt. No expense had been spared on her accessories. Precious gems blazed from an ornate headband, likewise the girdle at her waist. A dazzling collar of gold set with countless stones adorned Batya's long, graceful neck. Her slender fingers, sparkling with jeweled rings, stroked a spotted kitten.

At the foot of the royal throne, the party kneeled and bowed.

"Rise," Batya commanded softly.

With the others, Puah rose and faced Pharaoh's daughter. Some great secret flashed in Batya's dark eyes, yet the princess maintained a formal bearing and serious tone.

"I have summoned the Hebrew midwives, Puah and Shiphrah. Let it be recorded that their faithful service to the people of Egypt and to their own people is to be remembered and rewarded. I therefore declare them official midwives to the royal family. The house of Pharaoh protects them as their own. I order the Royal Treasury to distribute such funds and the Department of Building to provide workers as are needed to build both midwives homes that are suitable for their station. Let it be recorded and done. I order this in the name of my father, Khaneferre Sobekhotep IV, ruler of Upper and Lower Egypt."

Puah and Shiphrah stared at one another, stupefied. Just a few weeks ago, they'd faced death at Pharaoh's hand, and now the reigning princess ordered royal coffers opened to reward them for their work and faithfulness.

It took a few moments for Puah to realize

her mouth hung open in disbelief. She snapped it closed and smiled weakly at Batya, unable to speak. A wide smile lit Batya's face. She seemed to enjoy Puah's shock and amazement at her generosity.

Humility washed over Puah at God's goodness. She bowed before Batya. "You are too generous, my princess. I thank you most humbly. May the Holy One of Israel bless you exceedingly." Her voice broke as she tried to convey the depth of her gratitude.

"It is with great pleasure that we accept the trust of the midwives to the royal family." Batya nodded to Shiphrah, including her in the welcome. "May your seed flourish. Now, please join me in the garden. We shall have refreshments to celebrate."

Gracefully, Batya rose and withdrew from the throne room. A hushed silence followed as a guard closed the door behind her. Finally, Sennerfer's deep, unreserved laughter broke the constrained mood. Puah hugged Shiphrah and they laughed together until tears flowed. Soon the entire room was alive with a spirit of celebration.

A thin ray of sunlight beamed down from a high window, illuminating Moses' happy face. His contented smile turned into a soft gurgle of pleasure, and for an instant his eyes met Puah's. With innocent delight the babe gazed at her, but there was something more. Moses watched the young midwife with wisdom beyond his years. Many decades were to pass before Puah would understand.

XXI

You number my wanderings; put my tears into Your bottle; are they not in Your book?
When I cry out to You, then my enemies will turn back; this I know, because God is for me. (Psalm 56:8–9)

The children gazed at Puah, faces aglow with wide-eyed wonderment. Many nights had passed since she'd begun the story of Moses' birth and her own part in it.

"And as you know, the child that Batya adopted grew up to be our very own Father Moses. Through him, Pharaoh released our people as God promised. The tiny baby of whom God's messenger spoke grew up as an Egyptian prince, but he never forgot his people."

A small boy near the door leaned forward, his eyes bright with curiosity. "When did you know that Father Moses was the Deliverer?"

Puah sighed, once more reminded of her

oft weak faith. "God tried to show me many times, but my faith was never as great as Hattush's. God sent His messenger to encourage my husband. God protected Moses from the soldiers. Still, I didn't comprehend the full truth until Moses returned from Midian and began beseeching Pharaoh to let our people go. *Then* I knew."

"What happened to Princess Batya?" Hannah asked.

Puah looked at the child through sad eyes. "Princess Batya died of fever when Moses was a young man."

"Oh, Grandma´ma, you must have been very sad. Did Father Moses cry?"

"Yes, child, he cried. I also wept greatly when the funeral procession carried her body to rest in her father's tomb. God lightened my heart, though, as they placed her sarcophagus in the chamber. You see, she rested under the pale light of gold shaped by Hattush's own hands. By the time Batya died, her brother was king. Father Moses grieved deeply for his adopted mother. It was through Batya's mercy that he lived, and he was very thankful for her kindness to him *and* our people."

"Why was her brother such a mean king?" Ruben asked, wiping sleepiness from his eyes.

"From the very beginning Batya's brother was a weak leader," Puah said, her mind drifting back over the years. "He allowed the priests of Amun to guide him into the same wicked ways of his father, Khaneferre. I think in the end he was cursed with the same madness as his father. Had Batya maintained the throne, I believe we would've been allowed to leave in peace."

"So, Grandma´ma, was Batya a righteous woman? Do you think she is in Paradise with God?"

Puah smiled. Leave it to Hannah to get to the very heart of the matter. The aged midwife looked into the child's soulful eyes. Through her, Puah's descendants would see the Promised Land. In Hannah, she recognized a bit of her own independent spirit.

"Only God sees the heart, child. He sees the good and the bad in us all. However, in answer to your question, I *do* believe Batya embraced our God before her death. Although she was an Egyptian princess, we shared many quiet times together, and I came to count her as a dear and trusted friend. She freely allowed Moses to learn our Fathers' ways at Yocheved's knee."

Puah took a deep breath, trying to quiet her heart's erratic patter. "It's sad, you know. Only a few were as wise as Batya.

Egyptians believe that in eternity, in the Hall of Two Truths, one's heart is weighed for truth and purity. They are so close to wisdom, yet so far from it. If only they would reach out and embrace the One True God. Don't ever forget your Creator, children. He is all you will ever need. Even when troubles come, God will not let you down."

"And Shiphrah? What happened to her?" little Ariel asked.

Puah smiled, other memories flooding her mind. "Shiphrah continued to do some of the midwifery work with me, mostly training new midwives." She paused, feeling a tightness in her throat. "In my son, Baruch's, twelfth summer, she died peacefully in her sleep. I still miss her very much. She was a wonderful friend and a caring healer. Her gentle hands brought many of our people safely into the world."

Several of the children grew restless. It was time for bed. With a clap of her hands Puah signaled the end of the night's story time. She felt especially weary tonight. The heat made each passing day more difficult. It was good the tribes had camped early. All day long she'd struggled with her heart's irregular rhythm. It left her weak, her body covered with clammy perspiration.

"Goodnight, children. We have far to go tomorrow, and we'll need our rest. May your dreams be peaceful. If the LORD allows, I'll begin a new story tomorrow night."

Reluctantly, the children rose and left the tent, but not until each one planted a kiss on Puah's wrinkled cheek, thanking her for the story of Father Moses.

When the last child left, Puah found herself alone with Hannah. The girl curled up in Puah's arms and together they listened for a time to noises of the encampment. Earlier revelry around the cooking fires now gave way to quieter sounds, voices muffled by tent walls surrounding them in all directions. Soon, they slept.

The oil lamp flickered behind the rush of air from Daphne's entrance. Her soft touch startled Puah back to wakefulness. Hannah lay peacefully in her grandma´ma's arms.

"Goodnight, Grandmother. I love you. Do you need anything?"

"No child, just rest. I'll see you in the morning."

As gently as possible, Daphne scooped Hannah's limp form into her arms and disappeared into the darkness.

Puah poured some water from the skin and wet a scrap of soft cotton. For a moment she admired its fine weave. It would be a long time before the Hebrew women saw such fine fabric as this. Life in the Promised Land might be more difficult than many believed. Carving a new life was never an easy thing, and many enemies awaited the Hebrews along the way.

Yet, Puah knew who was in control of the matter — the One who'd given her the midwife's call and sent Hattush into her life.

Hattush. Endless seasons had come and gone, yet Puah still ached for him. Every night as she lay upon her bed she rested an arm on the place where he should be. More than eighty years had failed to quell the intense longing in her heart. God had given her a full and glorious life, abundant with adventure and challenge, trial and victory. Yet, she still hungered for her husband.

After washing, she changed into a fresh gown. The call of the ram's horn would come early for her weary bones. *LORD, please let me keep pace tomorrow. I don't want to slow progress. Your people are weary.*

Puah drank a small cup of fresh milk and nibbled on the remains of an emmer cake. After fluffing her pillows, she secured the tent flap. The night air would grow chilly before dawn. Easing back onto the pillows, she pulled a blanket around her and sank into the welcome softness.

Few sounds traveled across the crowded camp this late, save an occasional donkey's bray or baby's cry. A light breeze lapped at the tent flap, lulling her into a dreamy, near-sleep state.

Suddenly she felt the tightening flutter of her heart, then crushing pain. It felt as if a horse were treading upon her chest. For a moment she panicked, grabbing her chest, struggling for breath. Then, warmth, blessed warmth, spread over her and the pain receded.

Puah knew not if she dreamed as she flew along an endless expanse of stars, ten thousand upon ten thousand of them. Suddenly she saw Hattush beckoning, his radiant smile and amber eyes piercing her like the soft beams of morning sun. He seemed so alive, so real, the same as the day they'd wed, glowing with joy in his wedding raiment.

Puah rushed into his arms, hearing once again the sweet song of her heart as her beloved led the way toward a brilliant, irresistible light.

XXII

I call heaven and earth as witness today against you, that I have set before you life and death, blessing and cursing; therefore choose life, that both you and your descendants may live; that you may love the LORD your God, that you may obey His voice, and that you may cling to Him, for He is your life and the length of your days; and that you may dwell in the land which the LORD swore to your fathers, to Abraham, Isaac, and Jacob, to give them.
(Deuteronomy 30:19–20)

A scream shook Hannah awake, the same desperate sound she had heard the night the death angel passed through the streets of Itj-tawy. For a moment she lay there, clasping the covers tightly, hoping she'd been dreaming. She squeezed her eyes shut, wishing it away. The screaming stopped.

Then wailing filled the morning air. First one woman's voice sang the death song, then others joined in. Hannah pressed her hands tightly over her ears. She didn't like that sound! It made her sad and frightened.

Where was Mother? Why hadn't she come to wake her? The sun was already high in the sky. From afar, the deep call of the ram's horn trumpeted across the desert floor. Something was wrong! Usually by this time everyone was assembled and ready to travel.

Hannah slipped a sheath over her head. She brushed at the curls which fell into her eyes after a hard night's sleep. Mother would have to help with the braids. Quickly she laced her sandals, wiping a thick layer of dust from them, then stood. Grabbing her apron, she pulled back the tent flap and gazed out.

A soft haze formed a halo around the sun, but its brightness still required she shield her eyes from the glare. Hannah walked toward the cooking fire, but her mother wasn't there. A group of people stood near her great-great-grandmother's tent.

Alarm filled Hannah and she ran. As Puah's tent grew nearer, the wailing grew louder. *Something has happened to Grandma´ma!*

Hannah pushed past the group of women outside the tent door, dreading what she might find. She found her way to her mother's side. Daphne looked up at her with swollen, tear-filled eyes. The look told it all — her precious Grandma´ma was dead!

Daphne rocked back and forth, wailing the death song. Other women's cries filled the air with mourning.

Stunned, Hannah gazed down. *Perhaps Grandma´ma is only sleeping.* Puah lay on her back, her head cushioned on pillows, hands at her sides. Hannah couldn't pull her eyes from her great-great grandmother's face. Puah's lips were frozen in a pleasant smile. Never had the child seen such a look of peace.

Tears filled Hannah's eyes. Daphne reached out for her and she dove into her mother's arms. Together they wept for Puah. It didn't seem fair. How she had wanted to see the Promised Land! *Why would God take her now?*

After awhile some of the older women led Daphne and Hannah from the tent. Others busied themselves preparing Puah's body for burial.

Outside, Hannah hovered close to her mother, waiting. After a time, the women ushered them back inside the tent. Hannah's eyes grew wide at what she saw. There her sweet Grandma´ma lay, wearing her wedding dress of soft Egyptian linen. Many times Puah had shown it to her, telling stories of great-great-grandfather Hattush.

A commotion at the door of the tent caused everyone to turn. Hannah gasped as Father Moses ducked down and entered the tent. Aaron followed silently, leaning on his walking stick.

With deep reverence Moses knelt beside Puah's body. Then without warning he tore his mantle. He said nothing, but rocked in pained silence with eyes shut tight.

Every evening during story time, Hannah had noticed Father Moses near Grandma′ma's tent. He was always there when Hannah entered. Had Father Moses also been listening? Did he know how Grandma′ma had saved his life?

Moses rose and walked stiffly out into the morning air, then with a great voice spoke to the twelve tribes of Israel.

"Hear, oh Israel. The story of this woman shall not be forgotten. It will be written for a remembrance of our people for all generations. Great was her courage, and great was her love!"

Then the king of Egypt spoke to the Hebrew midwives, of whom the name of one was Shiphrah and the name of the other Puah; and he said, "When you do the duties of a midwife for the Hebrew women, and see them on the birthstools, if it is a son, then you shall kill him; but if it is a daughter, then she shall live." But the midwives feared God, and did not do as the king of Egypt commanded them, but saved the male children alive. So the king of Egypt called for the midwives and said to them, "Why have you done this thing, and saved the male children alive?"

And the midwives said to Pharaoh, "Because the Hebrew women are not like the Egyptian women; for they are lively and give birth before the midwives come to them."

Therefore God dealt well with the midwives, and the people multiplied and grew very mighty. And so it was, because the midwives feared God, that He provided households for them.

So Pharaoh commanded all his people, saying, "Every son who is born you shall cast into the river, and every daughter you shall save alive."

And a man of the house of Levi went and took as wife a daughter of Levi. So the woman conceived and bore a son. And when she saw that he was a beautiful child, *she hid him three months. But when she could no longer hide him, she took an ark of bulrushes for him, daubed it with asphalt and pitch, put the child in it, and laid it in the reeds by the river's bank. And his sister stood afar off, to know what would be done to him.*

Then the daughter of Pharaoh came down to bathe at the river. And her maidens walked along the riverside; and when she saw the ark among the reeds, she sent her maid to get it. And when she opened it, she saw the child, and behold, the baby wept. So she had compassion on him, and said, "This is one of the Hebrews' children."

Then his sister said to Pharaoh's daughter, "Shall I go and call a nurse for you from the Hebrew women, that she may nurse the child for you?"

And Pharaoh's daughter said to her, "Go." So the maiden went and called the child's mother. Then Pharaoh's daughter said to her, "Take this child away and nurse him for me, and I will give you your wages." So the woman took the child and nursed him. And the child grew, and she brought him to Pharaoh's daughter, and he became her son. So she called his name Moses, saying, "Because I drew him out of the water." (Exodus 1:15–2:10)

ABOUT THE AUTHOR

Brenda Ray began writing when life-threatening latex allergy ended her much-loved career as a nurse-midwife. She holds a Masters of Nursing from the University of Florida.

A member of Romance Writers of America and Soferet, an international collective of Orthodox women writers, Brenda is working on book two of the Hebrew midwife trilogy.

God has blessed Brenda with three wonderful sons, and the brightest, most beautiful grandchildren on the planet. Ms. Ray lives near Panama City, Florida, with her own hero husband, a teenaged son, a precocious peek-a-poo, and a silver-tongued Quaker parakeet. When she's not writing, Brenda enjoys quilting, gardening, and sailing the pristine waters of the Emerald Coast with her family.

For information on book signings and speaking engagements, contact:

books@karmichaelpress.com,
or visit Brenda's Web site:
www.manydaughters.com